MARVEL

A NOVEL OF THE MARVEL UNIVERSE

DEADPOOL
PAWS

A NOVEL OF THE MARVEL UNIVERSE

DEADPOOL
PAWS

STEFAN PETRUCHA

Titan BOOKS

Deadpool: Paws
Print edition ISBN: 9781785659607
E-book edition ISBN: 9781785659614

Published by Titan Books
A division of Titan Publishing Group Ltd
144 Southwark Street, London SE1 0UP

First Titan edition: May 2018
10 9 8 7 6 5 4 3 2 1

Deadpool created by Fabian Nicieza and Rob Liefeld

Editor: Stuart Moore
Original Design: Amanda Scurti
VP Production & Special Projects: Jeff Youngquist
Assistant Editors: Sarah Brunstad & Caitlin O'Connell
Manager, Licensed Publishing: Jeff Reingold
SVP Print, Sales & Marketing: David Gabriel
Editor in Chief: C.B. Cebulski
Chief Creative Officer: Joe Quesada
President: Dan Buckley
Executive Producer: Alan Fine

This edition published by arrangement with Marvel in 2018.

A CIP catalogue record for this title is available from the British Library.

Printed and bound in the United States

Dedicated to the Deadpool in all of us,
because if I don't, he might get angry.

BOOK ONE

WHAT PRICE THAT DOGGIE IN THE WINDOW?

ONE

SO here I am falling off a tall building and...wait.

WHERE THE #$%@ ARE THE PICTURES?

Now I have to deal with this? What is this, anyway—a really, really long caption? Come on! Comics are supposed to be totally in-your-face, in-the-moment, like TV, or...like TV! Get with the program. A picture's worth a thousand turds. Like, if I just *say* red, it's not as good as *seeing* red, is it? Don't get me wrong, I'm all for the chitty-chitty-chit-chat—they call me the Merc with a Mouth for a reason—but enough's enough. Like William Burroughs said, "Language is a virus from outer space."

Okay, yeah, he was a morphine addict, and there's no such thing as a naked free lunch, but still.

I know some of you out there already have smart-ass questions, like, if pictures are so hot, what about backstory? Exposition? How do you do that stuff? Okay, maybe you do need a curt sentence or two, but any writer worth his salt tosses that into the dialogue, like:

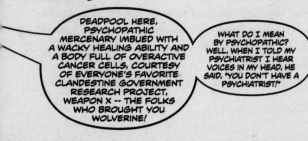

DEADPOOL HERE, PSYCHOPATHIC MERCENARY IMBUED WITH A WACKY HEALING ABILITY AND A BODY FULL OF OVERACTIVE CANCER CELLS, COURTESY OF EVERYONE'S FAVORITE CLANDESTINE GOVERNMENT RESEARCH PROJECT, WEAPON X -- THE FOLKS WHO BROUGHT YOU WOLVERINE!

WHAT DO I MEAN BY PSYCHOPATHIC? WELL, WHEN I TOLD MY PSYCHIATRIST I HEAR VOICES IN MY HEAD, HE SAID, "YOU DON'T HAVE A PSYCHIATRIST!"

None of that *Meanwhile, back at the ranch* crap. If you see a full-page splash of a bank vault, you don't assume the action's taking place in a convenience store, right?

So what's with all the verbiage?

Oh, wait. I get it. Book. It's a book. They really still make these things? Damn.

Okay, I got this. Just a little thrown. As I said, I likes me the talk.

I know you do.

By the by, meet my inner dialogue. If this was a comic, you'd be seeing that in a special-purpose yellow caption. As it is, we're going with that boldface thing, apparently.

Works for me.

Let's get this party started.

And italics for Inner Voice #2. Great. Just shut up for now and let me get on with the story already.

The sleek steel and glass of a Manhattan skyscraper warp into a haze as I careen along its chic frontage. Not being one of those flying types, or even a swinger like Spider-Man, I'm, well…plummeting. I'm flipping and flopping like a fish out of water. More specifically, a fish out of water that's been tossed out a window. I look for something in this big bad blur I can grab onto, anything to at least slow my fall, but there's nada. No flagpoles, no ledges, no gargoyles—just smooth sailing, first pavement on the right and straight on until mourning.

Things may look bad, but I've fallen lots. I've fallen

down buildings; I've fallen into mine shafts, criminal lairs, alien motherships, candy factories, women's bedrooms—you name it. I've fallen asleep, fallen in love, fallen in debt, fallen to pieces—but I've never, ever, fallen to my death. I have fallen to other people's deaths, but that usually involves better aim.

Here's the kicker, though: I'm not alone. I'm carrying the cutest Dalmatian puppy you ever did see. I just snatched this wee fellow from the fancy-pants penthouse way, way back up there. Things didn't go quite as planned, and boy is he going wee now.

I see what you did there.

Oh, aren't you clever.

His name's Kip, judging from the gold tag on his diamond-studded collar. But at this rate, it's going to be Spot when we hit concrete. Under other circumstances, like if he'd eaten a bunch of Cub Scouts and planned to go back for seconds, that might not bother me. Not that I don't enjoy killing, but Kip here hasn't done anything to deserve a premature demise.

So you like the little guy?

No way! He's cute, but cuteness is for lesser beings. I'm the hardened-heart type, keeping the warm fuzzies at bay. That means no man/dog bonding. But…he is so sweet with the rushing air currents pushing his vibrating eyelids wide open like that!

Ahem. That said, I am thinking—purely as a matter of principle, mind you—about how to keep him alive. I did see an online video last week about a puppy that survived a nineteen-story drop.

Sure you didn't imagine it?

Maybe, but it sounded good, especially the part about terminal velocity, how the upward push of wind resistance matches gravity's downward pull, blah-blah-blah. A small mammal like Kip here reaches terminal velocity much sooner than a big guy like me.

Which means…holding onto him should slow me down, right?

Wrong.

Since I'm still picking up speed, I'll give you that one. Kip's stuck with *my* terminal velocity. I can't have that, so I look into his wide, dark, terrified eyes.

"Time you were on your own, little fellow!" I chuck him upward. "Fly free, Kip! Fly free!"

Now that he's on his own, he'll be fine for sure, just like the dog in the video. Or was it a cat? I seem to remember a cat. And it was playing piano. Cat, dog, parakeet…what's the difference, really?

I continue to obey the laws of physics. Cumulus clouds spin above me like cream whipping in a blender. Mmm. Whipped cream. I'd grab a little nosh after I land, but the updraft carrying that oh-so-special city stench is ruining my appetite. The ground must be getting pretty close. I should probably look down, just to judge my distance to the pavement, maybe try to slow myself by bouncing against the wall or something.

Pavement, oh, pavement? Where are you?

There you are!

SPLAT!

I mentioned the healing thing, right? You know

how when Wolverine, that bad-attitude guy from the X-Men, gets shot or cut, the wound heals all by itself? I'm like that, only...more so. Unless I'm dunked in acid, or completely disintegrated, I grow back. Okay, yeah, most of the super crowd returns from the dead so often they should build a shuttle, but they at least have the *potential* to bite the big one. When one of them comes back, it takes a bunch of convoluted logic—or at most, a reboot.

Me, I'm effectively immortal. No matter how badly I get hurt, everything eventually grows back, cancer and all. Did I mention I have cancer? It's what made me sign up for the Weapon X experiment in the first place. Weapon X was run by the Canadian government, btw. Figured it might be a cure. Instead, the experiment made my cancer cells regenerate, too, leaving me with a body full of lesions and a head full of dreams.

Or was the word they used *delusions*?

Anyway, missing limb? A few hours, and it grows back. Flattened skull? Maybe a day or two. Sure, the brain being one of your more crucial organs, I sometimes wake up a little more confused than usual, speaking French, thinking I'm with the Bolshoi Ballet or whatnot, but bottom line? Despite what they say about death and taxes, I can't die, and I don't pay taxes.

Doesn't sound too bad, I guess, until it's *your* bones that are broken, *your* insides spilling out like an overturned Olive Garden garbage can. The problem is, I still *feel* every wound, every time. I could go on and on about the throbbing, stabbing agony that's coursing through my each and every neuron at this very moment, but I'm saving that for my next book, *You Think* That *Hurts?* For now, I'll close on the subject by quoting Ronald Reagan—who, shortly after taking a bullet, was heard to quip, "Ow! Ow! Ow!"

It does beat the alternative, meaning death. Take the two guys I landed on. You haven't even met them, and they're already no longer with us. Most people think I'm heartless (and gross, smelly, etc.), but I feel pretty bad about the hot-dog vendor. The stockbroker? Not so much, though I am impressed with his Patek Philippe wristwatch. It's still working even after I landed on it. Hey, he's not using it, and I've got just enough intact fingers to…

WHAM!

Kip lands in the pulpy center of my cracked chest, making a sound like a wet whoopee cushion. He's all startled, like, "What was that?" Otherwise, he's no worse for wear. The little guy yips and scampers off. Good for him. Sucks for me.

Nabbing that mongrel is the whole reason I'm here in the first place. Now I have to wait in agony until my body heals, then figure out how to find a puppy in the streets of Manhattan.

Is that a song? A puppy in the streets of Manhattan?

Nah. You're probably thinking about The Muppets Take Manhattan.

By the way, this whole scene? Perfect example of

the advantages comics have over prose. It would've been much easier with pictures. Two vertical panels and some motion lines, maybe a quick reaction shot from the hot-dog vendor and the stockbroker as they wonder why they're suddenly in shade, and we're done. Half a page, tops. And the slam when I hit? Much more visceral.

Oh, where will all those fools with their "book learning" be in our new post-literate world? Bwah-hah-hah!

Meanwhile, back at the story…

Yeah, yeah. Don't push me.

Before I can cry, "Here, Fido!" I find myself blessed with a visit from above. From the penthouse, not Heaven. Geez. The newcomer lands in front of me, not with an egregious splat or thud, but with the soothing, gentle rush of mech-armor jets. Why, it's none other than the wacky bodyguard who tossed me out of the penthouse in the first place! Never dawned on him I'd be fast enough to snatch up Kip as I went. Should've seen the look on his face.

I don't know if this guy's actually big and mean, or if it's just that high-tech suit he's wearing, but he nails his entrance. The snazzy final blast from his boot-jets whooshes along the sidewalk, sending the cart's still-steaming foot-longs rolling into the street. But that cool *vrt-vrt* noise he makes when he moves spoils it. Totally trademarked by Stark Industries. You can't just order armor like that from Amazon, so I figure he's sporting a Chinese black-market knockoff that his boss bought on eBay. Damn Internet. Doesn't anyone just carry automatic weapons anymore?

Iron Joe *vrts* a little closer. The suit does that thing where a missile launcher emerges from his forearm. Don't ask me how it's supposed to work. Unless the suit's made of something like Vibranium, which can absorb vibrations, the recoil on that thing should yank his whole arm off in the other direction.

But he doesn't fire yet. His helmet clicks back, showing me a broken-nosed face with a few miles on it. I can see it in his steely eyes: This man's street-smart, and he may even have been around the block once or twice. He's no hotshot wannabe out to prove himself. Probably has some combat experience that earned him the penthouse gig. I almost respect him.

Until he opens his mouth.

"Don't know how you survived the fall, and I don't care. Hand over the dog, or I'll decimate you!"

I laugh. "You're gonna destroy a tenth of me?"

His head twists in a how-dare-you way. "What'd you say to me?"

"Decimate, tin man, means to destroy a tenth of something. Don't believe me? That suit must have Internet. Google it. I'll wait."

"Freaking grammar Nazi." He raises the forearm bearing what I'm guessing is a smoothbore 37mm cannon. "I mean I'm gonna blow you up, okay?"

"Okay, but it's not a grammar issue, it's about semantics, as in…"

He nudges me with the barrel—which, given my

current state, hurts. "Where's the mutt?"

When he notices I'm lying on a gore pile too big to belong to only me, his face gets all sad. "You didn't...land on him, did you?"

I'd no idea I could actually *feel* my pancreas until he pushes that barrel under me like it's a shovel and uses it to lift me for a peek.

"Agh! Cold! Really cold! He's not under there! He ran off! He ran off!"

Relieved, the guard *vrts* his head up and presses a button on his forearm.

From his armor, a sultry synthetic female voice I wish I could hook up with announces, "Dog whistle activated."

The parts of my neck that usually let it move are shattered, so I can't change my point of view, but I hear puppy nails scrabbling along the cement behind me.

Vrt-man gets a smug smile, like he knew all along everything'd turn out fine.

"Kip, you little pain! There you are! C'mere, you flea-bitten dirtbag!"

His words are gruff, but there's a fondness in his voice that tells me he really cares about the hairy thing. Gives me a pang. Could be the pancreas again, but part of me wants to hallucinate a boy-and-his-dog montage with me as the boy—complete with stick, ball, and potty training. Now is not the time.

The bodyguard's not going to want to hear it, but there's something I really should tell him.

"Buddy?"

"Shut up." The scrabbling pup-nails get louder. "Here, boy!"

"What's your name, pal? Look at me down here. I'm good as dead. Might as well tell me that much."

He rolls his eyes, but finding the dog's got him feeling warm, so he gives in. "Bernardo."

Behind me, I hear quick, adorable puppy breaths and a lolling puppy tongue slapping the puppy sides of a puppy snout.

"Bernardo, *mi amigo, por favor,* listen very carefully. I know Kip's cute, I know it's your job to protect him, but you do *not* want to pick up that dog."

Before I can go into detail, I get a view of puppy junk and butt as Kip sails over my face and into Bernardo's waiting metal-composite arms.

"Here you are, you little meat sack!"

"Sure, it *looks* like a puppy, but trust me, it's really…"

The dog licks his face. Bernardo laughs, probably remembering a happy day from his childhood that never really happened.

"Hey, settle down, you!" Then the Dalmatian licks get a little harder. "No, really. Settle down! Kip!"

"Put him down, B. Trust me."

"I'll put *you* down."

The tongue moves faster. The dry, sandpaper feel gets coarser. It doesn't hurt enough to stop a rough guy like Bernie, but I can see from his eyes that he's starting to wonder what's going on. Rather than deal with the strangeness, he turns the anger my way.

"Who the hell are you, anyway? What kind of freak breaks in past a million-dollar security system just to swipe a kid's…"

And then the cute little tongue tears away its first chunk of Bernardo's skin, exposing the tendon and muscle beneath. Surprised—wouldn't you be?—B screams. Instinct makes him want to touch the wound to see how bad it is, but he can't because he's holding Kip in both hands. Teeny Kip, who's now gnawing a gory cheek in his mouth like it's a chew toy.

The welling pain racing his shock, Bernardo gets all nasty. All bets off, he holds up Kip like a football and uses his armor's augmented strength to chuck the mutt as fast and as far as he can. But the furry ball hits the sidewalk just right. Kip rolls, black and white, black and white, like a riddle, for half a block. As he goes, though, he also grows—and grows and grows, until his body's snowballing size mucks with the momentum and stops him short.

Then his body…how do I describe this? Well, it unfurls, sort of like a plant opening up its leaves or a bird unfolding its wings, but more accurately like a mutant monster that's growing, changing color and shape, expanding in seconds to a height of, oh, I dunno. It's not like I've got a ruler handy, so let's call it…forty feet?

Yeah, I'd say forty feet. Give or take.

And then the puppy-no-more cries out, its voice booming like something else that booms. Like, maybe what they used to call a boombox. Sure, a boombox, but much boomier. You know, like thunder. Yeah, like really loud rolling thunder:

"I am GOOM! Thing from the Planet X!"

Cheek-less Bernardo's eyes go wide. I'm disappointed. I thought the man had street smarts, but he loses a little flesh and suddenly he's some lame desk jockey who's never seen a giant monster before. He's easy prey, too busy staring to realize he should be running.

Me? My body may be broken, but with my heart and soul nestled safely in the burgundy mud puddle that is me, I yell to him: "Hey, Bernardo? 'Nardo, buddy?"

"What? WHAT?"

"Told you."

TWO

ALL this time, my healing factor's been doing its thing—sealing this rupture, regrowing that missing bit of internal organ, putting the gluteus back in my maximus. Can't walk yet, but with the good ol' sternocleidomastoid muscles in my neck mended (yeah, I know what they're called, what about it?), I tip my head back for an upside-down view of this creature that calls itself Goom.

Hoo-*wee*, he's a biggun'!

I mean that. Five floors if he's a story. His mottled skin's thick and stony. He's got a squat wrestler's body topped with a fat pumpkin-orange head and the prettiest little green eyes you ever did see. The innocent puppy I knew as Kip is no more. In his place…

"Goom lives!"

With his gaping maw stating the obvious right above me, I'm in the perfect spot to notice that he's got no upper teeth at all. He'd be a dentist's dream if it weren't for his two lower molars, which are big enough to mash up a bus like roughage. I'm ready to give him an eight outta ten for the monster look until I spot those lame-ass wings he's got flapping under his rocky armpits. They look like a box-store Dracula cape, size quintuple X, dyed orange to match his skin.

Should I say something about the tacky wings? I

never know what to do in these situations.

My bodyguard pal, bleeding-cheek Bernardo, finally makes all the appropriate neural connections. See dog? Dog gone. Monster here. Run, run, run! Bernie's out of my field of vision, but I hear him doing more than a few *vrt-vrts*—at least one of which, I suspect, is him soiling his high-tech shorts.

Me? All of a sudden I'm in shadow, like a building's falling on me (and yes, I know exactly what that looks like). But that's no building—it's the arm of my goombah Goom, casting major shade as he reaches over me. I turn my newly working neck in time to see him grab Bernado in his four-fingered King Kong hand.

Bernado plays his part, screaming like Fay Wray: "Aieeeee!"

"Goom hungers!"

Hard *not* to like a monster who lets you know where he's at. Not that I couldn't guess his masticatory intentions from the way he's smacking his lips and bringing B up toward his open mouth. Goom wants to get himself some more of that sweet cheek.

B's a good man in a pinch, perhaps even a delicious man, so I want to help him out. Not with force, since I can't move, but with something even more powerful: information.

"Bernardo? Hey, Bernardo?"

As he tries to squirm free, he calls back. "What?"

I wave my working fingers. "Hi."

Still flailing, he looks at me. "Are you crazy?"

"Bernardo? Bernardo?"

"WHAT?"

"Yes."

The four fingers tighten. The arm draws him closer. "Goom will devour you!"

I try to do a stage whisper, but I'm not very good at it. "I think that means he wants to eat you."

"For the love of…let me die in peace!"

I'd make a joke about how he's going to die in *pieces*, but Goom would need incisors and canines for that. It's more likely he'll be mashed and shredded.

"Sure, if you want, but…Bernardo?"

"What? What?"

My lip muscles back up to par, I smile. "Is that a cannon on your forearm, or are you just glad to see me?"

He looks pissed at first, but then a profound awareness dawns in his eyes. "Oh. Yeah."

Quick as a puppy-lick, he fires that smoothbore 37mm cannon. Guess what? Turns out Bernardo *is* wearing some Vibranium-free Iron Man knockoff *and* real-world physics are in play. The little-missile-that-could shushes one way and his armored arm snaps back the other, the recoil absorbed a bit by the suit. The limb isn't quite torn off, but B's not going to be signing autographs any time soon.

"Argh!"

I love a good *argh*. Don't you?

The missile leaves a trail so puffy-white it could be the clouds on the cover of a children's book.

Or a chemtrail.

When the missile hits the meaty part of the monster's chest, Goom goes boom! Monster-bits splatter across the wide avenue. The hand and arm holding Bernardo swing fast and low like a sweet chariot—their connection to Goom's torso just isn't what it used to be. Before the four big knuckles scrape pavement, B's out of their grasp.

Goom is down and out for the count, but do I get so much as a thanks? Nah. Bernie just pirouettes wildly in midair and grabs at his arm, screaming about how he thinks it's broken. Does he even ask how I'm feeling?

No, it's all, "Yie! Yie! Yie!"

Speaking of which, *my* arm's starting to feel pretty good.

When the spinning stops and he does talk, it's not about me at all. "Cripes. How am I going to explain this? The boss's kid loved that dog."

Having regained some upper-body wriggling capacity, I prop myself up on an elbow and raise an eyebrow his way. But he can't see that, because I'm wearing a mask.

You knew that, right? Do I really have to mention I'm wearing a mask? Black-and-red body suit? Doesn't this thing have a cover, at least?

"The kid, right. The kid. As if *that's* the problem here. Why not admit it, tough guy—*you* loved that hairy mutt, too, at least before it tried to eat you. But doesn't it growing into a giant monster mean there's only more to love? Face it—deep down, you're hurting because you had to put Old Yeller down."

The wobbly B hovers about ten feet up. He's quiet, probably unsure if he should say anything, or if our relationship has finally grown beyond words. But before he can even think to ask if I'm crazy again, he realizes I was right, in more ways than one.

There *is* more of Goom to love. Lots, lots more.

Goom's remains should've stayed a seething heap of oozing Lovecraftian putrescence. Instead, there's a whole lot of shaking going on. With a crinkly sucking noise, new tissue forms, body parts fill in like plot holes, and everything old is new again.

"Goom lives!"

Son of a bitch. It's got a healing factor like mine—only much, much faster. I'm shocked. I'm outraged. Mostly, I'm embarrassed. I look down at my pathetic body, still struggling to get a few internal organs going, and I *tsk*.

"Why can't you heal as fast as Goom? Why?"

But Bernardo's in trouble again, because, you know…"Goom hungers!"

In a panic, jets sputtering, B turns to me, the guy whose quick thinking saved his sorry ass the first time. "Now what do I do?" he asks.

I shrug, thinking, *Hey, I can shrug again!*

But then I say, "How the @&^# do I know? Swipe through your apps, find something that fires, and aim for the damn thing's gobbleshaft."

"The what?"

Gobbleshaft definitions aside, it's not as easy as it sounds. B's right arm is out of commission, and he's clearly not ambidextrous. His left hand fumbles about like that lady at the automatic checkout this morning who couldn't figure out where to put her pennies.

In the coin slot, you idiot! THE COIN SLOT!

You should've blown her up.

Instead of the machine.

Anyway, I cleverly suggest a daring shift in tactics. "Those wussy wings of his can't possibly work. Fly out of range!"

Nodding, he turns up the juice. The jets waver, like maybe there's a piece of Goom caught in the intake manifold. He doesn't zoom off, but he starts rising as the monster's paw reaches for him again. It looks close, but Goom's four fingers clamp on air.

"Fly away, little guard! Fly free!"

B's relieved. I can tell from his smug smile. I am, too, but only for about a second, because apparently those wings aren't just there to attract mates. Goom *can* fly. Pretty fast, too. He closes the distance in a flash and grabs Bernardo's legs. Rather than repeat his earlier mistake by telling us all again how alive and hungry he is, Goom pops Bernardo into his mouth.

Right there, in midair.

It's kinda like watching one of those nature films where the seagull thinks it's getting away from the shark, but the shark just jumps up and…

I'm about to offer B more advice, but there's

this...gnashing sound. Quality battle armor would give off a macho krunk as it collapses. This crap doesn't even squeal.

Wish I could say the same for Bernardo. "Yaghhhh!"

With a *vrt-vrt* here and a *vrt-vrt* there...he's gone.

By the way, if this had been a comic, his final exclamation would've appeared in what we call a BURST.

At least the big guy doesn't say, "Goom chews!"

Circle of life. Am I right? That's another reason I make it a policy not to bond with pets, or minor characters, or most things. You never know when they'll die. I mean, I barely knew Bernardo, and here I am, feeling all sniffly about...

Oooh! Look! A Patek Philippe wristwatch, and no one's using it!

I finally get my digits on the damn thing when a pained, wailing din intrudes on my opportunistic thievery. It sounds like a whole elementary school full of terrified, screaming children—because, yep, right across the wide avenue, there's a brown brick elementary school, full of kids. The brats are all gathered at the windows, pitifully wailing as Goom stomps toward them.

No "Goom swallows!" or "Goom wipes his lips!" Just: "Goom hungers!"

The reading material on Planet X must really suck.

The kids howl. Their brave teachers yank them

back from the windows. One pulls down the shade, as if that'll do something.

That's it. I don't care if he was a puppy once, now he's being piggish. I heave myself up, shake off a few steaming hot dogs, and snap out the twin katana I keep strapped to my back.

Unfortunately, I hadn't noticed that one of the swords healed right into my shoulder blade. Eep. Completely throws my iaido when I yank it out. Hurts pretty bad, too. Sorry, agony, no time for you now. Feet pumping, arms back and ready to strike, I head for the nearest bumpy orange ankle.

Goom raises his hand and arches his back, looking like he's about to take out the wall with a single blow. If I were a lot taller, I could hamstring him from here. Instead, I slash at his ankle, slicing out enough of a chunk to make him fall backwards.

Man, he goes down loud. The ground shakes. Asphalt cracks. Traffic's blocked both ways. Two cabs, a minivan, and an Acura all go crunch. A hydrant snaps, shooting water thirty feet into the air. In other words…

See? That's a burst.

Goom's on his back, disoriented, looking like a

papa who'd been playing with the baby on the living room floor and now can't quite figure where his little darling crawled off to. But then his great big pumpkin head (as opposed to Great Pumpkin head, which would be a Charlie Brown reference) turns my way.

By the time he narrows his twin greenies at my sweet self, the ankle's healed. Damn.

"Goom will destroy you!"

I give him a Bronx cheer. "Deadpool will duck!"

His hand comes for me. Despite my incredible reflexes, he's too fast for Plan A—which, as I said, involved ducking. I switch to Plan B and slice off a monster fingertip.

"Goom hurts!"

"Don't they have exclamations of pain on Planet X? Is it all just clipped self-reflexive narrative? 'Goom hurt?' 'Goom regret?' 'Goom enter shame spiral?'"

Before he can pull his hand away, I relieve him of another digit.

"Yeow!"

"Thank you!"

Turns out you don't really need all your fingers to swat something. Rather than take a minute of Goom-time to suck on his wounds, he backhands me. I go flying. It's not up, up, and away so much as across the street and into the stone base of the elementary school. Granite, mortar, and what looks like a time capsule from 1954 tumble around me. Bruised but not broken, I hop back out and angrily let loose with a stream of classic battle lines:

"Yippee-ki-yay, m***********! Go ahead, punk, make my day! I'm all out of bubblegum! Say hello to my little friend! You talkin' to me? I'm not locked in here with you, you're locked in here with me! I am the one who knocks! For hate's sake, I spit my last breath at thee!"

Goom sits up, the top of his head even with the third floor of the building behind him. His fingers already restored to their original, fabulous condition, he tries to grab me again, but I'm ready this time. I hop atop his index finger and rush along his arm.

So Goom can grow back pieces. La-di-da. Let's see if he can grow back his whole head.

Beneath the rocky folds of his cheeks, his neck is nearly invisible, almost like the narrator from *The Rocky Horror Picture Show*. But I can see it. Reaching the tip of his shoulder, I take to the air, katana out.

Goom is going down!

As I sail toward my goal, the world becomes a blur. I don't usually get much appreciation, and I try not to expect it, but this time I hear it, growing louder and louder: the wild roar of the crowd. All of a sudden, the whole middle-school audience is on their feet, cheering. And they're cheering for *me*, little Wade, the kid they all made fun of, because now he's going to win the big game! I've got the ball, seconds to go, and I'm soaring toward the net. It's going in, I tell you, it's going in! I see Sophie McPherson, the girl I love, shaking with excitement, squealing my name over and over, "Wade! Wade!"

"Look at me, Sophie! Look at me!"

Did I mention that sometimes I hallucinate at inappropriate moments? Never know when to bring that up. It's like trying to figure out how many dates in to mention having kids, or leprosy. Glad it's out there now. You'll get used to it, mostly. What causes it? It could be that as my accelerated healing repairs any head trauma, it interferes with my continuity of consciousness. Or maybe the experiment that gave me my power, coupled with the cancer, exacerbated some underlying psychological issues.

Could be something in the moment acting as an emotional trigger.

Yeah, remember how Dad used to beat you?

What? You think fighting a giant monster about to eat some children brings up a junior-high basketball game? Right. Whatever.

I'd like to say I can always recognize a delusion because eventually it fades, but—big picture—everything fades, doesn't it? Anyway, one minute, it's all cheering—and the next, my personal tweenage wasteland fades. No winning basket, no Sophie.

Instead, out to have the last clap, Goom slams me between his palms. He grinds his bumpy hands. I struggle, grunt, and shimmy, but it does squat to get me free. Then he throws me down very, very, very, very, very, very hard.

I go through the reinforced roof of a parked Humvee. I go through the upholstered seat. You'd think the chassis below that would stop me, but nope, I go through that, too—all the way down to the asphalt, where I lie in a brand-new, Deadpool-shaped pothole.

Like Bugs Bunny, only with blood.

Everything that took all that time healing? Broken again. Some new stuff, too. I think I have a working arm, but before I can use it, Goom lifts the Humvee off of me.

Clearly the finger-slicing is still fresh in his monster brain. Instead of grabbing me again, he tosses the car aside and jumps, planning to stomp on whatever's left of me with those gunboat feet of his. Gunboat *not* being a figure of speech.

Hey, I've survived all sorts of stuff: gunshots, arrows through my head, ingrown toenails. But even I'm not sure I can come back from being *totally* flattened. And like I said, it always hurts.

As I lie in the increasingly smelly shade of Goom's titanic tootsies, I contemplate not so much my mortality as what I'll be missing on TV.

Is the new season of *S.H.I.E.L.D.* on yet?

S.H.I.E.L.D.?

Oh, man. I feel like Dorothy when she finds out she had the power to go home all along (and frankly, I'd have kicked Glinda for holding back). I don't have to miss a thing, because I've had exactly what I need this whole time. With my one working arm, I withdraw the secret weapon tucked inside my stylishly small belt. I'd like to say it looks totally cool, but really it's just a fancy aerosol dispenser can.

Aiming up as Goom comes down, I give him a spritz. My current employers, the folks who gave me the can, call it a nano-catalyst. You know how most living things—aside from, like, amoebas—are made up of connected cells? The nano-catalyst I just sprayed breaks up those connections.

Is it fast-working? Just watch. Or…read.

As his rocky massiveness falls toward me, the Thing from Planet X melts into little gory Goom-gibs. It looks like he's splashing into a huge, growing water hole of himself.

Instead of getting squashed, I'm soaked in a gloopy pink rain.

I didn't even kill him, exactly, because he's not dead. No, I don't mean as long as we remember him. Since he can regenerate, each and every cell is still alive—even though collectively he's been reduced to a big pink puddle that sloshes and slurps along, each single bit less like Goom, the Thing from Planet X, and more like a Period, the Thing at the End of this Sentence.

THREE

IT ain't the first time a piece of the Big Apple has gotten itself chewed. The sirens of the first responders are already piercing the racket of yowling school kids, screaming pedestrians, honking cars, and chunks of still-falling concrete. Bet I'd have a real migraine right now if my ears weren't all clogged with the gunk previously known as Goom.

I try like the dickens to whack the gunk out, but it's in there deep. I'm still at it when an airy rush whines above the cacophony. Beating out the cop cars, ambulances, and fire trucks for "me first!" bragging rights, four hover-fliers set down around me.

What's a hover-flier? Well, it's like if a flying aircraft carrier laid an egg containing a rapid-response team of four or five field agents. For comparison, a flying aircraft carrier—A.K.A. a Helicarrier—has a crew of around 5,000, and you just *know* everyone isn't getting a window seat.

Both belong to S.H.I.E.L.D.

If you don't know S.H.I.E.L.D., part of me wants to threaten you with bodily harm. But hey, sometimes I can't even remember the names of all the voices in my head, so I'll let it go.

We have names?

Shh.

Once upon a time, S.H.I.E.L.D. stood for *Supreme Headquarters International Espionage Law-Enforcement Division*. In the '90s, they changed it to *Strategic Hazard Intervention Espionage Logistics Directorate* before settling on *Strategic Homeland Intervention, Enforcement, and Logistics Division*. But as Gertrude Stein said, A rose is a rose is a rose is a rose.

To me, they've always been *Supercharged Housekeepers Into Employing Lackeys for Dirty Jobs*. As long as they keep their groovy slogan (Don't Yield, Back S.H.I.E.L.D.!) and pay me in cash, I don't care what they call themselves.

Lift fans idle, hatches shoosh open, and the competent team leader hops out to assess the sitch. She's a good-lookin' African American; wife, mother, and ass-kicker. She's a robot, too. Some might say her synthetic body could stand to lose a few, but she likes it that way, because that's how she rolls. She's perfect—a textbook picture of efficiency and cool leadership—until she makes a face like she's staring at her kid's messy bedroom.

After rolling her eyes more than once, she gets all official into her comm. "I want a perimeter around that...that...goop, stat. Other than first responders handling the wounded, no one in, no one out until every drop of that stuff is secure."

A gender- and ethnically balanced group of fit agents wearing dark, Kevlar-enhanced bodysuits leap from the fliers, fan out, and work the scene.

After a few more whacks to my head and a little *plop*, I finally have one Goom-free ear. I give the lead agent a thumbs-up. "Hey, Preston! I didn't yield, 'cause I was backing S.H.I.E.L.D.!"

She rolls her eyes yet again. "Hello, Wade."

She gets to call me that because it's my name, Wade Wilson, and Agent Emily Preston and I are buds. Haven't got many. Buds, not names.

Speaking of names, to be honest, there is some question about whether Wade Wilson is my real name. My mental circumstances make it tough to remember my life before Weapon X—or during. Or after. Met this guy once who said *he* was the real Wade Wilson. Then again, I might have imagined that, or been staring in a mirror getting ready for a big date with Sophie, or something.

But hey, as far as *you* know, I'm making everything up, anyway. How could you possibly tell, especially without pictures? Pictures never lie. It's the word balloons you have to watch out for.

I had a balloon once. I think. Big yellow thing. I was so excited I was shaking, clutching it in my little hand, until my dad said, "Wade"—he called me Wade, since he was my dad, which I guess implies I really am Wade. "Why don't you see what happens when you let go of the string?"

And I...

Oh, God. Oh, God. Oh, God.

Was it a balloon on a string?

Or a puppy on a leash?

No. Never had a dog. Never. Far as I know. Only reason I'd want one as a kid would be to impress Sophie. Girls dig that cuddly stuff.

Anyway, Preston's one of maybe...three friends, I think? Hard to keep track. They keep dying or betraying me, or it turns out they don't exist and I've been palling around with myself the whole time. Come to think of it, *Preston* died for a while, which explains why she's got the robot bod now. Technically, it's a Life Model Decoy: a S.H.I.E.L.D.-designed re-creation of a living person. LMD for short. It looks totally human, which is more than a lot of people say about me.

Aside from Em, there's Blind Al, but she was sort of my prisoner. And Bob, Agent of Hydra. He was a big fan, but I tried to have him killed, he tried to kill me, and things got messy. Past that…look, if you really want to know all this crap, you can read all about it in my comic, unless you're all like, "Oh, I only read books, I'm so smart, la-la-la, look how smart I am!"

In which case, next time I break the fourth wall, it'll be on your head. Don't think I can't crawl out of these pages for a little chat about exercising your brain's capacity for conceptualizing spatial relations.

That's right, pal, I'm talking to you.

"Wade, who are you talking to?"

No one! Uh, why?

Damn. Forgot the quote marks.

"No one, Em! Uh, why?"

She heads toward me, brow mushed. "Never

mind. Don't need to know, don't want to."

"Careful you don't step in that Goom."

She looks down, wrinkles her nose, and waves over two agents. They trot up, carrying what looks like a high-tech vacuum-cleaner hose with a white metal snout mounted at the business end. All I'm-in-chargey, she snaps her finger at the ooze, and they aim the sucker (get it?) where she's pointing.

With the press of a touchscreen, diodes blink, air shushes, and what Jimmy Durante would've called the thing's *schnozzola* starts sucking up Goom-gore like it's cherry syrup with extra HFCS. The gunk gurgles along the hose and gets plopped into a big tank mounted on one of the hover-fliers. It's the size of that thing Homer Simpson used to store Spider-Pig's poops in the movie. Speaking of words that begin with "p," the thing's pretty picky for a power-vac. Slime goes in, everything else stays out.

Once the ground between us is clear enough to keep her boots clean, Agent Preston approaches. "You hurt?"

"Define your terms."

"More than usual?"

"Be up and at 'em in a few, not yielding 'cause I'm backing S.H.I.E.L.D.…ing!"

"Would you *please* stop saying that? No one's used that slogan since the sixties."

I'm having a little trouble hearing her, so I slam my head to try to clear the other ear. It doesn't work. Now my good ear's ringing because I just hit myself really hard. I can barely hear myself talk, let alone anyone else. So I shout:

"CAN'T BE AS EMBARRASSING AS HIRING ME TO KIDNAP PUPPIES BECAUSE THEY MIGHT TURN INTO GIANT MONSTERS!"

Em hisses like I farted in church. "Quiet down! As far as the public's concerned, S.H.I.E.L.D.'s only here to clean up *your* mess. That's the whole reason you were hired for this job."

I whack my head again. "WHAT'S THAT, EM? TIMMY'S TRAPPED IN A CAVE, AND I HAVE TO GO SAVE HIM?"

She narrows her eyes and nods at the agents. "Clean him."

They shove their nozzle my way—prodding this, poking that with a nudge-nudge here and a wink-wink there.

"OW! HEY, WATCH THE FAMILY JEWELS!"

"Every drop."

"Yes, ma'am."

"HA-HA! IT TICKLES! OKAY, PRESTON! I'LL STOP! I'LL STOP!"

I grab the nozzle and shove it against my ear. With a loud *thup*, a little bit of something-something shoots out of my favorite Eustachian tube, rattles along the twisty hose, and lands in the tank with a *clink*.

"He shoots, he scores!" I exhale a cheering-crowd sound, but it's a little sad without Sophie or the middle-school gym here. "Agent Preston, I have to report that, unfortunately, I may have had a piece of my brain sucked out. Warning: If it was the right temporo-parietal junction, my moral compass may be compromised. Do not use me if you may be pregnant or wish to be."

She crosses her arms. "You don't *have* a moral compass. Besides, the Gale Max 9000 only takes in biomaterial that's been compromised by the nano-catalyst."

I hold up my neat-o aerosol thingy. "My compliments to the chef for the most totally rad water gun I've ever had." I point it and make some laser-blast sounds. "Pew! Pew! Pew!"

Preston ducks. The other agents, who I'm really just not going to bother describing to you in any detail, scatter. "Deadpool! That stuff can liquefy *any* living thing, including you."

I twirl it a few times and plop it back in my belt. "Kidding. I know. I'm not stupid. I read the label. Most of it. Last resort only."

She looks around at the gaping holes in the street, the buildings, and the previously moving vehicles. "In this case, it looks like you could've resorted to it a little sooner."

"Had to make sure Kip was a threat, didn't I?" Healing factor's been chugging along, so I can pick myself up and stretch. "I tell you, Pres, it's the kind of story I see all too often on these mean streets. Goom lived, Goom hungered, Goom ate Bernardo, Goom lived some more, Goom got peckish and went after an elementary school. You'd think they'd have learned by now to store our most precious resource—children—underground."

Her brow does that mooshy thing again. "Did you say Goom? From Planet X?"

"Yeah, five times in once sentence. Why? You know him?" I arch my back. Something bony along my spine goes *krch*, meaning it's either back in place or it shouldn't have been there in the first place. "Did you date? Does hubby Shane know? Spill, girlfriend."

"It just sounds...familiar." Her groovy LMD eyes, which look otherwise normal, start projecting data out into the air. It's freaky, but I don't mention it because I'm polite.

She scans the info and scowls. The file she wants is locked. "Well, we knew whoever was working at that abandoned Weapon X lab was developing an apex predator with a canine larval stage. But we weren't sure *what* the pups would turn into. The real mystery's why they were shipped out to be adopted as pets."

I raise an eyebrow, but as I mentioned earlier, it can't be seen under the mask. "*That's* the real mystery? Have we grown so jaded we no longer take a minute to ask why someone would breed a cannibalistic monster with a larval stage that looks like a puppy in the first place?"

"Okay, maybe it's more the *immediate* mystery. But with more of them out there, there's plenty to keep us both busy." The data projection disappears. "I'll let you know if I learn anything else."

"You beep like that while you're sleeping? Shane is one patient dude."

"Yeah, but Jeff loves it when I read him holographic bedtime stories."

The suck-up crew finished, she waves them back to the hover-fliers. "One puppy down, but it's a long list, Wade. If any more of them transform, a lot of lives will be at risk. You'd better get on it."

"No problemo, kemosabe." I pull out my pad and scan the list.

That's a lot longer than I remember.

Even with the top one scratched off.

And we're gonna get beat up by all of them?

"Uh…Preston? Going with that whole acting-sooner idea, wouldn't it be easier if I *didn't* wait for them to do some damage? Y'know, even give 'em a little spritz *before* they change? Save time and money?"

Boy, do I get a look.

"No, it would not. I already told you, we pulled that list from a legit distribution center. The monster-larvae were mixed in with their regular shipments. We have no idea which of those are bio-engineered freaks, and which are real puppies."

"Point being…?"

Her eyes go wide. "Wade! I thought you liked dogs."

"Do not. I only said that for the book-jacket flap. Gives readers a reason to identify with me. I'm a detached professional. Never owned one, wouldn't want to. Besides, in some countries, dogs are considered a delicacy."

Her eyes go wider. Didn't know they could do that. Wonder if it's an LMD thing.

Before she breaks an eye-widening servo, I get my

foot up on a concrete shard, put my elbow to my knee, and stare off into the distance for a quick monologue. "Sure, I had a thing for Snoopy when I was a kid, but if I bonded with a mutt these days, we'd both get hurt in the end. It'd start innocently enough: game of catch, cold nose nuzzling my neck, some sandy tongue-licking. Next thing you know it's sleeping at my feet, warming my toes, and providing 24/7 unconditional love. Where would that leave me?"

She smirks. "Uh…happier? Quit the BS. I know you. You wouldn't hurt a real puppy in a million years. Would you?"

I put my hands behind my back, look down, and kick at the ground. "No. I guess not."

She smiles. "Didn't think so."

"But it would be more efficient."

She gives me the wide eyes again. "What did you say?"

"Nothing."

"You want the money for this job, don't you?"

"Yes."

Her hands shoot to her hips. "Look at me. Look at me right now. Do you *want* me to fire your ass?"

"No. But I thought you *liked* it when I kill bad guys."

"I do not like it when you kill *anyone*. And talk like an adult, will you? Or whatever it is you are."

I clear my throat. "What about when I shot that Hydra assassin who was trying to hurt your family?"

"That was different—you saved our lives. Unless

those puppies transform into an immediate threat, you are not saving lives. And will you quit talking to me like I'm your mother? It's hard enough being your friend."

"Fine. Can I be excused?"

She waves me away like I'm a big red-and-black fly. "Go on. Get out of here before what's left of my sanity returns and I take that aerosol can back. Remember, you've only got this job because I said you're not as totally crazy as you seem. Don't prove me wrong."

I trudge off, thoughts ping-ponging in my skull.

You wouldn't hurt a dog.

Would you?

Some folks were worried how this whole inner-dialogue thing would work in a book. Jury's still out, but I'm starting to wonder how much I need it.

Wait.

What?

Well, what do you guys do, really? It was fun in the comic, but even there you do, like, three things:

1) Provide juxtaposition between fantasy and objective (or at least consensus) reality. But I just did that with the basketball-game hallucination—no voices needed.

Yeah, but...

2) Distinguish between what I say to myself and what I say aloud. But since I'm narrating this mess, we know that only the stuff appearing in quotes is out loud—like in my chat with Preston.

Still...

3) Express multiple personalities, like Good Wade/Bad Wade, Crazy Wade/Less-Crazy Wade

That's it! That one.

That one you can't do without us.

Wrong. I don't actually have separate personalities. I *know* you're me. Besides, multiple personality disorder was rejected as a legit diagnosis years ago—so screw you, *Sybil* fans. These days, psychologists think it's more like role-playing, only you lose track.

Don't we keep it real for you on the inside?

Please. If a tree fell in a forest and no one was there to hear it, would it make a sound?

Yes.

Oh? How do you know, smart-ass?

Same way you know a tree fell in a forest with no one there, dimwit.

Hmm. Oh, I can't stay mad at you guys! Okay, you can stick around!

FOUR

PRESTON'S got nothing to worry about, puppy-wise. Not for the touchy-feely reasons, but I've got limits. I do like me some killing, and I'm good at it, but I only whack proven murderous scum that totally deserve it. Sure, I think about it plenty, talk tough to keep up my image. But when it comes down to it, I wouldn't hurt a Komodo dragon with a sneaker dangling from its venomous maw without proof there'd been a foot inside that sneaker. Couldn't look at myself in the mirror otherwise.

Not that I do anyway, what with all those pus-oozing cancer lesions. Some people wear masks to conceal their true identities, others to protect loved ones. I do it to keep my face from sloughing off.

Second place on the list is Playful Pete's Pet Potpourri up in Yonkers. The pet store's unwittingly received an Alsatian that might be a kaiju (that's Japanese for strange creature, genre fans) in disguise. Knowing the breed doesn't do me a lot of good. I have no idea what an Alsatian looks like, and I'm too lazy to look it up on my phone. Is it the one that looks like a puffy German shepherd, or the one with the wrinkly face?

Eh, I'll work it out when I get there.

And I won't be driving or taking public

transportation, either. S.H.I.E.L.D.'s got hover-fliers, Michael Knight has KITT, Roy Rogers has Trigger (who he stuffed after death, by the way—talk about creepy). Me, I've got a teleporter built in to that thin and stylish weapons belt of mine. So with a song in my heart, a cool wind bracing my face, and my spandex riding up my crotch, I click my heels, slap my buckle, and say, "Bamf!"

I only say *bamf* 'cause I hate the *buzz* the 'porter makes. It's like an annoying alarm clock. It never makes *any* sound on my arrival, which makes it great for sneaking up on people. This time, though, there's this unexpected, gaudy flash of light—and it doesn't go away.

Maybe the 'porter was damaged in the fall back in Chapter 1? Nope, it's working fine. Reality, as usual, is the problem. All that trashy flash is coming from Playful Pete's lit plastic sign right above me.

This is no mom-and-pop shop—it's one of those big-box stores. Instead of the usual collection of inanimate goods meant for conspicuous consumption, Pete's supplies a wide variety of life forms that are bred, packaged, and sold for the emotional support and amusement of our planet's currently dominant species.

It's big even for a big box, taking up most of a strip mall right across from Yonkers Raceway and a stone's throw from the Hillview Reservoir.

Not that this is foreshadowing or anything, but boy, wouldn't it be dramatic if that water supply was endangered at some point? I mean, Hillview supplies millions of Manhattanites with potable hydration. Can you imagine?

Russian playwright Anton Chekhov once said, "Remove everything that has no relevance to the story. If you say in the first chapter that there is a rifle hanging on the wall, in the second or third chapter it absolutely must go off. If it's not going to be fired, it shouldn't be hanging there."

But he's dead, I'm here, and I'm telling you not to make *anything* out of the fact I'm packing a nano-catalyst that can reduce any living thing to gloop, and I happen to be near a reservoir.

And the raceway? Nothing to do with anything.

To review: no horses and nothing going on with that reservoir, capisci? This chapter is all about the potential danger lurking within Pete's—and me, Deadpool, the right man for the right job, in the right place, not in my right mind.

With an energetic leap, I bound onto the automatic door pads, because I still get such a kick out of it when doors open by themselves. It's magic! When they part, Pete's lives up to its name: A potpourri of animal fecal odors assaults my nostrils. Barks, trills, and chirps tickle my eardrums—and that's just from all the kids promising their parents they'll take care of their new whatever, no matter how their room looks, *oh please, please, please!*

"Can I have a dog, Dad?"

One side, you've got your mega-wall of bubbling

fish tanks. On the other: squawking birdies who really don't give a crap that you *think* you know why caged birds sing. Farther up, all the mice and other rodents are busy fornicating in front of their offspring and yours. Next to them we have the predatory reptiles, eyeing the higher-maintenance mammals, like ferrets and sugar gliders, and wondering how long each would take to digest. To the right, my target: a whole lot of yipping puppies.

There are lessons here for all of us. It's here that our processed-food-fed young learn the cycle of life, here that the adults learn the cycle of commerce, and here that college grads learn the cycle of underemployment.

But I know something they don't—that beneath this seeming utopia of cages, wood chips, and readily available nutrition lies a potential time bomb. At any moment, Pete's and all within it could be torn apart by a rampaging behemoth masquerading as a puffy pillow of love.

Or not. Could just be a real Alsatian puppy.

So what's my move? Kip made the shift right in front of me, but that might've been a fluke. For all I know, the transformation could take place over days or weeks. But my list is long, and something tells me I'd better move fast to flush out the lurking horror before it quits lurking and gets all horrid. Not sure what the "something" is. Probably one of the voices in my head.

Don't you dare blame me.

Or me.

Hm. Kip changed right after a fall from a tall

building. Maybe a sudden adrenaline rush triggers the change.

I think that's an informal logical fallacy there.

Post hoc, ergo propter hoc. Just because something happens after something else, you can't conclude it happened because of it.

So all I have to do is create a little adrenaline rush, and see what comes of it.

Katana are great when you don't want attention. For this, I hop up on a seasonal display, slip out my Glock .45 GAP pistols, and start shooting.

Ptaff! Ptaff! Tzing!

Bits of cheap ceiling tile and plasterboard fall. Shoppers screech. Employees race for cover. Goldfish dive into faux castles, never to be seen again, and best of all, the freaking birds finally shut their beaks. Lest anyone misinterpret, I speak loudly and calmly:

"Don't worry, citizens! I'm a crack shot! No one will be hurt! I'm just trying to rattle a monster to get it to show itself!"

Packeta-pack! Pwee!

But do they listen? Do they notice I'm just making patterns in the wall? No. It's all panic, panic, panic, run, run, run. Man, Sherlock Holmes shot whole words into his Baker Street wall, and Mrs. Hudson barely blinked. I don't get no love.

Tkak-pow!

At least the manager keeps his head. He ducks his way up to me, swinging one of those aluminum thingies they use to grab stuff off the high shelves.

"Stop! Stop!"

He shakes it at me like it's a bat. I could point out that even if it were a bat, it wouldn't be particularly useful against two guns. Instead, I cast an admiring glance his way.

"It takes balls to walk up to a masked guy shooting up a store, sir, and I respect that."

I keep firing, but with respect.

Dakka-dakka-dak!

"You maniac!"

"Sir, the details are very hush-hush, but I'm afraid you and your patrons may be in danger."

He swings. "From you, you freaking lunatic!"

His aluminum picker crumples against the display, and he gets all sad. Could've told him those things make crappy weapons, but he didn't ask. To take his mind off his troubles, I keep him talking.

"Sir? I'm looking for an Alsatian puppy that was shipped here two days ago, but—and this is a little embarrassing—I don't know what an Alsatian looks like. Think you could describe one for me? It doesn't have to be lengthy in terms of word count, but I will need you to try and be evocative."

Ptaff! Ptaff!

He gets all red-faced. "An Alsatian?!"

He tries to grab my feet, but the poor guy's an inch too short, which explains why he was walking around with that picker in the first place.

"No need to take a tone, sir. I'm doing the best I can."

Beads of sweat join the red on his face. "You're shooting up a packed store for nothing!"

"It might seem like nothing, but as Orwell said, 'Those who abjure violence can do so only because others are committing violence on their behalf.'"

Pwing! Takat!

"You idiot! We just *sold* that puppy!"

Packeta…

"Oh."

The Glocks are empty, anyway. I point them at the ceiling and eject the magazines. Given my faux pas, the move doesn't look as cool as I'd hoped. Plus, one of the mags bounces off the manager's head and lands in a ferret cage.

"Uh…how long ago?"

"Like a minute before you came in! Look at this place! My God! My God!"

Feeling a tad sheepish, I look around. There are holes in the walls and holes in a few pet-supply displays, but not so much as a crack in an aquarium. I want to say something about having to break a few eggs to make an omelet, but my ears prick up at a familiar sound: sirens.

"Why, sir! Did you call the police?"

The stalwart, height-challenged manager isn't listening. He's busy hustling the last few customers and employees out the back.

I wave. "Godspeed to you, sir! Godspeed!"

And I am alone, alone with my thoughts; alone with my failing memories, my imperfect perceptions—

and a few hundred animals. Hey, that means I'm not alone at all, am I? But who are the real animals here? The helpless creatures we define as pets? The humans who, as if they were gods, buy and sell these lives? Or the crazy guy with the smoking Glocks?

Guy with the Glocks.

Definitely.

There is much to consider. But now—with plasterboard dust and kitty litter settling all around like gray, mass-manufactured snow—I hear something else above the sirens, a plaintive cry that pierces the night:

"Help! Help! Help!"

Somewhere a soul is in distress—an innocent endangered, a monster being born.

And I know in my heart I must answer.

FIVE

CAPTAIN AMERICA—Super-Soldier; hero of the Second World War; a man who, despite the intervening decades since his fateful encounter with the serum that gave him his great abilities, still remembers what it's like to be weak, and so truly understands what it means to be strong.

CAPTAIN AMERICA—the first Avenger, a man so entwined with the stars and stripes adorning his proud costume that even those closest to him are never quite sure where his lofty ideals end and the flesh-and-blood man begins.

CAPTAIN AMERICA—Champion of Democracy, Sentinel of Liberty, Bodyguard of the Bill of Rights, a man out of time, a man trapped in a modern world that moves so quickly it sometimes seems to have outgrown the very principles that brought it so far so fast.

CAPTAIN AMERICA…is NOT in this book.

Fooled you. Being psychotic means never having to say I'm sorry. It's all up for grabs, kiddies. Even that last sentence.

But enough of that.

Blood rushing, legs pumping, and _____ (something faster than lightning) reflexes peaking, I head for the exit of the decimated pet store.

That's right. I destroyed a tenth of it, give or take.

I'm poised for action, prepped to propel myself into whatever perilous puppy-themed plight awaits. But you know what? In this hectic modern life of ours, it's important to stop and smell the roses. So I pause to jump up and down on the black pad in front of the doors, making them open and close. I *love* how that works.

Uh, monster?

I'm on it. Once outside, I hear that panicked voice cry out again, "Help! Help! Help!"

I look left, I look right, I look behind me. I look under my shoe. Nothing. Nothing I want to touch, anyway. Don't blame me. Humans suck at audio-location. That's why you only need one bass speaker, because most of us can't tell what direction the low-frequency sound's coming from.

"Help! Help! Help!"

Hm. Could it be a cry from within?

Nope.

Not here.

Having exhausted all other options, I look in the only direction remaining: up. Whaddaya know? There's my screamer! Hm. He's not much to look at. Could be a dad who picked up an Alsatian puppy to surprise the kids, or a lonely businessman who wanted *something* to greet him when he came home at night. I could give you his hair color, age, height, or weight—or some clever evocative metaphor (face sour as a squeezed grapefruit)—but really, in the end, he's boring. I'd much rather go back and describe all those

S.H.I.E.L.D. agents. And his dialogue is totally lame: "Help, help, help!"

No hint of character, or even any info to keep the plot moving. How about, "Eek! I'm being kidnapped!" Or, "My new puppy has transformed into something huge, and I have reason to believe it means me ill!" Or even, "Aiee! The world has been upended! What once I held in my arms now holds me!"

On the other hand, the creature holding him way up there? Now *that's* interesting. My, my, my! Someone get me my silk folding fan, the one with the black sequins, because I do believe I am feeling faint!

Sporting much-better-than-Goom wings, it flaps along about twenty yards above Central Avenue, clutching the shrieking Mr. Dull in its…shall we call them hands? Overall, it looks like a big old gray stone building—but you gotta figure it's not really a building, because buildings can't fly, right? Thanksgiving Day Parade balloon? Nah. It isn't T-Day, and why would anyone make a giant gray balloon?

Heart all aflutter, I clamber onto a parked van for a better look. From the hewn-stone gray of its skin, craggy features emerge, rising like the tree-hidden faces of U.S. presidents on a diner placemat. And those wings? Oh, mama. These are vast, bat-like suckers. Stylish, too—their sharp bony tips are a perfect match for the big pointy ears rising on either side of its classic goblin face. You'd think something that looks like it was chopped out of granite wouldn't need clothes, but it's wearing shorts as gray and lumpy as its skin, covering up privates that probably don't exist.

Unlike Goom, this fellow looks just like one of those…whaddaya call the statues that sit on ledges to carry water away from the roof? St. Romanus fought one in the seventh century? There was a cartoon show? It's on the tip of my tongue.

"Now the world will feel the might of Gorgolla, the Living Gargoyle!"

I snap my fingers. "Gargoyle, that's it! Thanks! But Gorgolla? Dude, that sounds like some kind of cheese."

The monster either ignores me, or he's too far up to hear. No problem. I am poetry in motion. An expert leap to a fire escape's bottom rung, some quick climbing, another jump, a midair twist, a landing roll, and I'm on the roof of Pete's running right alongside the wing-flapping beastie.

"Help, help, help!" the helpless victim screams.

Yeah, yeah, whatever. I'll alert the press.

I'm out of roof, so I leap to a multiplex next door. The place is still under construction—and what a mess, let me tell you. So much trash around, I'm wasting my time zigzagging around open crates, unused bits of ventilation shaft, and general detritus. In the first draft, I even stepped on a rake that slapped me in the face, but everyone agreed that would be ridiculous. There's a chute leading down to a dumpster all set up, but do they bother to use it? No.

With no small effort, I do manage to catch up

with Gorbachevolla. I wave my arms at his flying enormousness.

"Hey there, Gargy-boy! Can you hear me now?"

He looks ahead, like I'm not even there. I chuck a brick at his nose, and he turns his eyes my way long enough to correct me: "I am *Gorgolla*! And I hunger!"

What do you know? He *was* ignoring me. Guess I hurt his feelings. As long as he's holding Yawn-Man, I can't use the spray, so I cleverly poke at his weak points.

"Hey, Gogo-ooh-lah-lah! Sensitive about the puny humans getting your name wrong, huh? You want to project strength. I get it. But if you *really* want the world to, as you say, *feel your might*, I gotta ask why a Living Gargoyle such as yourself would ever be caught dead carrying Mr. Monotonous in his big strong claws? What does it say about you? We are all, like it or not, judged by the victims we torment, aren't we?"

He raises the screamer and gives him a look. "Help! Help! Help!"

I can tell from his disgusted gargoyle expression that he agrees.

"If I were you, I'd trade up, go for someone more attention-grabbing, someone who'll make the world sit up and take notice. Someone…" I puff out my chest, about to say, *like me*—but before I can finish the sentence, the plan works. He drops the screamer.

Because you're *that* good.

And smart, too!

I already said you could stay. You don't have to brownnose me.

Anyway, while Gouda the Poppadum flaps off to look for that special someone, I have to take my eyes off the prize and deal with the victim.

And yes, he screams, "Help! Help! Help!" on the way down.

Feh. I'm not some super zero who goes out of his way to catch every poor shmoe about to go boom on the cement, but he'd still be safely exclaiming in Gorgollapalooza's clutches if I'd kept my mouth shut. It's my bad, so I gotta do something.

Since what I do best is aim and shoot, I pop some caps into the dumpster chute's supports. A few snap, and the slide twists, catching Dull-Boy mid-"help" and saving his dull ass so he can live out the rest of his dull life in dull peace and relative safety.

Because…wait for it…

You're *that* good!

Got that right.

It's a perfect save. Not a hair on his…

Well, maybe not. He hits the slide harder than I expected, and now he's rolling down like a rag doll— or perhaps more accurately, a limp corpse. I *think* he's okay, but it's hard to tell since he's no longer repeating, "Help!"

Damn. Now I have to check on him.

My mistake. No sooner do I get down into the dirty dumpster than he jumps up, wraps his arms around me, and buries his head in my shoulder. And what does he have to say for himself after this life-altering experience?

"Thank you! Thank you! Thank you!"

Awkward.

I pry his nondescript hands off the costume. "Really? That's *all* you've got? Even your gratitude is boring! Just…get out of here! Go! And don't you ever *dare* have an original thought, because it'd just make you see how utterly hollow you are if you did!"

Hands up like it's a bank robbery, he backs away. "Okay, okay, okay!"

"Come on! I mean, you couldn't even keep a *hungry monster* interested!"

Speaking of which, the Brobdingnagian Gorgolla is taking my advice to heart while choosing his next target. Remember that racetrack? The one I said had nothing to do with the story last chapter? Turns out, it has plenty to do with this one.

"Gorgolla hungers!"

And when hunger calls, who am I to wait for the machine to pick up, hoping it will leave a message at the sound of the tone? Sure, maybe it's just a solicitor, but how can I be sure? No, I say to you, sir and madam, when hunger calls, I do not sit on the couch; I go running, joyfully, toward the sound.

Ahem. Yonkers Raceway, over a century old, is part of the fabulous World Casino—a name that sounds like it's from a comic, which is appropriate, since it looks like a bit of Vegas that fell from the sky. Complete with rainbow lights a-flashing, the complex boasts full-service gambling, lush restaurants, and Manhattan-style comedy nights. But it's the multicolor artsy-fartsy webbed canopy hanging over the entrance that attracts our attention-seeking gargoyle.

The colored lights make for a nice contrast with His Grayness (wish you could see it!), but I hear him smacking his lips when he spots what's beyond it. He's over that canopy..and headed for the half-mile oval track on the other side faster than the babysitter's boyfriend when the parents' car pulls up.

What's the draw? The first harness race of the evening, already in progress.

Harness racing?

That a Fifty Shades *bondage thing?*

Can you get my mind out of the gutter for a second? Harness racing is like Ben Hur, only sitting down, with the jockeys riding two-wheeled race bikes called sulkies. To Gorgolla, it's meals on wheels.

Ignoring things like entrance fees and security guards, I make for the track. I'm in eyeshot just as eight gorgeous Standardbred trotters thunder around the last turn into the home stretch.

And what a race it is! Two of the horses take turns nosing into the lead. One second, Bringing the Bacon pulls ahead! Then it's Daddy's Debt! Hold on—odds-favorite Tasty Cornballs is coming up from the inside. He's neck-and-neck with Daddy's Debt! The finish is seconds away, folks. Or is it?

Can you believe it? Gorgolla the Living Gargoyle, A.K.A. Fifty Shades of Grey, swoops down behind the pack, his outstretched wings raising a major dust cloud. In a seamless partnership between man and beast, the jockeys and their animals look back and see Fifty Shades nipping at their shod heels!

The lead horses pass the finish line and keep going. The race is on again!

And the crowd goes wild! Not like you'd think, either. I expected them to run off because of, you know, the monster. Nope. They're either one tough group, or they're so used to special-effects extravaganzas they think this is part of the show.

They're clapping their hands and cheering their horses.

Who can blame them? Look at those nags move! It's like they're running for their lives. Because they are! Even long-shot Vegemite Sandwich, in last position, is giving it her all. Fifty Shades may have started out strong, but going into the first turn, he's flapping like crazy just to keep up!

No. Looks like the Garg was holding back! He's gaining. Vegemite Sandwich pours it on, staying inches ahead. Coming out of the turn, it looks like she's gonna make it, but...

Oh!

Too slow.

Fifty Shades grabs her like a gummy horse, pops her in his mouth, and has her for lunch.

Vegemite is down under.

Like you didn't see that coming?

Lucky for the jockey, Vegemite's a mouthful. The horseless sulky spills, but the little guy gets up quick, like his pants need to dance, and hightails it out of the way before Fifty Shades can swallow.

I thought Gorgolla was more about showing his might, but I guess munching living flesh is a thing with these monsters. Maybe their mutated metabolism is unstable. Not that the desire for world conquest is a sign of stability.

That aside, unless I'm misinterpreting the moral impetus implied by the current scenario, we've reached that special moment where ethics not only allows me to snuff the oversize Boulder-Boy—it practically demands it.

Yay, ethics!

I heave and ho the slo-mo spectators, making a path for myself as I slip the nano-catalyst into my hand. What with all the brouhaha, getting a clear shot is tough. But after a lot of bobbing and weaving, I've got it. One quick squeeze, and Googly the Search Engine that Could will be a big, wet puddle of love.

Rats. It's never that easy, y'know? There's always some *but* or *until* or *suddenly*. In this case, I'm about to do the hero thing when some thick-armed hippophile comes up and grabs my arm. When I say thick-armed, I don't mean muscular—I mean fat. We're talking hogzilla ham hocks. I have no idea how he stuffed those suckers into that shirt, let alone the vest. And adding to the porcine aura, he's got this short, scratchy hair on both his head and face, like a pot-bellied pig.

Not that this is about fat-shaming. He carries it well. It works for him. But then this reject from *The Island of Dr. Moreau* actually grabs my *hand*. He gets his shower-gel smell all up in my face and asks, "What're you doing?"

What am I doing? I've done *lots* of things I think need explaining, but trying to save a bunch of people from a rampaging behemoth isn't one of them. I'm so gobsmacked that instead of coming up with a clever retort, I point at the big gargoyle, like it's not obvious, and spell it out.

"I'm going to stop that monster and save those horses."

Hogzilla shakes his big-ass head. "I bet my mortgage Daddy's Debt is going to do three laps before that thing gets to him. Let 'em finish the race!"

Overhearing, a tall, thin, coiffed hairdo with angry glasses shakes her bony fist at me.

"Yeah! Let 'em finish!"

Next thing I know, I'm surrounded by a crowd that makes *me* look sane. I don't know if they're sleek pro gamblers, mad-eyed addicts, or tourists who just like shouting. Their hands are all over me, like *Night of the Living Debt*, or *Day of the Locusts*, or *Afternoon of the Airheads*. They're all angry, and they're all shouting:

"Let 'em finish! Let 'em finish!"

I'm hallucinating, right? Like the basketball game with Sophie?

No.

Don't think so.

If I'm the voice of reason, we're in trouble. "Hey, I'm as much for collateral damage as the next guy, but even if you set aside the poor horses, don't any of you care about the jockeys?"

They stop and stare. Maybe I got through to them, awakened their better angels, slapped them sensible, verbally kicked them into catharsis. Only they're not staring at me—they're staring at the track. They only stopped shouting to watch another Standardbred get turned into a horse d'oeuvre. I only hope Tasty Cornballs lived up to her name.

The losers wail their loss. The rest, Hogzilla and Angry Glasses among them, cheer their still-charging nags.

You *sure* I'm not hallucinating?

Your guess is as good as mine.

Time to get my hands dirty. In other words, I start shooting. (Yeah, okay, not *at* anyone, but the loud bang-bangs get the idea across.)

"Everybody *out* of the gene pool!"

Most of them scatter like good little primates with a functioning survival instinct. Not Hogzilla. He's still staring at the race. Sheesh. This guy's got a major monkey on his back.

That reminds me: I always wondered why a monkey on your back is a metaphor for addiction. Those little guys are as adorable as puppies. Don't you wish we still had organ grinders, publicly cranking their boxes while their well-dressed simian pets collect coins?

I know I do.

Hogzilla—bulging eyes locked on the track, tickets clenched in meaty paws—is not budging. I could go around, but like a mountain, he's there, so I climb over him. Reaching his peak, I give him a kick.

That gets him moving. "Keep running!" I tell him. "It works!"

I jump the rail and plant myself center track. Once Daddy's Debt passes by, there'll be nothing but dusty air between me and Gurgles the Garbanzo. He's coming, wings outstretched, arms reaching down.

"When they see how powerful I am, the Earthlings will be easy to enslave!"

Clearly a Living Gargoyle in his prime. Not so much on the clear thinking. "Look, Geegle, putting aside the fact you've got a piece of horse stuck in your teeth, are you sure you're dug in on the slavery thing? Economically, a free market with a thriving middle class would provide many more eager, educated consumers."

Ah, he's not listening. He's too busy watching his previously gawking crowd hoof it toward the parking lot.

He veers toward them. "Humans! Behold my might!" He sounds a little sad.

Mindful of the irony, I hoot and cheer. "Run, you crazy bastards, run!"

And the race is on! After a quick stop to place some bets, I rush over to watch. Look at 'em move! It's like they're running for their lives! Even Hogzilla is giving it his all. And there goes Angry Glasses, taking down anyone in her way, leaving others in the path of certain destruction just to buy herself a few more precious seconds of life, sweet life.

Hogzilla tries to edge ahead, but Angry Glasses trips him and runs right over him! Recognizing that she may be that special someone, Fifty Shades gets closer. But, man oh man, she pours it on. It's Angry Glasses, inches ahead. Angry Glasses, almost at the door of her SUV. Angry Glasses, pressing the key fob and unlocking the doors! It looks like she's gonna make it, but…

Oh!

Fifty Shades almost had her, but she dives and slides *under* the SUV! What a move! And it's not over yet. He grabs the whole dang car and lifts. Angry Glasses tries to crawl away, but there's no place left to go!

Mrrr. Can't really let this happen, can I? No, really. Can I? Pretty please?

No.

You can't.

Oh, fine. You know you're both starting to sound like Preston?

I make for a streetlight near the fracas and then hand-over-hand my way to the top. From there, it's a dazzling leap onto Gumby the Lady Gaga. I land on his broad back, latch on to the rocky nape of his neck, and plunge my katana into his thick, turgid flesh.

"Feel *my* might, Gargles?"

Wounded, at least for the moment, he roars. As he twists, I ride him like a mechanical bull—a really big, gray mechanical bull. Say, I'm pretty good at this! What the hell. I toss one hand up and shout, "Yee-hah!"

Never underestimate the beast you're riding. When I yell, he lurches forward and I go rolling like water off a gargoyle. I hit a Prius that still has the sales sticker in the window. Lucky for me, those hybrids are pretty soft. The car crunches, absorbing most of the impact.

The Living Goebbels is pissed. So pissed, his priorities are shifting. Now he's less into showing his might and more into killing me. He rushes toward me, but I've got the nano-spray out, and I'm sure as hell close enough to hit the target. Finger on the button, I'm about to end this race for good. But (there's always a *but…*) Gurgles doesn't like what he sees. Sensing the danger, he stretches his wings to the max and gives them a great big flap.

Whoosh!

Not being aerodynamically correct, I go flying backwards off the car and down to the ground. Not being aerodynamically correct, either, but much lighter, the nano-catalyst goes flying like a piece of paper caught in a tornado. And where, oh where, does the deadly aerosol of annihilation go flying, pray tell?

Remember that reservoir I told you about? The one providing fresh, clean water for millions? The one I *swore* would have absolutely nothing to do with that chapter, like the horses and the raceway?

Yeah, it's headed that way.

Turns out Chekhov was right, even if he is dead.

SIX

GORT the Gitchee-Gumee wants to crush me ever so badly, but big airborne monsters don't turn easy, so I've got a few seconds before I have to deal with him. I flip to my feet, because sometimes simply standing isn't enough, and put some distance between us by bouncing car-to-car all parkour-like.

Making my way across the parking lot toward the gleaming waters of the reservoir, I spot the nano-catalyst, glinting as it tumbles. I track it down, down, down, until a patch of junk pines blocks the view.

It's either landed in the trees, which I guess would be okay, or it's on the reservoir access road on the other side, which wouldn't be too bad, or it's *in* the reservoir, which could be really bad. If you're fond of people.

I'm an optimist, so I head for the pine patch first. It's so dark, I can't see the can for the trees. I'm on my knees like I'm looking for a contact lens when Googolplex fixes the lighting issue by flying *through* the trees, uprooting a swath of tree trunks. Between the dangling roots and brown dirt, a treasure trove of shiny things shakes loose.

"Gorgolla will decimate you!"

No time for semantic corrections now. I start sorting. Beer can. Beer can. Soda can. Gum wrapper.

Aerosol nano-catalyst. Beer can. Beer can. Beer bottle. Classy. Shroud of Turin? What's that doing here? Beer can. Beer bottle *label*. Wait! Hold it! What was the fifth thing I said?

Gorgolla's shadow over me, I snatch the gleaming metal cylinder, spin onto my back, aim up at His Rockiness, press, and…

…nearly cut my finger off on the bent pop-top.

Damn. Beer can.

"Feel my might!"

Where the hell…? I turn to look. Oh, there it is! Got it. But you know what they say about turning the other cheek? Not always a good idea. As I twist back to take my shot, my other cheek meets a big, gray fist.

Powerful blows come and go in my line of work, but this is a good one! Long before the pain registers, I'm up out of the dirt and into the air. I see pulsing lights, the kind you get when you close your eyes and stare at your eyelids. Mine tend to be cherry red. Gorgolla says something about conquering our puny race as soon as he has another gnosh, but his voice is muffled and distant, consumed by rushing air.

My vision clears in time to see the lovely neighborhood of brick houses I'll be dropping on shortly. Nice digs. A couple have in-ground pools. Not the one I land in, though. That one has an attached greenhouse.

Crunk!

Used to have a greenhouse, anyway. The broken

glass and ceramic pots barely sting, but the pain from that punch catches up with me.

Oh boy, that hurts.

Pain isn't the only thing catching up with me. Gorgy-Boy takes a shortcut through the house. And when I say *through* the house…all that's left is a smoking pile of brick, mortar, splintered wood-frame, and select crackling electronics. Good thing no one was home.

I'm ready for him. While he's busy shaking house dust from his eyes, I'm eating the distance between us with my blades out. I shove both my bad boys so deep into his rocky gut that my hands and arms almost go in with them.

For my effort, I get a startled "Yearghh!"

I want to hit him again, harder, but first I have to get the swords back out. While I'm up on him, bracing my feet against his abdomen and pulling at the hilts, he tries to swat me again. I see it coming far ahead of time, so I cleverly position myself so that his titanic blow (*Thud!*) sends me shooting right back where I came from: the patch of fallen trees where the nano-catalyst landed (*Whoosh!*).

No, really. I wanted that to happen.

Sure you did.

If you say so.

Smart-asses. Sure, the landing was rough, but if I didn't plan it, how'd I wind up on my feet all the way over here, halfway to the nano-catalyst with the Living Git all the way back there wondering where

I've gotten to? Tell me that, why don't you?

Sometimes I wish I could pull you both out of my head so I could slap you.

Trust me, there's plenty of self-abuse going on in here.

And harness racing!

I go for the can. Gorgolla, already healed, decides against flying and makes like the Hulk, jumping on over in one huge leap. Pretty good aim, too. One foot lands to my left, the other to my right. I don't want to tell you what I see when I look up.

Okay, I will. It's rocks. All rocks.

His flapping wings cause another rumble and rush, and *again* the freaking can goes sailing toward the reservoir! With no trees left to stop it, it flies up and over the water.

Some days you just can't keep the drinking water safe no matter how hard you try.

Luckily, there's a fenced walkway stretching diagonally across the water. I know, I know, but really! It's totally there, I swear. Check it out on Google Earth. The can hits it, bounces, and rolls.

Never turn your back on a Living Gargoyle. With a hearty, "Feel my might!" Gorgolla picks me up and makes for the sky. In seconds we're alone at last, the stars above, the twinkling lights of Yonkers below. I look down, trying to see what the can's up to, but my date keeps going up, up, up. The air gets colder. I think he's planning to fly to the moon.

He can't do that, can he?

Why not? Cartman's friends once built a ladder up to Heaven.

Gotta get to the can quick. And yes, I know what that sounds like. I let loose a flurry of punches—a flurry, I tell you! Gargoyle pieces fly. I keep at it, pummeling his granite skin with such a steady beat I suspect it'd be fun to dance to.

Wincing, Gargolla draws me up so we're face-to-face. "I will annihilate you!"

I flash an *okay* sign. "There you go! Annihilate works! Not so hard to pick the right word when you try, is it? But uh…how exactly are you gonna annihilate me? Squish me? Won't work. Punch me? You tried that already."

His brow furrows. It even makes a noise because of the rocks. He's not sure.

I get smug. "Eat me?"

Uh-oh. The Merc with a Mouth does not know when to shut up. Gorgolla's eyes go wide, and he sucks my arm into his mouth like it's a piece of ziti.

"Hey! I was kidding!"

I yank it out, but not fast enough. Stony teeth clamp on my wrist. The arm comes free, but I really don't like the flesh-and-bone-tearing sound it makes when it does. Next thing I know, I'm staring at a bloody stump.

"You bit off my hand! What is *wrong* with you? Spit it out! Spit it out, now!" No rolled newspapers around, but I glare at him to show him I mean business.

He just swallows and smacks his lips.

"You ate it? You *ate* my hand? You are going to be *so* sorry you did that!"

Can't use two katana, but I can still use one. Faster than Jiminy Cricket can wish on a star, I cut into the stone where his right wing meets his back.

"Eat this!"

The ensuing "Aghhh!" is satisfying. I particularly enjoy the part where he arches in agony and lets go of me. One-handing the hilt, I let my weight pull the blade until the whole wing detaches. As I hook onto his shoulder with my bent legs, I watch the wing drop down, down, down, twisting like a helicopter seed from a maple tree, only gray and vaster.

Reeling, Gorgolla grabs at the cut. "Foolish Earthman! We'll both plummet!"

He makes a good point, but I'd prefer a less sexist term, like *Earthling* or *Earther*. I do indeed notice, though, that we're moving faster toward the ol' home planet.

"I admit I wasn't really thinking things through, but dude, you *ate my freaking hand!*"

The stars spin in celestial indifference. Less indifferent, but also spinning, the giant gargoyle tries to yank me off his back. I make myself like that itchy spot you can't reach. I need my one hand to keep hold, so I can't punch him, but I can kick. I sheathe my katana, then wrap my fingers tight around his pointy ear and let loose with my combat-trained tootsies:

Kick-kick-kick!

Not really hurting him, but it bugs him. Bugs him so much, he cries out: "Stop it! Stop it!"

Kick-kick-kick!

He tries to return the favor, but Gringold the Grinch can't get his feet up high enough. I try to stay on top so I'll land on him; he tries to stay on top so he'll land on me. And there we are, accelerating toward that terminal-velocity thing discussed earlier (there will be a test!), locked in an exciting, madcap dance. But like Tommy Smothers (or John Lennon, or Allen Saunders) said: Life is what happens when you're busy making other plans.

His missing wing grows back. It's sort of like time-lapsed flower petals opening to the morning sun, or super-slo-mo footage of a corn kernel popping in a microwave. Once it's whole, he spreads both wings wide, slowing our momentum with a dizzying loop-de-loop.

I hold on with my three whole appendages, but it's not the same anymore. I'm totally self-conscious again. *My* hand won't be back for hours. Why does *he* get to regenerate faster than me? Why? Why?

Oh, honey.

There will always be those lesser and greater than yourself.

No! I'm special, too! I am! Sophie! Look at me! Look at me! I'll get a dog, I swear!

Lest a certain middle-school-basketball hallucination return, I keep my focus on my stump. I grunt and strain.

"Ungh! Come on, hand! You can do it! Urgnnnghh! Grow, damn you, grow!"

All I get is a blood spurt from a severed artery. Adding insult to injury, it shoots up my nose. The monster—that big bully—laughs at me.

"If that's your best, Earth will be easy to conquer!"

I hide my bloody stump behind my back. "Stop watching me! I'll show you!"

On the reservoir walkway below, death in a spray can rolls. Slowly, yes, but surely—like that one last turning pig in Angry Birds. Closer and closer it gets to the water, ever closer, closer still, and closer yet again, until...

SEVEN

DON'T you hate books with really short chapters, like this one?

EIGHT

GRAY monster = huge.

Nano-catalyst aerosol can = small.

But is it the size of the wand, or the magic it performs?

His Stoniness all but engulfs my field of vision. Right now, one of my hands, my *favorite* hand (sorry, Lefty, it's just true), is being digested by whatever acidic juices Gorgolla's internal organs produce. I'm in the middle of a battle royale—all pow, bam, and smack, all…

"Feel my might!"

"No, you!"

But it's that can, that itty-bitty, teeny-weeny can, way, way down there—battered, dented, but still round enough to roll—that seems so much bigger than Gorgolla. The struggle between its fading momentum and the growing inertia feels like the groaning of a world.

The suspense is killing me. I'm really into it. I even give Gorgolla an extra turn at smacking me so I can watch the can longer. How many turns before the end? One? Two? As many as it takes licks to get to the chewy center of a Tootsie Roll pop?

I try not to blame myself, but it's tough to blame Gorgolla. He's just doing what monsters do. It's even tougher to blame the can. Not being connected to any neural or mechanical network that would allow it to actualize its desires, it clearly lacks agency.

Then again, maybe it does have a will of its own. Some say information *wants* to be free (mostly to justify illegal downloading). Tree-huggers believe the Earth is conscious (and what they're smoking is mostly legal these days). We speak of hive minds, group minds, Minecraft minds. Why not a can mind? What might it be thinking?

Roll, roll, roll. Roll, roll, roll.

Or: *Oh, no, I'm going to kill millions! Sure wish I could stop myself!*

Could it ask itself the big questions? *A canner can can anything that he can, but a canner can't can a can, can he?*

Most important, could I make it feel guilty?

In any case, there's no way I'm getting to it in time.

But I gotta try. I crawl over to Gorgolla's shoulder like he's a Living Jungle Gym, and he gets all prissy.

"Cowardly Earthling! Instead of daring to face me, you go behind my back?"

"Duh! But there's madness to my method, G. From here, I can get my one and only hand around the base of your left wing—like *so*. And with a little stretch, wrap my ankles around your right wing—like *this*. Now, I twist my mighty fine body sideways— like *that*—and whoo-hoo! You're going down! Okay, technically, *we're* going down!"

Rocky couldn't care less. "Talk all you like, Earthling—"

"Thanks, I will. Blah-blah-blah-blah!"

"—even if you force me to land, what will you do then?"

Good question! If the nano-catalyst has rolled into the water, I could try to steer us toward the drink and jump off at the last second. But hey, what do you know? There's the can now.

And it's not alone.

Preston and the S.H.I.E.L.D. cavalry? Nope. The deadly nano-catalyst has somehow found its way into the slender black-gloved hands of an incredible hunk of drop-dead feminine pulchritude. She's got exactly the kind of body I think about on lonely nights.

That is one hot MMFF (Mysterious Masked Female Figure) I'm falling for.

Or toward.

She's got an oh-so-tight black bodysuit with tiered cape and red highlights that covers not only her body, but also her face. With a bod like that, how can she possibly not have a great face to go with it? With a bod like that, who cares? Not that I'm shallow. I swear I'll love her no matter what she looks like. If she looks like that, I mean.

Better yet, soon as we're close enough, she raises the can and zaps Gorgolla.

"Feel my…"

One second I'm grabbing rock; the next, I'm in the middle of a big old bloop of gooey pink goodness.

It goes splooshing down into the—ahem—potable water. I make an acrobatic flip that lands me on the walkway.

Yeah, all that stuff went right into the reservoir. I think Preston said something about the nano-catalyst being rendered inert once it bonds with a target, but that might've been something I heard on TV. Oh well, I'll deal with that later.

Right now, I've got a rocking lady to impress.

I strut on up to my rescuer, nonchalantly flicking goo from my suit. I'm all full of nasty ideas about how to express my gratitude should she provide consent.

"My, my, my! Pierce my ears and call me drafty! Have I died and gone to heaven? Because you look like an angel. Who might you be?"

She aims the nozzle my way. I try to be sensitive to subtle body signals, so I take this as a sign I should slow down and give her space.

"And…uh…why are you pointing that at me?"

Even though she didn't ask, my hand shoots up in surrender, because that's the kind of thing a lady shouldn't have to ask a gentleman to do when she's threatening his life.

"Call me…Jane." Her voice is like music, only without any recognizable melody. So in fact it's nothing like music.

"Jane. That's a lovely name. Means divine gift. You know, Jane, I realize we just met, but I want to make it absolutely clear that you're holding like the only thing on the planet that can kill me."

Probably shouldn't have said that out loud.

Damn. I'd have gone with, "You know, that won't have any effect on me."

"Can we start over?" I put my hand down, step backwards, and strut toward her again. "Well pierce my ears and call me drafty! Who're you?"

She lowers the can a bit. I think she smiles. "I'm not here to hurt you, Wade Wilson. I admit, I find men who fall from the sky and try to flirt appealing, but trust me—I'm the last person you want to be involved with."

"Who's the first? I mean, why would you say that about your…?"

I take a half-step closer. The nozzle shoots up again, inches from my nose.

"Forgive my caution, but I can't let the dizzying rush of pheromones between us distract me. There isn't much time. I have to make sure you hear me out before your S.H.I.E.L.D. employers arrive."

"Hear you out? Deal!" I sit down on the walkway, cross-legged, and put my chin to my stump. "Talk to me, girl, I'm here for you."

She sighs. "It's Dick."

"Isn't it always?" I nod sympathetically. "Testosterone can be so…testy."

"You don't understand. Dick and I were involved. He used to be…" She turns away shyly. "…my partner."

"We all have baggage. It's part of being alive."

"*He's* the one behind the canine mutations. I

thought I knew him—I thought we shared the same goals—but now he only cares about using his monster army to take over the world. I'm…I'm…afraid of him."

I stand up. She turns my way, and our eyes meet. There's electricity between us. Not Electro-electricity—the romantic kind. I take her hand, the one not holding the can, in mine. She resists, briefly, then gives in, trembling.

There's a relieved little laugh in my voice. "Oh, Jane. The past's not important. The only thing that matters is how we feel about each…wait. If Dick wants these monsters to form some sort of army, why did he ship them out to pet stores?"

"Allergies. He plans to collect them once they've changed, but—"

"Did he consider shots?"

"That takes years. He said there wasn't enough time, but—"

"I'll bet he's secretly afraid of needles and doesn't want to admit it. They have this cream that numbs your skin—"

"Will you stop interrupting? I want to—"

"Sorry. I won't do it again."

"You just did. The thing is, I need to ask you—"

"Yeah, but that was the last time. I swear."

"I WANT TO HIRE YOU TO FIND DICK AND KILL HIM!"

I take a step back, put a pinky in my ear, and wriggle it. "You don't have to shout. I don't do that hired-killer kind of contract work anymore. I don't kill anyone or anything unless they really deserve it. Not even for you."

Beneath the mask, her eyebrows twitch. "If Dick lives, his monster army will kill millions of people. Deserving enough for you?"

I shake my head. "No, not if I stop his monsters as planned."

"I'll pay you twice whatever S.H.I.E.L.D. is paying you."

"I don't care about money."

She steps closer. The fabric covering our lips touches.

She whispers, "I'll do whatever you want."

"I want a retainer and my spray can back."

She hands me the nano-catalyst and a thick envelope. I have no idea how she managed to keep it hidden under that skintight outfit—but hey, I carry two katana, a pair of Glocks, a teleporter, and the nano-catalyst, so who am I to throw stones?

I open the envelope and rifle through the bills inside. I pretend I'm counting them—but hell, I'm so taken with Jane, I don't even know if they're real or counterfeit. I mean, what year was Salmon P. Chase president?

I look up. "Where can I find this Dick?"

I hope you're not asking us.

Girl's gone, dude.

So she is. That was fast.

I mistake the sudden wind for an ache in my

heart. It's the S.H.I.E.L.D. hover-fliers arriving on the scene. Two of them skim the reservoir's surface with those vacuum-hoses, sucking up the gooey badness left by Gargy's water landing. The third hovers right in front of me.

I barely have time to hide the cash in my costume before the door opens and Agent Preston leans out. Always a pro, she expresses her displeasure with my performance by screaming very loudly. "In the *reservoir*, Deadpool? The reservoir? Thank heavens the nano-catalyst binds with the first bioform it contacts! What was I thinking letting you run around with it in the first place? Hand it over."

To ease the tension, I launch into my best Jimmy Stewart impression. "Now, now, hold on, hold on just a cotton-picking minute, there, Emily! If it *binds* with anything, can you really call it a catalyst? I mean, I always thought a catalyst causes a chemical reaction without undergoing any change itself. You see what I'm saying here, don't you, Emily?"

It doesn't help. "Shut up! I didn't name the damn thing. It's part nanobot with a modest artificial intelligence, which is more than I can say for you! There's security-camera footage of you trying to bet on which fleeing civilian is going to make it!"

Now I'm hurt. "What're you, like Captain Renault in *Casablanca*, shocked to see that there's gambling going on at a racetrack? I saved all the people, didn't I? And I have to say, I don't care for your tone."

"Plus you lost three horses!"

I think about doing John Wayne—but seeing how well Stewart went over, I decide against it. "It's not like *I* ate 'em. I didn't even so much as use an *I could eat a horse* joke. I wanted to work one in, but there wasn't time."

"Hand it over."

I put the can behind my back. "Hand what over?"

The hover-flier weapons system clicks as it locks on me. Won't kill me, but it could be very inconvenient. I hold out the can.

"Oh. You mean this?"

"Yes. That. Now."

I toss it to her. "Come on, Preston. We both know you wouldn't have shot me."

"You're right. I couldn't risk destroying the dispenser."

"That's cold."

When she looks over the dents in the can, her face goes from worried back to angry. "Think that's cold? How's this? Your ass is fired, Wade. I don't care what I owe you, or how good you are, the crazy is just too much. Even when you mean well, you're dangerous. I'm not risking the public's safety or my job for you anymore. Jeff's barely eight, but he'll graduate school eventually, and S.H.I.E.L.D. has a tuition-benefit program I can't afford to lose."

"Fired?" I show her my stump. "I lost a hand over this! You mean I'm on probation, right? Like I have to attend an anger-management class even though we both know I should be teaching one, right?"

"No, Wade. I mean you're fired. Like this."

With an airy *fsh* (as opposed to a mechanical *vrt*), the door closes. The other hover-fliers retract their hoses, and then all three zoom off.

I am alone, surrounded by water once again rendered potable.

As alone as you get.

You should probably be thinking about how you could have done a better job here.

But you're not, are you?

No. I'm thinking about Jane.

NINE

NOT only am I glum—'cause I lost my hand, my job, and the first woman I instantly fell in love with since Sophie—now I discover that the guy writing this book is out of it today, too. Maybe my gloom's catching, but he's all, "Here I am, in my fifties, no job security, why don't my books sell as well as Stephen King's?" Boo-hoo-hoo.

Hey!

You're ruining the suspension of disbelief!

Really? *That* ruins it? I talk meta-this, meta-that, break the fourth wall from here until Ragnarok, and mentioning the book has an author *ruins* it? The readers know the deal. It's not like the title page is a carefully guarded secret. What the hell difference does it make *whose* head I'm a voice in?

I just think you're pushing your luck.

Enough is enough.

Don't you tell me what to—

Guys, guys, can we get past this? I'm sorry I'm moping, but I've got a deadline.

You keep out of it! How many fonts are you going to use in this thing, anyway? It already looks like a mess.

I just thought…

Yeah, you just thought. That's your problem, just

thinking. Go have yourself some frakking coffee for pity's sake. Let the professionals handle the being-fictional thing, okay, Mr. I've-Got-a-Real-Life?

Fine. I'll…I'll…go.

Who was that?

Never mind.

Point being, don't blame me if this chapter's a downer. A long depression requires an emotional consistency that ain't in my playbook. The hand? I already feel some bubbling at the wrist. She'll grow back fine by morning. Getting in good with S.H.I.E.L.D. and finding my beloved MMFF? I've already got a good idea how to make it happen.

Right! We still have the puppy list, so all we have to do is take down the next monster by the book.

And S.H.I.E.L.D. will be sure to take us back!

Huh. I was gonna try searching for Jane on social media, but okay…sure, let's go with your idea about the puppies. Let's see. Dalmatian, Alsatian. Hey, that rhymes! Next is a rough collie pup. I know that one. Isn't that Lassie's breed? This one went to…Charleston Hospice in Astoria, Queens.

Funny—they called the torture chamber where they dumped us Weapon X rejects a hospice, too. But that's like calling John Wayne Gacy's basement a daycare facility.

The dog's probably being used as a comfort animal for the terminally ill residents. Big comfort if it goes all extra-special giant-sized. I'd better get on it.

A quick press of my 'porter, and I'm in the pleasant, walled-off courtyard of a modest, tan brick building. From its looks, it could be a place where people are born just as easily as a place where they go to die. Surrounded by night, I keep hidden in the well-tended shrubbery hugging the wall. Not a lot of security. Why would there be?

I peer through a picture window into some sort of communal room. And here I am—deadliest merc in the multiverse, able to heal from any wound—kind of afraid to go inside.

Not that it reminds me of the Weapon X hospice. After I killed the wrong guy, my keepers stuck me in that torture chamber along with all their other failed efforts to weaponize human beings. At least we could still be used for experiments, right? We dropped like flies. Even had a "dead pool" going to guess who'd be next. In my case, the name stuck. Good times.

So this place isn't that—not by a long shot. It's packed with patients and puppies. Despite the tubes in their arms, the fading strength, and the ebbing days, some are smiling. A teenager—out of it, probably from his meds—absently pets a corgi. It prods and licks his long-fingered hand like it's trying to wake the kid up. An old man looks on alone, patting his knees and laughing—probably thinking if he has to go, now's as good a time as any.

A girl—maybe eight, skin thin and pasty— tosses a ball to an eager German Shepherd. The dog's completely thrilled by everything she does. Then there's a woman whose sharp eyes sparkle as if no disease could ever touch them. She's bald from chemo, sitting in a wheelchair like Professor X's twin sister, and cradling a Labrador in her lap. She looks like she's pouring her heart out. The dog stares back with incredible sympathy.

Guess sometimes it's easier to talk the tough things over with a dog. Makes me wonder what I'm missing. What I missed. Did I miss it?

Something about the scene feels familiar. Did I have a dog and forget? No way.

Why can't I just go in and get on with this, then? Not sure. Maybe it's the sheer normalcy—all the friends, family, and staff trying to make the residents' last days comfortable. Maybe it's because the sense of finality here is less horrific than the Weapon X facility, and somehow that makes it *sadder*. I don't know any of those people in there, but for a sec I wish they were the ones who could live forever, not me.

I said this chapter would be a bummer, didn't I?

It's also the last place you'd want to see some freaky monster, like A the Living B, or C the Thing from D—so I can't keep hanging out here getting all weepy.

Spotting the only rough collie is easy. She's got that narrow head and long coat with shades of tan and a band of white. Extricating her without a fuss will be the hard part. The sweet thing's a favorite—the belle of the ball getting passed from lap to lap.

First step: ask her out and treat her like a lady.

Wait.

That's the MMFF.

Right. First step: Get inside. Already mentioned the lack of security. The nearest side door is propped open by a brick—probably by some orderly planning to grab a smoke, or a resident who thinks a last few ciggies won't make a difference anymore. Walking in puts me in a dark, empty hall right outside the main event.

Second step? Dunno. I'm out of my comfort zone. I want to impress S.H.I.E.L.D., so I can't go in guns blazing or making clever comments on how short life is. But there is something that might work.

I take off my mask.

I already mentioned how I'd hoped Weapon X would cure my cancer, but it didn't. The big C can't make my organs fail anymore—but *it* regenerates, too, leaving my mug a colorful combo plate of scar tissue and pulpy lesions. Some people can wiggle their ears. I can make my face ooze. Without the mask, I figure I can pass as a particularly ugly hospice resident. Once I talk my way in, I'll take a turn with Lassie Jr., offer to walk her in the courtyard, then vanish into the eerie stillness of the night.

I shove the mask in a pocket, cover the costume with a hospital gown and booties, and step into the community room.

I thought it'd smell bad—like the pet store, or at least puppy pee. Nope. Other than a faint antiseptic odor, it mostly feels warm. At first, no one takes their eyes off the puppies. I clear my throat, but everyone's doing that.

Finally, the old man who was slapping his knees spots me. He waddles over, either nearsighted or doing his best not to look horrified.

"You must be Jeff, the new resident. I'm Bill Sloan, pleased to meet you. Sit! Sit down!" He mutters the next bit under his breath. "You poor, poor man."

Hands on my shoulders, he gently pushes me into a chair. "Say hello to Jeff, everybody!"

Slowly, they pivot my way, everyone trying to be polite, everyone trying to hide their reaction—except the little girl. She shrieks and grabs her German Shepherd like she's afraid I'll drip on it.

It gets real quiet. Guess no one feels like asking, "So how you doing?"

The sooner I'm out of here, the better, so I break the awkward silence. "Uh…can I get a puppy?"

Bill moves fast for an old man. He grabs the nearest dog and shoves it into my lap.

"Here."

"Actually, I was hoping to have some time with…"

The woman with the Labrador wheels up and gives me her dog, too. "Take two. You need it more than me."

"She's a cutie pie, all right, but I'd really like…"

"Here, take mine, too."

One after another, they pile on the puppies until I'm buried in cold, burrowing noses, warm foreheads, and tickly snouts.

They're probably trying to cover up your face.

Nah, I really think they're just being nice.

Heh. It does feel pretty good, being surrounded by all this squirming, fuzzy, tickly goodness. The puppies don't care what I look like, who I am, or what I've done. And all this attention from oversized eyes on little bodies isn't a delusion, or even a bunch of Big Eye paintings.

I feel…

Happy?

Dad, can I have a dog?

Where'd that come from?

Dad was a son of a bitch, a military man with a fast hand. Didn't understand me—or like me very much. Did I ever dare ask him for a dog? Do I remember him saying it'd help me learn some discipline? Or am I imagining that?

Between the yips and nuzzling, I almost see his face, almost hear "yeah" coming from his lips.

A dog? Really? For me?

No! Must be strong! Must…escape…sense…of joy!

Hey, where'd the damn collie go? Crap! It was here a second ago. See what I mean about distractions? See?

I jump up and send the dogs flying. Can't say it feels good to shed the puppy love, but this baptism of callousness is definitely more familiar. I scan the room. The door is closing, but before it does, I catch a glimpse of the collie trotting down the hallway like she knows I'm after her.

I hop around the puppies, pushing them out of the way when I have to. The girl shrieks again. A male nurse moves up to me, talking at me like I'm a rearing horse.

"Whoa! Easy, fella! I'm not sure you should be walking."

He gets a good look at my face and backs off.

I hit the door so hard, the force hurls it off its hinges. There's a chorus of gasps and barks behind me, but I can't worry about that now. Matter of fact, I doubt I'll worry about it later. As the door hits the ground, the collie looks back, sees me, and dives out an open window.

She *does* know I'm after her. Or it could be my face.

Either way, I follow. Throwing myself out the window and into the courtyard, I land on an attendant and a doctor. Both are knocked out by the impact.

Lassie? Oh, Lassie? Where'd she get to?

Common sense will tell you dogs can't climb trees. Their legs are too long. They don't have claws to speak of. They're not like cats. YouTube says different, though, and so does the collie. Moving like the dickens, she scrabbles up a Japanese maple's low-hanging branch and in a burst of flying bark jumps the brick wall.

Skipping the tree, I hit the wall and try to spot her course. From here there are only two basic choices. Dead ahead you've got four lanes of Hoyt Avenue, followed by six lanes of 278 and another four lanes of

Astoria Boulevard. That's a grand total of twelve lanes, all packed with jockeying Friday-night traffic. Escape route two? Treelined streets to the left and right—all with tight-packed family housing, and a rat's nest of interconnected alleys and backyards. Smart dog could hide there for weeks without being found.

And which way does the nimnode go? Straight into the big, bad street. Could be that narrow skull pinching her brain, but I've made better choices with an arrow in my head. She ducks the first few screeching cars, and keeps going until a couple of heedless SUVs make her scramble back a lane and wait for an opening.

It's just like *Frogger*.

Now what? If I *knew* she'd change into something ginormous, I might be inclined to think, "Would it be so bad if I let a car hit her while she's still vulnerable?"

What would that be, morally?

A sin of permission?

But I *don't* know. So I run into traffic after her.

All the honking and flashing headlights nearly start up the hallucinations again. I get a flash of faces: my dad at home, Sophie at the basketball game, a broken phone. I don't get the connection.

Further complicating things is the dog's desire to flee from me at all costs. When she sees me catching up, she throws caution to the wind and dives into the next lane. A speeding New York cabbie, who you'd like to think wouldn't be thrown by a sudden obstacle, swerves so quick his cab nearly goes up on two wheels.

The brakes squeal like Wilbur from *Charlotte's Web* if he'd lost that fair and wound up being "some" dinner. The cabbie skids across not one, but two lanes. The first is occupied by a fancy new Acura, the second by some junker I can't imagine getting past inspection even if you bribed the guy. It all makes for a great three-vehicle fender bender. Or as we say in the comics:

WRONK!   (THOK!)   CRASH!

Fun's not over. Car bits are flying, airbags deploying. I spot a tractor-trailer heading straight for my little doggie. I want to say she's frozen like a deer in headlights, but she's a dog—so, really, she's frozen like a dog in headlights.

I leapfrog along, crunching hoods as I go, until I get to the trailer-truck cabin and yank the wheel hard. This surprises a very sleepy driver. When his scruffy cap falls from his scruffy face, he looks at me, I look at him, and we both scream.

The tractor-trailer doesn't stop—because, you know, momentum—but it does jackknife, making a nice V shape around the collie. The moan of creaking metal and screeching rubber snap her out of her high-beams staring contest. After nearly getting ground into—that's right—dog food by the wheels, she leaps up onto the grill.

When the truck finally does come to a halt, she looks so much like a cute hood ornament that the driver and I smile at each other. Then he starts screaming again. Before he can compare me to some nightmare, I conk him.

It's better this way. Now he won't have to see all those cars smashing into his rig. There are so many, I won't even bother with all the sound effects. As long as I'm waiting for all the crashing and shaking to stop, I pull my sporty red-and-black mask back on and lose the hospital gown.

As one of the few costumed types who looks *less* freakish in his suit, I'm hoping this will calm the pup long enough for me to get my paws on her. I kick the windshield just right so it flops forward and slides to the street. As I'm crawling onto the hood, the dog does this acrobatic leap onto the roof of a westbound FedEx truck—because, you know, it absolutely, positively had to be there.

As it speeds off, she looks back at me. She's pleased as can be—ears perked, fur ruffled, tongue lolling. She thinks she's smart, but I'm one up on her. I know dogs are communal animals, engineered by evolution to be part of a pack and obedient to the alpha dog. I put on my most commanding voice and shout, "Get over here, now!"

Didn't work with Gorgolla, doesn't work here.

"Yip!" she says, turning away to enjoy the breeze.

The tractor-trailer driver, awake again, crawls out on the hood toward me.

"Yes, sir."

"Not you!"

Now I'm chasing a freaking truck, like *I'm* the dog. I stop—partly to maintain my own dignity, partly because I can't run as fast as a truck. A taxi squeals to a halt behind me. The cabbie, face sour as a grapefruit, sticks his head out.

"Hey, buddy, what's your problem?"

I put my hand on his hood. "I don't have a problem, buddy. You do."

I climb onto his roof and hold onto the "Off Duty" light like it's a surfboard tip. I howl to the driver and the world, "Follow that collie!"

You'd think cabbies wait their entire lives to hear something like that, but this guy goes so slow that— well, choose one:

a)   The zombies will catch up.

b)   It'll take us two hours to watch *60 Minutes*.

c)   We'll get a parking ticket.

I shake the suspension. "Faster, you fool! The villain is getting away!"

"I'm already twenty over the limit!"

"Speed limit? We don't need no stinking speed limit!"

I drive a katana through the roof, avoiding the driver (except for a little of his pants leg), and stab the pedal to the metal. The engine revs; the axles turn.

Now we're moving! I roll my mask half-off so I can loll *my* tongue out the side of my mouth. Always wanted to try that. It tastes like…victory!

Below me, something wakes within the dormant cabbie. Summoned by a law far deeper than speed limits, he obeys. No longer afraid, a mad glint in his eyes, he wheels wildly from lane to lane, cutting off Audis and Hondas alike.

Trouble ahead? Not for this man. Despite seemingly insurmountable odds—and a pair of pimped-out Humvees—he bounces up on the median and back down mere yards from the FedEx truck.

We pull up alongside. I can see the driver. He's just a kid, fresh out of school, trying to do the right thing, caught up in this lousy, stinking war. His eyes stay dead ahead, his mind on his job.

I have the cabbie give the truck a little nudge to get his attention.

Now he sees me. "Slow down and pull over! It's really important!"

But being a one-handed guy in a black-and-red costume riding atop a speeding cab doesn't get you the same deferential treatment it used to. Instead of slowing down, the truck driver speeds up, veering toward an exit ramp marked "Ditmars Blvd."

All the while, mini-Lassie is looking at me, smug, satisfied, doubtless thinking:

Woof! Woof-woof!

Pulling ahead, the kid makes the exit without so much as tapping the brakes. We stay with him as he tries for a left on 23rd. Fans of the NYC Metropolitan Transit Authority will recognize the Ditmars Boulevard Station as the last stop for the N and Q elevated trains running along 23rd Street. Fans of physics will know that taking a sharp turn too fast while speeding in a top-heavy vehicle runs the risk of a rollover. And boy, are we all surprised when it happens!

The FedEx truck flips sideways. Screeching, sparks flying, it rams right into one of the El supports. Behind him, headed straight for the truck, the cabbie laughs madly.

"Good a day to die as any!"

What a loon.

I yank my katana from the accelerator and stab the brakes. Deciding to steer, the driver narrowly avoids the crash. But I go flying over the FedEx truck—and into the girder.

Ow, oh, ow! I sing an ode to ow!

For nothing hurts like pain itself.

And so, I sing to ow!

I'd like to say I leave a Deadpool-shaped outline in the steel, but it's more like there's a girder-shaped outline in my skull. The freaking puppy, meanwhile, is utterly unfazed. She rushes up the steps to the train platform.

I toss the cabbie some bills from Jane's envelope—probably ten thousand—pinch his cheek, and hightail it up to mass transit. Train's cheaper than a cab, anyway, especially when you hop the turnstile. Of course there's a train waiting. Yes, the puppy gets on. And yes, the doors close right before I reach them. I bang on the windows, but that never works. She looks at me, panting, then pretends to read a paper like I'm not even there.

With that weird elephant-fart hiss, the train starts to move.

I run along the platform ahead of it, jump on the track, and run backwards frantically waving my hand. The operator's pretending to read a paper, too. The big hunk of steel on wheels picks up speed. In short order, I'm turning around and running forwards, trying to keep the choo-choo from running me down.

No. Wait, wait, wait. Screw this. No dog's making a monkey out of me. I force my blade into a track and pry a rail from its rivets—just enough to be a pain.

Seeing this, the conductor goes wild-eyed.

"Paying attention to me now, huh?"

The brakes engage. The train doesn't go all screechy-sideways like in *The Fugitive*. By the time it hits the bent rail, it's slowed enough so that it only creaks and twists like it's tired and needs to lie down for a minute.

It's still moaning along a bit, but I climb up on the side and pry a door open.

The collie looks up at me through the flickering lights.

"Nothing personal, but I gotta get you someplace safe in case you turn into a monster."

She twists her head, all *Why didn't you say so?* And hops into my arms.

Sheesh.

Pup under one arm, I climb out and take in the scene. There's a little more metal-on-metal squealing and a few sparks before the train halts, but no one's hurt. In the streets below, the cabbie's gone, off with his next fare, our time together just a memory. I do see a certain young FedEx driver jumping up and down as his truck bursts into flames.

To the east, I see smoke and a few fires from some of the wrecked cars.

And I hear a sound, one I hear so often it should be on my playlist: sirens wailing.

But at least the puppy's all right.

"Isn't that right, girl? *Who* made this big mess? You did! *You* did! But you're such a sweetie, I'm gonna put you in a box and gift wrap you for Preston. If I forget the airholes you just tell me, okay, baby? One look at you, and S.H.I.E.L.D.'s gotta take me back, right?"

Right.

You bet!

TEN

AS I pat the doggie—mushing her fur, wriggling her head, walking my fingertips along her snout—I wonder how long it will take S.H.I.E.L.D. to notice the carnage we've caused. With street cameras everywhere and folks giddily uploading everything they pick from their noses (#checkoutmysnot), it shouldn't be long before they figure out it's not just any ten-car pileup/subway derailment. Don't like all that surveillance? Chuck out your cell phone and cancel your Internet. Can't blame Big Brother if you keep yanking your trousers down in front of him while he's trying to read, now can you?

I can imagine how it'll play out back at S.H.I.E.L.D.: A pimply-faced MIT grad, black shoes clicking against the hard floor, puffs his way down an insanely long hallway with recessed lighting and the hum of bad electrical wiring. Arriving at the last office and grasping a paper file as a prop, he shouts to his beleaguered section chief:

"I think I've got something, sir!"

They'll be here any minute now.

Any minute.

Huh. Guess all that TMI is tough to sort through. But hey, the DP—meaning me—can't be waiting around all night with a rough collie in his hand. I've things to be, places to do.

So I 'port over to Preston's office at the NYC branch. The room's so dark and cool, compared to the smoking train station, that the collie practically falls asleep. The room's also a little on the austere side. The only personal touches are a family photo of Em with hubby Shane and son Jeff, and a tasteful two-tone print that says, "BREATHE."

Ironic, since I don't think LMDs breathe.

Em, sitting at her desk in an ergonomic chair, is focused on the multiple screens her brown robot eyes project in the air. Hot cup o' Java in one hand, scratching her cheek with the other, she hasn't even noticed me. I tiptoe up and shove Li'l Lassie's wet nose right into her ear.

"Aiee!" she says.

I love it when she says "Aiee!"

Before the hot coffee can hit her vulnerable lap, I snap a pic of her priceless expression and post it on sundry social media.

Better yet, when that coffee hits, I get a second "Aiiee!"

"I'd get some seltzer before that stains, Em. But look, look what I got you!"

I hold out the puppy. The collie and I look at her expectantly.

"I'm rehired, right?"

Before she can answer, we're surrounded by flashing lights, howling sirens, and a digital voice warning that an intruder has somehow breached S.H.I.E.L.D.'s top-notch security. Lockdown is initiated. Metal shielding slams down. Protocols are actualized.

Preston pants a few times before hitting a big green all-clear button. Wonder what the blue one does. Seconds later, a boss-type voice comes over the com. Could be Phil Coulson, or maybe Nick Fury himself. I don't keep up with the continuity. Whoever it is says one word:

"Deadpool?"

Preston closes her eyes. "Deadpool."

The lights and sirens stop; the protective walls recede. And then the yelling starts.

"YOU," Preston begins. "I don't even know what to call you! Dangerous is an understatement, careless is a compliment, and lunatic would be redundant!"

"I know! I put the 'z' in 'crazy,' right?" I try to reassure her. "Don't even try. You'd just sound like a stereotypical police lieutenant chewing out his best cop 'cause he goes outside the lines to get the perp. But look, look! A dog!"

She buries her head in her hands. "Sometimes, Wade, I swear, if it weren't for Jeff and Shane, I'd jump off a building just to avoid dealing with you."

"You don't mean that. Look at the dog!" I hold her out. She yips and wags her tail. The dog, not Em. If Em did that, it'd be weird.

Finally, Em looks.

"From the list?"

"Charleston Hospice, Astoria. This one hasn't gone all monster, but that doesn't mean she didn't put up a fight—right, girl?" I make her paws do a boxing thing, like she's punching. "At least I've been calling her a girl. I never really looked." I lift her up to check. "Yep. Girl. Y'know, in the films and TV show, even though Lassie was supposed to be female, they used male collies 'cause they were heavier and looked more impressive. Some of the stunt doubles were female, though. So…can we test her to see if she's a normal puppy?"

Em shakes her head. "From what we know so far, the transformation's triggered at a sub-cellular level—it literally rebuilds the DNA. Until she actually changes, she'd test as a dog."

"Huh. And who knows how long that'll take? Maybe she just needs a little encouragement." I shake her a bit and hold her up to my ear. Nothing but the pitter-patter of frantic puppy heart.

I tug on her teeth. "Grrr!"

Preston waves her hands at me. "Wade, stop! Just stop! Even if that did work, I wouldn't want her changing into a monster here in my office. Bad enough I've got *you* here."

Just then, a pimple-faced, out-of-breath intern rushes in, prop-file in hand. "Special Agent Preston, I think I've got something!"

Em gives him a look. "Astoria, Carl?"

"Uh…yeah…"

Noticing me, his shoulders slump, and he walks back out.

Preston sighs. "I keep telling him he should just

text or email. I think it gets lonely down in Data Collection."

"Before I pretend to be sympathetic, can we get to the elephant in the room? Am I rehired or what?"

A multitude of expressions ripple across her face. There are a few I've never seen before. "I want to say 'no' in the worst possible way. But the thing is, I was about to contact you."

I do a little dance. "Ha! Nobody else right for the job, huh?"

"Not exactly." She grabs some napkins and starts dabbing the coffee on her outfit. "Tactical analyzed all the footage from the security and traffic cams in Yonkers. They concluded that while your methods weren't…coherent…given your superhuman accuracy, a S.H.I.E.L.D. team might've actually caused more collateral damage. So we had a meeting—department heads, brass. Despite initial appearances, they think you played within the rules."

Rules?

There are rules?

She rolls the napkin into a ball and leans over to toss it into a wastebasket. "Are we gonna find the same true in Astoria?"

"How the hell would I know? I mean…sure!"

Still hunched toward the basket, she looks at me sideways. "Given your unique skillset, the fact that you're considered expendable…"

I bend over to make my head even with hers. "As if I *could* be expended!"

She closes her eyes. "…and the unique level of deniability your public image provides…"

"Denial is a big river in Egypt! That's me!"

"…they decided that the single-agent strategy remains preferable, and that you remain the preferable agent."

I'm so excited, I pull her up to a standing position. "Brace yourself, someone's about to get a hug!"

Usually when I move in for a friendly squeeze, even Galactus can't stop me. Preston keeps me back with a single finger. "HOLD ON. We were still left with one big-ass question: How can we possibly trust you with the nano-catalyst when you almost dumped it in the reservoir?"

"But you backed me up on that one, right, buddy?"

"I was the one who raised the issue."

"Oh. Ow." I take a step back. "Well, if that's how you feel, maybe you should get your own Netflix password for your streaming needs."

"You never gave me your password."

"Yeah, but I could."

She taps her temple, indicating her eyes. "Got all the video I can handle, thanks. But the boys in Tech did come up with this." She turns toward a hard metal case on her desk, which I didn't mention earlier because the writer made it up just now.

She clicks the latches and it opens up, revealing one sweet-looking weapon. It's slick and white—the iPod of guns. "We should've thought of this in the first place—the circuitry is similar to what we used on the Gale Max. But things have been happening so fast, we were forced to improvise."

"So if I get out of line with the nano-catalyst, you'll shoot me with that? You know that trick never works."

She hefts it. "This would. It's a new housing for the nano-catalyst. Our acronym-happy techies call it an ADD: Aerosol Dispersal Device. It's strong enough to withstand a .44 fired at two paces. There's laser targeting, which you probably don't need, but here's the important part." She touches a little grid above the nozzle. "The firing mechanism is only enabled when this sensor detects monster DNA. Point it at anything else, it won't fire. We may actually have found a way to keep the public safe from you."

"Relatively." I nod appreciatively. "Given what you said about the transformation, I couldn't even use it on a potential monster pup—only the big guys. Well, I can't say I like what it says about our trust level, but fair enough. It sure beats the crap out of that spray can when it comes to looks. You sure it works?"

Before I can so much as "Aiee!" she aims it my way and pulls the trigger.

Click.

"Yeah. It works."

"Whoa! Geez, Em. I'm holding a puppy here! What if it didn't?"

"Ha!" She smiles for the first time since I showed up. "It's not loaded yet. Sure was nice to see you jump, though—especially after you shoved that dog in my ear."

"Good one." Remembering my advance from Jane, I bring up another awkward subject. "Long as we're having a laugh about my possible mortality here, how about a little raise? Wouldn't want another employer stealing me away, would you?"

"No."

"Not even like a carpe per diem?"

"I don't even know what that means."

BOOK TWO

OUT,
DAMNED
SPOT.
OUT,
I SAY!

ELEVEN

FOREST Hills, Queens, looks like the love child of the city and the suburbs. There aren't any mega-skyscrapers for me to fall from, but it does have lots of streets with six-story brick apartments on one side and freestanding Tudorbethans on the other.

WTF is a Tudorbethan?

What am I, a dictionary? Go use the Internet.

No McMansions, either, like you'd find in Westchester. Here it's mostly stuff built back when men were men and bricks were bricks, and it was cheaper to build houses out of bricks than men.

Now that I'm back in S.H.I.E.L.D.'s good graces, I'm visiting what the cops once called the "snooze" precinct to track down a Maltese. I did look this one up. It's not the falcon—this one's a snowy white member of the Toy Group, A.K.A. a lapdog. Hate 'em, love 'em, or have 'em for lunch—in dog world, it don't get smaller than a lapdog puppy. Unless it's a mutant, or you're using a shrink-ray, in which case all bets are off. If it starts out that small, I'm hoping it'll change into a smaller monster—like Teeny, the Thing from Under the Cushions.

The target address is on a particularly quiet street. It's a humble one-family that looks cozy even from the outside—exactly the kind of place you'd love to have someone else raise your kids. The sun's just a-rising, garbage men stretching and yawning to greet the day. If the occupants are still in slumberland, it'll make for an easy in and out.

But that wouldn't be fun to read about, would it?

With the collie safely back at S.H.I.E.L.D., I'm on my own. My hand's about grown back, too, but you wouldn't want to look at it. I get a side window open, like a good little second-story man. The residual smell of last night's home-cooked dinner wafts out. Sadly, there's no time to raid the fridge for leftovers. The front door creaks and wobbles open, and I hear the high-pitched chirp of a lapdog.

Bingo. That's not the name of the dog, BTW—as far as I know.

A patient, elderly female voice answers the bark as if she's speaking to a rambunctious great-grandchild.

"Oh, settle down, B. Don't want to wear yourself out before we get to the park."

B. Maybe it *is* named Bingo. Or Bill. Or Bernardo—remember him?

I creep along the roof for a closer look. Creep. Creep. Creep. There's my mini-mutt. The collar's almost bigger than it is. And, man, that's one sweet old lady holding the leash. We're talking *the* little old lady from Pasadena. She's like Ruth Buzzi from *Laugh-In*, an archetypal crone carved in flesh and blood. She looks so frail, I'm afraid if I just nab the dog it may give her a heart attack. Once more, I'll need a subtler approach. Which means, basically, any approach other than my own.

I hop down in front of her, gentle as can be, and give her a gentlemanly bow. "Excuse me, ma'am, I couldn't help but notice what an attractive Maltese you have there!"

Well, that didn't work. I'm not sure who looks more terrified, the lady or the dog, but she screams loud enough for both of them. "Eek!"

My hands shoot up. "Oh, ho! Sorry! You okay there? Didn't mean to startle you! I only…"

Her back arches. Her arms go out, like she's taking some sort of freaky AARP battle stance. For a second, I think *she's* going to turn into a monster.

"Who are you? Get away from me!"

I back up. "Uh…the dog…it's…so sweet. Can I…hold onto him for a second? I'll give him right back. Promise." I cross my heart, pinky swear, but even the mini-mutt doesn't look like it believes me.

While the Maltese yaps at me, the old lady snaps it up quick as a lick and holds it to her chest. "Get away from me, you horrible man! Help!"

I try to laugh it off. "Horrible? You should see me without the mask. Look, I'm not here to hurt you…"

But the feeling isn't mutual. Grandma doesn't hit me with her purse, but the Mace-in-the-Face (Ultimate Strength for Long-Lasting Deterrence!) she sprays in my eyes stings like a sonofabitch.

As soon as I can see again, I'm done being nice. "Gimme that dog!"

She's already making for the door, moving

like Usain Bolt. "You stay away from Benny! Help! Someone help!"

I stomp after her. "I *am* trying to help, lady!"

"Help yourself to my dog, you mean!"

"No! I mean, yes, but you don't understand what you've got there…"

Her Tru-Shot Taser (Why Be Half-Sure?) hits my chest like a cobra strike.

Gzt.

Ow. Not the same as being riddled with bullets—but it's got a kick, *and* it leaves a nice metallic aftertaste in my mouth. Having shrugged off worse, I get my hand on the dog's collar and tug. This lady isn't just feisty, she's strong. She yanks back, I yank again, and all of a sudden we're in a puppy tug o' war. At least she can't mace or tase me while we're both holding Benny, but I'm stuck. I can't pull too hard. The dog could break—or even grosser, the old lady's arm could pop out of the socket. While she seems to have the wherewithal to try to beat me senseless with her own detached limb, she doesn't strike me as the regenerating type. So I try to be gentle, which totally isn't my thing.

"Let go!"

"You let go!"

"No, you!"

Next thing I know, I'm on my ass about five yards away. For a sec, I think Granny emitted an AARP shockwave—some secret, last-ditch defense mechanism for the retired. Only she went flying, too, in the opposite direction. Something threw us *both*.

The dog?

How would a little dog do that?

Wait for it.

Oh, right. Monster dog.

Granted, the Maltese seems extremely pissed. Its tiny body is shifted forward, its tiny tail stiff, its tiny muscles tightened, and its teeny pink gums bared—but that's typical dog-about-to-attack stuff. The deep-throated snarl that rattles the pavement and the way it sends pieces of concrete flying as it scrapes its paws against the sidewalk are not so typical.

It *is* changing, but not nearly as fast and furious as Goom or Gorgolla. Whatever it winds up being, I can't let it run loose in this nice family neighborhood. When it charges my way, I draw my shiny new ADD.

"Lady, close your eyes. Trust me!"

Hm. If she keeps them closed long enough, I can turn Benny to goo, quick-'port to a pet store, buy another Maltese, and hope she doesn't notice the difference.

The mini-mutt almost on me, I hit the button. Nothing happens. I try again. Zilch. Nada. The Big Egg. The ADD won't fire. The darn dog's changing so slowly, the sensor doesn't recognize it yet.

"YIP!"

The top of Benny's surprisingly thick skull (I mean, how do you even fit a brain in there?) hits me square in the chest. Three ribs crack, and bone shards press into my lungs. My arms fly out; my feet lift off. I go zooming in a kind of sitting position until my back hits one of those classy old wrought-iron streetlamps. With a creak, a crunk, a thunk, and the shattering of its glass and my bone, the lamp falls across the peaceful, tree-lined street.

Somewhere, a sleeping baby wakes and cries. Somewhere, a misophonia sufferer, not knowing the source of the racket, wishes she'd turned on her white-noise machine. Somewhere, a car owner will soon wonder what happened to his Mercedes.

Me? I've got to deal with what's in front of me.

"Never mind, lady, keep your eyes open. It'll be easier for you to run!"

But it's not like she's listening. She's too busy grabbing her chest and crying out: "Mercy!"

She's going down!

TWELVE

SENIOR citizen with a health crisis, Maltese slowly transforming into a predatory brute…

Somebody's gotta do something!

You?

You betcha! Feet akimbo to solidify my stance, I shake my finger at the as-yet-still-small dog.

"Play dead!"

Gentle wisps of white fur crisscross its coal-black pupils and yellowed corneas as it glares at me.

"Play dead, damn you! Play dead!"

It won't. It won't play dead.

I heft a piece of the fallen lamppost and chuck it.

"Fetch!"

It doesn't. It doesn't fetch. It doesn't want to play anything.

Its chest puffs. An ancient need, forever young, wells within it—the same placeless urge that first dragged life from the peaceful sleep of the primordial ooze into the searing violence of being. Heeding its implacable summons, the cottony white Maltese comes toward me.

"Stay! Stay!"

It's more a plea than a command. Even if morality *does* exist—even if compassion matters not just to ourselves, but to reality's very design—right here, right now it doesn't matter. For in the dreadful terror of this moment…the bad dog has won.

Who're you supposed to be now?

Not sure, but I think I'm on a roll.

"Bad dog! Bad!"

The space between Maltese and Merc vanishes as if it never were. We go *mano a pata*, immutable Wade meets irresistible pooch. It bites me—*rar!* I bite it—*grr!* Neither of us tastes like chicken. It spits out a bloody Wilson-gib. I spit out a chunk of fur that's already growing back.

We go at it again. There's a punch, a kick, a scratch, another kick, more biting, and a heartfelt shouting of unsavory names. I'm shouting, anyway. A second petite headbutt takes me to the ground, but not before I throw the little sucker all the way across the street. My first mistake. On this page, I mean. It lands on all fours and, concrete crunching 'neath its paws, races toward a peaceful playground in the idyllic park at the end of the block.

A playground? Didn't we just have an elementary school? Why are there so many *kids* in this freaking city?

I hurl myself across its path and land sideways, skidding with my hand supporting my head like I'm lying on a couch. It's a cool look.

"Hey, cutie. Where *you* goin'?"

Before I can nab it, it's up on my skull, licking my face really fast, really hard. Normally I'd love it. They say dog saliva, even if it's not antiseptic, is cleaner than human. Think about that next time you're swapping spit with someone.

Are you saying we should kiss dogs instead of people?

That's gross.

No, don't go kissing your dog! Geez. Especially not this one. The coarse-grain-sandpaper tongue shreds the mask in no time. Getting my hands up and under its snout slows the lapping, but it's still licking away, tearing off chunks of flesh like my head's the business end of a chunky Deadpool ice-cream cone. Just like poor Bernardo.

Screaming some guttural variation on *ow-ow-ow*, I twist away and get a look at myself in a storefront window. For a second, I think the missing face-bits make me look better, but that's probably just the mind-numbing pain talking. Makes a fellow think, though. I've been around, gone toe-to-toe with every major character in the Marvel Universe—heroes, villains, sidekicks, and supporting cast—and this is what I've come to? Licked to death?

Yawn.

What's up with the old lady?

Pardon me for paying attention to my own agony. She's back up, standing in front of her house. One hand's clutching her chest like she's trying to keep her heart from escaping; the other's up on her chin, fingertips touching her lower lip. Dentures agape, she runs through a litany of phrases better suited to the Roaring Nineties:

"Heavens to Betsy! Stars and garters! Jumping jiminy! Crikey! Bless my soul! As I live and breathe! Jinkies! Black goat of the woods and her thousand young!"

(Okay, I threw in that last one, but she was saying it with her eyes.)

Meanwhile, I'm trying to push off her beloved Benny before he hits bone and starts gnawing. It's not getting any easier. He still looks the same, but he's getting heavier. My arms feel like they're gonna buckle any second.

I rally for a big shove, only to hear a sharp *beep-beep-beep*. Someone's texting me? Now? Nope. It's the ADD. That flashing green light means it's finally figured out this thing is not really a dog, after all.

Goody! What with me not completely sure my whole head can grow back (and really, would I still be me if it did?), I figure I'm entitled to the use of some deadly force. Slight problem, though: If I take one hand off the pooch to grab the ADD, there won't be much holding Benny back. I've got to be fast, so no pausing to check for messages.

One, two…

I'm about to skip three and make my move when company arrives. No, it's not S.H.I.E.L.D. I haven't done nearly enough damage for that yet. It's a super-hero guest star! You know super heroes, right? If not Squirrel Girl or Throg the Frog, then at least the really big names, like Spider-Man? Remember what I said about Captain America not being in this book? He isn't, but Spidey is.

Amazingly, a flash of red and blue swoops in. I don't even want to ask what that web's attached to. I'd call him poetry in motion, an arachnid Astaire, but he's more like one of those hopping wolf spiders—still as a statue one second, followed by a lightning-bolt move. Not a water spout in sight, he lickety-split leaps to a brick wall, waits a sec, jumps to a tree branch, waits, grabs a car hood, waits, hits a lamppost, waits…

And me, I'm lying there like an idiot, watching him with what's left of my face as he grabs the dog.

I'm fast. I could certainly kick your ass and have you home before you knew what hit you. But this guy? By the time I belt out "Spidey, wait!" he's over by the old lady, handing her the dog.

"Here's your pet, ma'am. Hefty little guy, isn't he?"

Benny's no fool. He plays it to the hilt, going all limp, panting and whimpering. It's the old lady who does the snarling: "Get away from my dog, you awful Spider-Man!"

She jabs him with that Taser. *Gzt!*

I thought his spider-sense was supposed to warn him of danger, but it's like he has a blind spot for old ladies—or this one, anyway. Next thing you know, that awful Spider-Man is crouched sideways on a lamppost, rubbing his boo-boo.

FOURTEEN

YEAH, that's right. Chapter 14. I'm skipping 13, like in an elevator, because it's unlucky. Deal with it, sequential freaks.

Meanwhile, back in fictive reality....

Little realizing that her furry ball of love has become as dense as lead, the sweet old lady tries to lift him into her puny arms. Not happening. Her spine cracks like a bunch of banging billiard balls. I hear it all the way from over here.

My trusty ADD armed and out, I trot over, ready to do my good deed. "Back away from the puppy, ma'am!"

Startled by the *je ne sais quois* of my muscular form barreling at her—or maybe by Benny's increased mass—she staggers far enough away to give me a clean shot. Now if everyone will stay right where they are for a sec, I can shoot first and answer questions later.

The monster spray once seemed a quick and easy solution, but in practice that hasn't always been the case. With a *thwip* and a *thok*, a web snags the ADD. I *hope* that stuff doesn't come out of Spidey's body. I really, really hope so. I know it's all Adamantium-strong and stuff, but it sure as hell looks like there's a fist-sized glob of snot oozing around my nice clean ADD.

Before I can say *ew!* the web-sneezer pulls it out of my hands.

I don't even merit a decent spider-quip. "Wilson, I'd ask what the hell is wrong with you, but there isn't enough time in the world to hear the answer. Just get away from the dog, get out of the city, and we'll call it a day."

I'm stunned. The original teen-angst super hero steals my gun, and then he goes all cranky old man on me like a Frisbee landed in his front yard? He is not being friendly or neighborly in the slightest.

Hoping I don't come across like some kid whining, "He started it," I point at the lady and her lapdog. "You don't understand, that's really a monster!"

Sideways on the streetlamp, he rears like I've insulted his momma. "That's no monster—that's my aunt! I mean…it's a harmless old lady!"

Before I can begin to parse the psycho-dynamics inherent in that odd utterance, the aforementioned harmless old lady gives Spidey a look that makes *me* shiver. By now, even I know to give Madame Mace & Taser some deference. Sure, in my head I may call her old lady, biddy, crone, or what have you, but out loud? That's asking for trouble.

"You come down from that pole, you whippersnapper, and I'll show you who's old!"

I put my hand to my mouth in the universal gesture for *oh my!* Spider-Man puts up his hands in submission, which looks really odd since he's still sideways.

"Sorry, ma'am, sorry! I meant senior citizen. Is senior okay?"

Her eyes become angry slits. He looks around all nervous, like he's sussing out an escape route from the Rhino.

Since my costume and wacky behavior are no longer getting the attention they deserve, I clap my hands real loud. "Hey! Over here! Much as I'd love to grab some popcorn and watch this sad display of political correctness, I wasn't talking about *her*. I was talking about the dog!"

All three—Spidey, the senior, and the dog—twist their heads at me. It's pretty cute, all of them with the same expression like that. A nice family shot.

"Benny…a monster?" says the Amazing One. "Give me a break."

I cross my heart and raise two fingers. "I swear, any second now, that pampered snowball is gonna swell up so big it wouldn't fit on a Jumbotron if you pulled back for a long shot. And I'm not just talking big—I'm talking an insatiable taste for living flesh. Can't you tell yet? Look at it!"

They do. They look at the puppy. It's licking its crotch. I can hear the crickets.

"Okay, maybe not *any* second, but it will, I swear! Why would I lie about something like that?"

Ever the wit, Spider-Man shoots back, "Because… you hallucinate?"

Good point.

You're not helping! How'd you like a punch right

in that bold face of yours?

You keep talking to yourself like this, you'll only make his case for him.

Right. Outside voice. "C'mon! Didn't you see it attack me? And you both felt how heavy it was, right? They heard her back crack in Times Square! For Pete's sake *and* the love of Mike, what else could make a toy dog weigh in like Tyson?"

Mr. Great Power/Great Responsibility shrugs. "She overfeeds him?"

She *tsks*. "I do not."

Having had just about enough of our costumed shenanigans, the nice lady bends over to hook her leash on Benny's collar. She starts to rise back up, but her expression's changed. The wheels in her head have started turning. She's thinking about something. By the time she's fully upright—which, you know, takes a while—those scary eyes are glinting like the metal on the edge of a knife.

"How do you know my dog's name, you awful Spider-Man?"

"Oh…uh…you just said it, didn't you, ma'am? You called him Ben…or Benny?" His head starts a-twitching, like he's looking for that escape route again. "Something like that?"

Benny perks up at the overuse of his name.

His owner's not amused. "I did no such thing!"

He digs himself in deeper. "Sure you did. Back me up here, Deadpool."

"Sorry, bro. Neither of us have used that name

since you got here. Come to think of it, how *do* you
know?" I put my hands on my hips. "Spider-Man!
Have you been stalking this poor woman?"

He nearly leaps out of his costume. "No! I…"

Guess I hit a nerve. "Relax, compadre. Maybe
J.J.J. calls you a menace, but I'm not here to pass
judgment. Like I always say, before you take the
splinter from someone else's eye, you have get the log
out of your own eye first. That way, you've got a log
you can smack him with. Get me?"

"No, not really."

Me neither.

It's a tactic! I'm playing for time, hoping the dog
will get going with his strange change already. If this
mysterious Dick guy is behind it all like Jane said, he's
got a real quality-control problem. Or maybe granny
here *does* overfeed the dog.

"Guys, I don't want any trouble. I love you,
Spidey—and ma'am, you should really consider
joining the X-Men. But I've got a job to do, and it's
actually in the public interest for a change. Can't I
please just have the dog for a little while—just to
make sure he doesn't turn into a monster?"

They both shout, "No!"

With a *tsk* and a *harumph*, Miss America 1776
yanks Ben's chain to resume the morning walksies
and gives us her back. Gotta hand it to her—
snubbing two big-power types like Spidey and me
takes guts. But hey, the little guy really looks like
he has to go. Grunting endearingly, he pulls hard

against the leash, tugging her forward.

At first it's a few steps, but then…bang, zoom!

Ben's off like a streak, dragging grandma with him. Too freaked to let go of the leash, she flies behind him like a crappy kite, not even touching the pavement. Go granny go!

Wonder how high she'd get if that leash were longer. Doesn't matter. Looks like it'll be a short trip—the tear-assing pooch must be getting fur in his eyes. He's headed straight for the cornerstone of one of those six-story brick apartments.

Scratch that. His coconut-sized head takes out a chunk big enough for him and the old lady to plow through.

"Aunt May!" Spidey screams.

Hold it. What? He knows *her* name, too? I didn't know he was psychic! OMG, does that mean he can hear *my* thoughts, too? That would be so embarrassing! It's not like I spell out my every passing whim and fancy for all the world to see. Spidey, can you tell me what number I'm thinking of? Come on, do it! Tell me!

No go. His spider-sense is probably too busy being spider-shocked. For those of you out there in our audience wondering—yes, it was seven.

But fear not, Aunt May! Spider-Man's swifter than swift, with wild reflexes. Like a streak of light, he can arrive just in time. So he's stunned, yeah, but only for a microsecond.

That happens to be long enough for a quick-thinking merc such as myself to snatch back the ADD. *Snatch!*

Weapon of choice in hand, I'm hot in pursuit with a hearty, "Told you so! Told you so!"

(To be clear, ladies, the DP is always hot. This time it just happens to be in pursuit.)

Remaining dogged in appearance, but not deed, Ben races through Forest Hills. When I say through, I mean *through*—parked cars, street vendors, residential structures, dragging the hapless Aunt May behind all the way. Given all the crashes, bangs, and flying debris, you can't really call it the Snooze District anymore.

I play catchup, bounding off this, twisting around that, ducking debris, closing the distance, and trying to look cool while I do. Spider-Man? He's got that web-swinging down like he's been at it since 1962. (Anyone ever tell him spiders don't actually travel that way?) He's past me in a blink.

To avoid complete humiliation, I pick up the pace, gaining until I'm close enough to kiss the old lady's free-flying foot (though I have no idea why I'd want to do that).

You're probably sick of all the wrecked cars, but really, what else is there to hit in New York? Ben splits a parked limo in a postmodern symphony of rending steel, ripping polymers, and careening composites. It barely slows him down, but barely's all I need.

As limo pieces hurtle past me, I make this incredible move. It's a *peak* moment—maybe not in terms of sheer strength, or even speed, but as a zen-like exercise in technique. I'm totally going to ask Agent Preston to check the traffic cams for a shot of this. I'm telling you, it'd make a *great* splash page. Picture it drawn by your favorite artist, a signed print available in a numbered limited edition: With one hand on the sundered limo's deploying driver-side airbag, I push myself up and over Aunt May. My other arm's already out, aiming the ADD smack-dab at the perilous pup.

But…along comes a spider. With no waterspout in sight, he slams into me, probably thinking *he* deserves the splash page. From a purely marketing standpoint, he may be right.

"Don't shoot, you maniac! You might hit her!"

He swings past, leaving me to rant at the red spider shape on his receding back.

"Oh man! This sucks! Come on! Hitting the target is what I do!"

Rather than mope, I pick myself up and get back in the race. The path of destruction is easy to follow. It's narrower than, say, what the Hulk might make if he had to get to a bathroom real quick, but the rubble's every bit as good.

Spidey's moving above, looking for an in. Since he hasn't found one by the time I reach him, I figure now's as good a time as any to clear the air.

"Y'know, wall-trawler, if she gets hurt because you blocked me, it's *your* fault."

He slaps himself in the head. "Like I don't have enough guilt!"

"This whole thing with you and her is kinda

strange to begin with. People get older, they get sick. Sometimes they get dragged off by a monster puppy, but eventually they do die. Circle of life, my friend. Don't you think it's time you just…let her go? As Faulkner said, 'Ode to a Grecian Urn' is worth any number of old ladies."

"Shut up! It's not a Grecian urn, it's a monster dog! And that's no old lady, that's my…!"

He stops mid-sentence. I hear his teeth gnashing behind the mask, like he almost gave away his secret identity or something. Then it dawns on me:

"I know that one! That's no old lady, that's my wife! Henny Youngman, right? Wait, that's your wife? Dude, that is so…wrong."

"She's not my wife!"

"You're just using her? I know commitment can be scary, but if you're never tied to anything, can you ever really be free?"

"Aghhh!"

He veers off from his desperate chase long enough to smash my chin with his heels. It hurts. Not only physically—though I do see stars. It really hurts deep down inside, where I keep my feelings and my porn. But that's okay, I know it was for my own good. I know it'll make me a better man, a better son. I know I should leave Daddy alone when he's drinking his adult juice. I know…

Daddy? Daddy? Why don't you love me? Why? A puppy would love me. A puppy could…

Look at me, Sophie!

Hallucinating.

Okay, then. The traveling circus family of Deadpool, Spidey, May, and the Astonishing Ben exits the residential section for a bit of tended greenery. While Spider-Man hovers like a helicopter parent watching his kid's first steps, Ben and May burst through the stone wall of a dog park. Along the perimeter of the poop-filled grass, pet owners look up from their smartphones to see their world turned upside down: A dog is walking a human. They scatter, but their pets are into it, awed at the sight of one of their own breaking the grass ceiling. They bark joyfully at the mighty Maltese, as if to say:

"I'd sure sniff *your* butt if I could!"

Before the Benny-train reaches the other side, Spider-Man spots his opening. Using that endless supply of web gunk, he fashions a zip line running from a high tree branch to the far wall. He rides down spectacularly and scoops Aunt May into his arms.

But May still has her knuckles wrapped around the leash, and Ben's not stopping.

"I've got you! You can let go!" he cries.

It's looking like Spider-Man may wind up being dragged along himself. Frankly, that'd be pretty funny. But she does let go—so she can tase him again.

Bzt!

"Ow!"

"Put me down, you awful Spider-Man!"

Awfully *amazing*, she means!

While Spidey tries to justify saving her life, Ben

hits the streets again, and (finally, finally, finally!) he grows. Wish I could say he snowballs into a horrendous beast, because that image would match his coat, but it's more like a big rocky orange thing comes bursting out of a little furry white thing. His dog features don't vanish so much as fold into a larger picture.

It may seem strange, but I feel really good about this. Here it is: proof that I'm not lying or crazy. Well, not *just* crazy.

My first instinct is to grab Spider-Man and turn him around so he can see, but Aunt May's busy swatting him with the leash. Besides, Ben's transformation is already causing problems. Of course a growing galoot like that is going to block traffic—how can he not? More specifically, he's doing his business right in front of a speeding bus.

And—you're not going to believe this, because even I don't—it's packed with nuns.

Seriously, with the world the way it is, why bother hallucinating?

Force of habit?

Practice?

Nuns. I suppose I should be grateful it isn't kids again. At least they look like nuns, what with the wimple-and-veil habits, but it could be a flash-mob performance of the 1992 Whoopi Goldberg vehicle *Sister Act*. That feels like a stretch, so I'm going with real nuns, none of whom seem to realize how close they are to an unscheduled meet-and-greet with the Big Guy in the sky they've devoted their lives to.

The driver does. He honks. I dunno, maybe he thinks the swelling rocky mass hasn't seen him yet and will get out of the way when it does. It doesn't, though. It turns toward him, all angry and monstery. The driver screams so loud, I hear it over the horn.

The nuns are just starting to look up as the beastie proudly announces:

"I am GOOGAM, son of..."

Whatever.

I spray him. He goes all puddly. The end.

THIRTEEN

SCREW it. Here's Chapter 13. This is the 21st century. I'll be damned if I'm going to kowtow to some lame superstition. Pardon me while I toss some salt over my left shoulder.

The danger's gone, thanks to me (and whoever invented the nano-catalyst), but I don't get so much as a "Thank you, you beautiful psychopath!" before Spidey heads off to lick his old-lady wounds and Aunt May leaves to ponder a goldfish for her next pet. Me, I can already guess how the conversation with Preston will go ("How did you even *find* a busload of nuns?").

I figure I may as well vamoose before S.H.I.E.L.D. gets here.

Felt longer, but the Benny incident took all of fifteen minutes. A little luck and I'll be able to scratch-and-sniff another doggie name off the list before the sun's done rising.

Upper East Side, here we come. My 'porter makes the trip a done deal. No muss, no fuss. Y'know, teleportation can be a pain for writers. If a character can zap anywhere, whenever they like, where's the drama? That's why there's always some intergalactic whatsis interfering with the Heisenberg compensators. But that's not a problem here, me not being what they call a rational actor. As already seen, I'd *never* use my 'porter to ruin an exciting battle sequence. I'm more likely to 'port myself into a *worse* situation, or surprise everyone by dropping the plot completely to chill on a nice sandy beach. (SPOILER ALERT: I do that later. Watch for it!)

It does come in handy for eliminating the boring bits we can all do without, like me catching a cab or earning stares as I ride the subway. I don't want to go through it, you don't want to read about it, so…poof.

This time, I pop myself into a cozy bedroom. Wafting window shades with heart-shaped patterns, drawn closed against the growing morn, cast wavering shadows on the walls, whose whiteness is interrupted only by a few cheerful self-stick Disney characters. The child-small furniture is a matching white, with pink borders. A few dolls with unrealistic body proportions are scattered on the plush rug.

It's either a little girl's room, or some clever bait set out by a pederast.

(Now there's a type I could kill with impunity…)

But there's no grisly creep waiting to strike. The only sounds are the soft rhythmic breaths of the two sole inhabitants, the cherubs asleep in the princess bed: an innocent child and her Labrador puppy. Her arms around him, his around hers, foreheads touching, eyes closed, they dream their dreamy dreams of rainbow unicorns and butterflies. It doesn't get sweeter than this.

Which means it's downhill from here.

Quiet as a Mouseketeer, I try to slip the Lab

out without waking either of them. They wrinkle their noses, but I pull him steadily along, slow and gentle. Nice and easy, nice and easy. One nail on a neatly clipped back paw catches a loose thread on the comforter. I keep moving back—steady, steady. The thread gets tighter, tighter, until it snaps silently and drifts off like a tethered snowflake.

They both go right on sleeping, she under her quilt, the Lab in my hands.

Arriving via 'porter is quiet, but it pops when I leave. I figure I'll put some distance between us before I zap out, so at least she'll have a good night's sleep before she's traumatized by the missing pooch.

Got the drapes pushed aside, one hand on the window, the other holding the Lab. Through the cloth of my costume, I feel a morning breeze against my man-teats. The scamp feels it, too, and he starts scrabbling his legs in midair. He doesn't wake up. It's more like he's sleep-chasing a butterfly. Awwww! He's *special*.

And not a big problem—until he twists and nearly falls out the window. I hop back to keep him in the room, and he slips free. Now he's sleep-trotting, bumping into anything that doesn't happen to appear in his dream.

Isn't this peachy? Me, chasing a pooch on tiptoes. I put my finger to my lips and make the "Shh! Shh!" sign without the hissing, but a) he's asleep, and b) who knows if a puppy'd understand that, anyway? Full of that freaky boundless pup energy, he hits a standing lamp, bounds across a shelf full of picture books, and headbutts an 8x10 of him and the kid in a heart-shaped frame that probably came free when he was delivered.

Everything goes falling, but I manage to catch it all—each and every appliance, book, and tchotchke—before they can hit the ground and wake the sleeping child. Why? Because no matter how many people I kill, no matter how much blood I spill…you know, I'm not really sure why. I should have 'ported out when I had the chance. Now I'm balancing all this kiddie crap, and the freaking mutt is still jumping around like a backup dancer in a Michael Jackson video.

I try to put it all back where it came from, but for every popup book I get back in place, Sir Happy-Dance sends two more flying.

Now I'm so fed up I want to chuck the pile at the wall. We've all been there, right? Stuck in traffic, waiting for an elevator, trying to defuse a nuclear bomb. You'd just grit your teeth and suck it up, right? But in moments like these, I don't do what you do, I do what I feel like. That's part of my appeal.

So I chuck that precious pile of belongings right into those nice clean walls.

The girl shoots up to a sitting position. Even her terrified gasp is endearing. The Lab can sleep through anything, though. While I run around after the skittering somnambulist, the kid gawks at the red on my suit with all her wide-eyed glory.

"Are you…Santa?"

If she's going to throw it over the plate like that, who am I not to swing?

"Sure," I say. "It's August, but hey, why not?"

I grab the dog. She rubs her eyes. "What are you doing with Mr. Snuffles?"

"Mr. Snuffles?" I look at the dog like I'd forgotten he was there. The double take makes the kid giggle. About time someone laughed at my jokes. "Well, honey, Mr. Snuffles is broken, see? So Santa's gonna take him to the North Pole and fix him for you."

That's from some kids' book, right?

She pouts. "But mommy said the vet already fixed Mr. Snuffles."

"Yeah, well, he broke again. See how his legs are moving around even though his eyes are closed? That's pretty freaky, isn't it?"

"Oh, no!"

"You don't want a broken Mr. Snuffles, and Mr. Snuffles hates being broken, so now he's got to get himself fixed again."

Fixed in this case likely being a euphemism for dead.

"And you'll bring him right back?"

I give her a thumbs up. "You bet!"

My fake grin is so sincere, I think about taking off my mask to show it to her, but that wouldn't be pleasant for either of us. I do feel kinda bad about lying. If Snuffs *doesn't* change, maybe I can bring him back. If he does, maybe S.H.I.E.L.D. will let me send her the goop in a jar. It'd be like a Sea-Monkey, only pinker. Picture that at show-and-tell.

My guilt assuaged by vague promises, I turn to the window. But you know kids.

"You won't hurt him, will you?"

"Not if I don't have to. I mean…of course not! I'm Santa. Don't you trust Santa?"

She nods. "I sure do!"

I turn away again.

"Santa?"

"Oh, for… What?"

"I'm thirsty."

"Kid, it's very early in the morning, and Santa's had a rough night, so he's a little cranky. If I bring you a glass of water, will you promise to close that freaking pie hole under your button nose and go to sleep? Otherwise Santa might punch a few holes into your pretty walls. Get me?"

"Okay."

Sleepwalking dog under one arm, I make it into the kitchen and pour her a tall one on ice (filtered water, you freaks!). I stick in a straw and leave a stern note for the parental units suggesting they tell their child about stranger danger sooner rather than later.

She takes like half a sip and sets the cup aside. Thirsty, my ass.

She snuggles under the covers, I pat her warm head and make the puppy wave bye-bye with his paw. Since she's already awake, I use the 'porter to take myself to the roof, like I should have done in the first place.

Kids. Sheesh.

FIFTEEN

WE'VE already had Chapters 14 and 13—so 15, right? Look, just read the damn thing in page order, okay? It's all one story, more or less—with a subplot or two. Stay with me. One sentence after another. There you go!

Sun creeping up behind me like a big bald head, I stand on a flat roof, listening to the vents rattle as I give Mr. Snuffles a look-see. Like all Labradors, he's got this floppy skin a size too big for his frame. It bunches into small wrinkles when I hold him up, making him look newborn and a million years old at the same time. He's still lightweight, like a puppy should be—and also still asleep. I can tell he's not faking. His eyeballs are moving beneath his furry lids in doggie-style REM.

Can't help but wonder what he's thinking. If he's feeling as free and happy as he looks.

Awwww! He *is* special!

No! I will not lose myself in warm fuzzies. I will not nuzzle him. I will not bond. I will not bond. I will not bond.

I should dump the mutt with S.H.I.E.L.D. like I did the collie. Their biochemists are the ones who'll have to figure out what to do with the duds. But this hit went down so fast, Preston's probably still on cleanup duty in Queens, and she's the only one I trust there. Can't have Mr. Snuffles wind up in the hands of some raging infomaniac whose rallying cry is, "Hey, how does this life-form work?" Having gone through that myself in the Weapon X hospice, I wouldn't wish it on—yep—a dog. But I can't keep him, either.

"Can I, Dad?"

It isn't real Dad I see. It's imaginary Dad, better Dad, Dad who might have let me have a dog. Hey, not all the fantasies can be basketball games. Sometimes you have to keep even the dreams real.

It's a narrow galley kitchen. He takes up most of the table. Rest of the place is small like that, too. He fills every room he's in. Everything is always underfoot. Ice clinks in the glass as he shuts his bloodshot eyes.

With his head bowed low over the broken Formica surface of the table, most of what I see of Dad is the top of his military crewcut. That's pretty much how I really remember him—in pieces. Top of his head, his arms, his belt. To remember his eyes or his face, I'd have to look at pictures of him. (Same with Mom. Back then I'd have to be sure he wasn't around while I was looking at her photo. Mom died of cancer, like maybe I should have, and any reminder—like a photo, or me—put Dad in a bad mood.)

"That thing craps or sheds anywhere in my house, I'll put it to sleep myself."

Imaginary Wade is much more eager to please than I ever was. Half the beatings I got, I asked for. Half.

"You won't know she's here. I swear it."

When Dad stops moving, I think he's some version

of asleep. But then he starts cursing. Not at me—at nothing. He slams his fist so hard into the table, his glass spills—even though there's barely anything left in it. He hits the Formica again and again with one hand, but the slams fade out like he's losing a boxing match. The arm twitches and settles. He takes a few deep, rattling inhales and starts to snore.

Sometimes I have trouble remembering who's who in these things. For a sec, I'm the one with my head down on the table, smelling old food stains mixed with scotch, ready to pick a fight with the air. But it's *my* delusion, so I force myself back into being good little Wade, watching the top of his head. I mop up the booze so he won't mistake it for dog piss in the morning. I try to imagine leaving him there like that, drooling on himself, but I can't seem to exit the room.

And there's no dog. No dog anywhere. The place is too small.

A wet belch (his or mine?) takes me halfway back to the rooftop. Mr. Snuffles is still breathing peacefully in my arms, every bit as alive as Eternity or an amoeba. But some delusions are stickier than others.

"I'll put it to sleep myself."

Given the way the world is, maybe mercy killing is the only kind there is. What with Snuffles likely a monster, where he's at now could be as good as it gets. I raise him a little closer and whisper, "Oh, Mr. S., one day, one way or another, sooner or later, you're going to die. Would it be more merciful to put you down now, before the world steps in and ruins you?"

It's funny because it's true.

He makes a little growl, almost like a snore.

"Damn it! Who am I kidding, Mr. Snuffles? I could never hurt *you*!"

I give him a hug. Nothing big—just enough to let him know I'm sorry.

Thought you weren't going to bond.

It's not bonding! It's an apology. The hallucination weirded me out, okay? It's not like I'm going to adopt him. I'll pass him on to Preston as soon as I can. Watch.

I prop the esteemed Mr. S. behind my back to make it look like he's photobombing me, take a selfie with my cell phone, and shoot it off through the intertubes.

Takes a sec before my cell rings.

"Did you mean to post that shot to Pinterest?"

It's good to hear Em's voice. "New phone. Really got to change the defaults on this thing. I may have tweeted it, too. You still in Queens?"

"Yeah. Where're you?"

"Upper East Side rooftop. Got a nice view of the FDR and the sweetest little Lab y'ever did see. Goes by the name Snuffles. That's Mr. Snuffles to you."

"Wade, don't name the dogs."

"Why not? So I don't bond with them?"

"No, because Mr. Snuffles is a ridiculous name."

"Tell that to the precious little girl who gave it to him."

"Little girl? Tell me that's one of your multiple personalities."

"No, she's real—I think. I really need to start

wearing a bodycam when I work. Gonna yell at me for the mess in Forest Hills?"

I can tell from her tone she won't. "Tough call. You've actually got a busload of nuns as fans. By the way, they want you to know there's forgiveness to be had. The big problem this time is Spider-Man's involvement. How'd you manage that?"

"It's not like I invited him. Why's that a problem?"

"Because fights between costumed types attract attention. The media was already all over you after Midtown—now some stringer named Peter Parker snapped you and the wall-crawler fighting over a puppy. Not like I'm your PR manager, but this isn't the best time for you to be posting a selfie with *another* stolen dog. You never know who's gonna see that."

"That was the idea, wasn't it? Don't blame S.H.I.E.L.D., blame me?"

"All I'm saying is, get ready for some blowback. I'd suggest you keep out of sight, if I thought you knew what that meant."

For a moment, the world gets the shakes.

THUD!

"Em, could you speak up? Sounds like they're blasting for the 2nd Avenue subway again."

"Right. And you're losing bars 'cause you're driving into a tunnel. Don't BS me. I've got your location right in front of me. The readout confirms there's no construction going on for blocks."

WHAM! The rooftop vents rattle like tin cans.

"Really? Maybe I've got a headache?"

Nope.

Nothing in here.

THUD!

I wonder if I'm imagining Dad punching the table in the kitchen again, but even Mr. Snuffles picks his head up at that last one. We scan the roof, the buildings. Nothing.

"Deadpool! Pay attention. I've got some news for you on Goom, Googam, and Gorgolla."

"Cheeses, right?"

"No, that's what the creatures called themselves."

"Oh, yeah."

"They're also the names of real monsters."

KWOOM!

Mr. Snuffles barks, but I ignore it. "Real monster names? Puh-lease. Frankenstein—now *that's* a real monster name. Come to think of it, actually, it isn't. It's the name of the doctor, not his creation. Though in the original James Whale film, he does refer to the monster as his Adam, so technically you *could* say the monster's name was Adam Frankenstein—but I think that's a stretch. How about you, Mr. Snuffles?"

"Focus!"

BOOM! Mr. Snuffles' ears go straight up.

"Hey, Em? Sounds like my fake excuse to get off the phone is getting closer."

"Huh. I heard it that time, too. Let me get some sat data."

"Focus yourself, Agent P. You were saying about the monsters?"

"Had to have my security clearance upgraded to get this information, but S.H.I.E.L.D. used to work with a whole team of…well, monsters, to assist in paranormal containment."

"Wait, wait, wait. Stop. Rewind. S.H.I.E.L.D. worked with monsters?"

"Hired *you*, didn't we? The group was codenamed the Howling Commandos…"

"And you have trouble with the name 'Mr. Snuffles'?"

"While the Commandos were active, we ran tests on all the members, took samples. The servers storing their DNA patterns were breached a few years back. The working theory—and it's a good one—is that their data wound up in the Weapon X lab and was used to create these creatures."

"Did the originals eat people?"

"No. That seems to be a bioengineered response peculiar to these cloned versions. Maybe it's meant to compensate for all the energy the transformation consumes. Whoever designed them probably figured that the nearest food source available in large supplies would be…people."

WHOOM!

It's real close this time—like right in front of the building. Mr. Snuffles and I peer over the side. Both our hearts go pitter-pat. "Don't worry, fellow, I've got you. Oh my. See that down there, Mr. S.? A big hole in the street, a crushed car, and a fallen lamppost—all making a line headed our way? Uh, Preston, has some doggie monster maybe done the change thing without me?"

"Hang on. Sats out of range. I'm accessing the street cams nearest your location, and…"

In the background, an excited voice calls out. "Agent Preston, I think I've got something!"

"Is that Carl? Say hi, will you?"

"Wade, get out of there, NOW!"

"Chillax. If it's another monster, I've got the ADD. One spray and…"

"It's *not* one of the monsters, it's…"

KROOM!

The building shrugs. The dog yelps. The phone nearly flies out of my hand.

"Em? Hello? Don't tell me *you* went into a tunnel? Hello?"

I look down again. A blur flies up toward us. I want to say it's moving impossibly fast, but it's not only possible, it's also crazy thick and crazy muscled, with green skin and shredded purple pants. I stumble back barely in time to give it the space it needs to land in front of me. The impact nearly throws me off my feet, and its weight almost collapses the roof.

Mr. Snuffles clings to me. Aw!

Our next surprise guest star isn't Goom or Gorgolla big, but he *feels* bigger—a massive powder keg perpetually ready to blow. Worse than Dad. Especially when he starts yelling at me, too. It's like…like… y'know how all caps in an email or text makes you feel as if the writer is shouting at you? This is kind of like that, only more, so I'm going with boldface, too:

"HULK NOT WANT SEE PUPPIES HURT!"

SIXTEEN

WE ALL know the Hulk: brilliant, mild-mannered scientist Bruce Banner, belted by gamma rays, wrecking the town with the power of a bull. Ain't he unglamorous? You won't like it when he's angry, 'cause the madder he gets, the stronger he gets.

Any of this ringing a bell?

Longtime Hulk fans know that sometimes he's sort of in control of himself, and sometimes he's just a plain old rage machine. Pretty sure we've got the latter here.

Mr. Snuffles under my arm, my hands out in a sign of abject supplication, I stare into those big green eyes and try to do what is for me the most difficult thing in the world: talk sense.

"Easy, there, Hulky. I know what it looks like, but I'd never hurt a—"

Then comes the punch. It's not like he can manage a sucker blow with that fist—it's broadcast like crazy. I can hear the trashcan-thick muscles tense when he pulls back his arm, giving me sweet, sweet time to try to get out of the way. I almost make it, too. Matter of fact, I'm not sure if it's actually the unyielding flesh and steely bone of his fist that makes contact with me, or the air ahead of it, so compressed it feels like a concrete beach ball. Whatever it is, my gut curls around it, my tootsies leave the roof, and once again we've got liftoff!

In a comic, it's easy to control the passage of time. A falling droplet can stretch across several panels, centuries skipped with a single caption reading, "A thousand years later…" Here in the first-person, present-tense prose world, it's trickier. But as I watch the Hulk get smaller and smaller while his blow sends me sailing far and away, indulge me, if you will, in some brief and perhaps needless time expansion.

Remember, the events you are reading took less time than they appear.

We begin with the pain of the moment: "OOMF!"

Hoping to soften the impact of our landing, I struggle to wrap myself around the hapless Mr. Snuffles. First we hit the enclosed stairwell leading back into the building. No rolling downstairs for this dynamic duo. We crash through like a fist through an empty tissue box—plaster, wood-frame, and all.

Take it from a guy who's gone through a lot of walls—usually, it slows you down. Not an issue here. If anything, I feel like we're moving faster when we come out the other side. We pass over the ledge and head into the open air: free, free, free.

Except for the whole gravity thing.

By the time we cross 2nd Avenue, the pull of good ol' Mother Earth tugs us just enough so that we hit the slightly lower roof of another building. The Lab tight against my belly, I spin backwards like a ball—not so much because I'm a skilled fighter who knows the best way to land, but more because I'm an object caught in the grip of physics, and that's how I roll. (Get it?)

Fortunately, this roof is bigger and more crowded than the one we left behind, so after pinballing off a few air-conditioning condenser units, we do slow down enough for me to stop us before we tumble off the ledge.

Though I wouldn't tell him to his face, the Hulk can't fly. Small comfort, since he can cover miles in a single jump. I'm barely up, doing a staggering Fred Astaire dance thing, when the big green machine lands. He's still pissed, but not shouting quite as loud, so we'll do away with the boldface:

"HULK SEE YOU HURT DOGGIE ON YOUTUBE!"

The Hulk gets Internet? How incredible of him. No time for questions about his choice of ISP. This time, I'm pretty sure it *is* his actual fist that connects. Gives you an idea of how mad he gets. If he was really worried about doggies, he'd have given me a chance to put Snuffles down, but *you* tell him that. The wacky guy's all feeling—wears his heart on his sleeve.

Or is that *my* heart on his sleeve?

We cross another street, hit an office building, go through the wall, fly across a desk or two, and then it's out the window and down a mere four stories. I'm tough, not invulnerable, but it's mostly scratches and bruises so far. I cleverly slow our descent by slamming into a few jutting window ledges.

I hit the sidewalk. Mr. Snuffles hits my chest, making the cutest little sound as all the air is forced out of his lungs. Can't get it exactly, but it's kinda like "Rrrrrunnfff!"

With all the grace and savoir faire of a plummeting aircraft carrier, Greenie lands a few yards away. I hope he'll do the thing where he claps his hands to create a devastating sonic wave, because that probably won't hurt as much. But no, he punches me again. Right upside my head, where I keep all those... What do you call them? Oh yeah—thoughts.

Often I'll slip gently into hallucination, barely noticing when it happens. This is more like when you get a different station every time you hit a broken television. Images scramble, audio mixes. In the "real" word, I think the trajectory takes us over a subway vent blasting steam, because I feel this gush of warm air that reminds me of the hot wind on a summer day.

One day in particular. I'm on a baseball field in a park, making fun of some chubby kid for striking out. Sophie's watching. I'm trying to impress her with my wit when I unwittingly cross some bully-etiquette line. The kid, who's a head shorter, is furious, red-faced, straining and shaking like he's constipated. He doesn't know whether to burst into tears, or to try and beat the crap out of me. With all the other kids watching, he makes a stand and pummels me, popping his fists against my chest.

"I'll kill you! I'll kill you!"

It's the old-school rule: Take the biggest guy

down, and the others will leave you alone. Only he's got like zero strength, so it's like being hit by extra-soft Q-Tips. It's so pathetic, I laugh. That only makes him more frustrated and ashamed.

"I'll kill you! I'll kill you!"

So he punches faster and faster, harder and harder. But no matter how fast and hard he punches, it doesn't hurt. I laugh harder. I can't control myself. I double over. Everybody's laughing. Sophie, too. Even the kid's parents. It's *that* funny. Tears stream down his puffy red cheeks, but he keeps at it.

"I'll kill you! I'll kill you!"

But then it changes. Next thing, *I'm* the stupid chubby kid doing the punching—only I'm not hitting myself, I'm hitting the Hulk. And he's not laughing. And it doesn't tickle. I hurt all over: snapped ribs, broken femur, squirting blood, the works.

He picks me up over his head, ready to toss me.

"YOU HURT PUPPY!"

Despite the swirling spots before my eyes, I get an idea. I've pretty much met everyone in the Marvel Universe, which means I must have met the Hulk.

"Hulk, listen! You remember me?"

He thinks for a second. He's kinda cute when he thinks. No. Let's say cut*er*.

"DEADPOOL HURT DOGGIE! HULK CRUSH!"

"Deadpool! That's right. I'm Deadpool. That means that no matter what you do to me, I'll still heal. You *can't* crush me. Not forever, anyway."

That one puzzles him. "HULK *CAN'T* CRUSH?"

He drops me. "Ow. Yeah. So if you think about it, what's the point?"

He squints. He lowers his voice. "Hulk can't crush."

He stomps on me again—just a little—to make sure.

"Nrgh! See? Still…here…"

"Can't crush. Can't crush. What Hulk do?" He scratches his head. "Not crush…not crush…"

"You could…listen to me…"

His eyes light up. I'm sure he'd snap his fingers if he knew how, 'cause he looks like he's had himself an epiphany.

"HULK SIT!"

"No! I didn't… Wait…"

I'd move if I could, but I can't even manage to squirm before that big green butt and its accompanying two tons of meat mass plops itself down on what's left of me.

"Eeeg! No! Nooooooooo…!"

"Hulk sit until you promise not to hurt doggie."

I suppose there's something to be said for the fact that he's not hitting me anymore, but I'm not sure what that might be. Hope he hasn't eaten any chimichangas recently. I look up past his crotch into that big green face, so terribly pleased with itself.

"Hulk…listen…I don't *want* to hurt any dogs, but some of 'em might be monsters."

He tilts his head. "Dog monster?"

"That's it. And the monsters might hurt people."

"Hurt people?"

"Yes! You are *so* smart, Hulk. You got that right away. That is *so* good. Now, if the monster might hurt some poor people, it'd be okay for me to hurt the monster so it couldn't hurt the people, right? The same way you hurt me—really badly, I might add—because you *thought* I was hurting real doggies."

He scrunches his brow and purses his lips.

"Am I right, Hulk?"

But then he clenches his fists, rattles his butt, and snaps a few more of my ribs.

"DOGGIE NOT MONSTER, DOGGIE DOGGIE! Hulk sit until Deadpool promise not to hurt doggie!"

It goes on like this for a while—so long I'm wondering where S.H.I.E.L.D. or the first responders are. With the Hulk immobile, they're probably watching from a safe distance, laughing their asses off.

Mr. Snuffles has stayed with me, though. The sweet, special thing even tries to drag me out from under. Sometimes it feels like that dog is my only friend—and I've known him for less than an hour.

We humans cause so many of our own problems, don't we? Look how long it's taken me to realize I can just lie to the big green idiot.

"Okay, Hulk! You got it! I promise never to hurt any doggie ever again so long as I live. Cross my heart!"

He looks at me suspiciously, but then gets up. My right arm lifts along with him. I'm afraid it's stuck between his clenched butt cheeks, but it comes loose. The oppressive weight gone, a few of my bits rise back into place with a disturbingly rubbery sound. The rest is gonna take a while, but the healing has begun.

The loyal Mr. Snuffles wags his tail and yips happily.

Which, of course, Greenie notices. "Doggie! Hulk want pet doggie."

The average dog understands 165 words. From the terrified look on Snuffles' face, he's caught the Hulk's gist.

"I'm not sure that's a good—"

"HULK NOT HURT DOGGIE! HULK WANT PET!"

It's not like either of us can stop him. The green giant plucks him up like a hairy grape. Mr. Snuffles gets all stiff and saucer-eyed. I try to apologize to him with my eyes, since they're among the few body parts I can still move, then I just hold my breath and watch.

Hulk pats the head. "Nice doggie! Soft doggie!"

So far, so good. Awkwardly, like a big toddler, he moves his hand up and down the furry body. Maybe this'll calm the Hulk down, change him back to his human form.

Only then he gets a little…eager. He starts moving his mitt faster and harder.

"Hulk will pet you and pet you and pet you and…!"

"Easy! Gentle! You don't want to…"

Uh-oh.

"Doggie?" Eyes widening, the Hulk looks down at the motionless animal in his hand. "Why doggie not move?" He turns to me, big green lips trembling. "Why doggie not move?"

Like I'm going to tell him. "Uh…"

He prods Mr. Snuffles with his finger. "Wake up doggie! Don't be…don't be…"

Eyes watery, he lays the limp Mr. Snuffles by my side. "Hulk didn't mean it. Hulk not bad."

Never heard the Hulk actually *cry* before. It's… creepy.

He leaps off, screaming, "HULK NOT BAD! HULK NOT BAD!"

And he keeps right on jumping until the sound of crunching pavement fades in the distance.

SEVENTEEN

MR. SNUFFLES! We hardly knew ye. Sob.

Still no sign of S.H.I.E.L.D., but with all the big green excitement over and the workday clock ticking, the city's daily commute gets going. More and more people wander by. Sure, they stare. Can't help it, I suppose.

They say New Yorkers are unfriendly, but it's not true. In a hurry? Yeah. Assertive? Sure. And yes, you have to *know* how to hail a cab. But ask for directions, and any one of them will help you out. Just keep your stupid questions quick and to the point. Haven't got all day.

The gawking crowd gathering 'round is a perfect representation of the great melting pot: white, black, Hispanic, Asian, male and female, old and young, working class and execs, single parents and same-sex couples. Ignoring their differences, they stand shoulder-to-shoulder, pressing in for a better look.

Not ten feet away, two homeless people are huddled in a doorway, clothes and skin as gray as the street, and no one gives them the time of day. What's unusual about that? Now, a guy in a red-and-black suit, beaten to a pulp, lying next to a dead Labrador puppy? That's news.

The smart phones come out like forks at a feast.

Memory chips being cheaper than minutes, video is recorded with abandon, despite the fact neither of us is moving.

If any of 'em had really, really good hearing, they might hear my body stitching itself back together. As it is, I must seem pretty bad off, lying here in a stew of my own pureed organics. Mr. Snuffles looks more natural, but that only makes it sadder.

One eagle-eyed gal in a business suit pushes to the front and gets a particularly horrified look on her face. Maybe she'll finally suggest calling an ambulance?

Nope. That's the other thing about New Yorkers—they're full of surprises. She points at me like I came out of the dog's butt.

"OMG! That's the dognapper from the news! He killed that puppy!"

"Did not! And he wasn't just any puppy. *Sniff.* They called him…Mr. Snuffles."

Surprised I'm still alive, the ad-hoc group gasps and takes a collective step back. You'd think most people would take a talking gore pile at its word. I know I would, but when assumptions run rampant, the accusations come free of charge.

"How could you do that to a poor helpless puppy, you freaking loser?" says a bike messenger. He takes off his coat and uses it to cover the dog.

"Couldn't tell you since, like I said, *I didn't do it.*"

"Murderer!" the first woman shouts.

"Well…sure, depending on your definition, but…"

A pencil-thin older guy in a three-piece shakes his rolled-up *Wall Street Journal* at me like he's gonna swat my nose.

"I don't believe in the death penalty, but in your case, I'd make an exception!"

"You're entitled to your own opinion, but not your own facts. I didn't do it!"

He sneers. He's heard it all before. "Why would you even say something like that, unless you're guilty?"

This is worse than talking to the Hulk. Mobs are all about selective hearing. One idiot shouts something incendiary, someone else agrees, and before you know it, they've hit this funky tipping point. Suddenly, everyone's in tune, and they all magically know the same lyrics and choreography—like in an episode of *Glee*.

"He can't get away with this!"

"We should do something!"

I'd say mobs are like sheep, but sheep don't get angry, even when you take their wool and eat them. Lemmings? Nope. Despite popular belief, they don't *really* commit mass suicide. That's just an urban legend that got traction when a nature-film crew faked it by tossing the little buggers off a cliff for the camera. But you don't see anyone forming a mob around *them*, do you?

"Let's do something!"

"Yeah! Let's!"

I'd love to get up and beat the crap out of everyone for being stupid. But until I heal, all I've got is this lame honesty thing: "Didn't do it! Didn't do it! DIDN'T DO IT!"

Hey, my throat's healing, getting stronger. If I'm loud and adamant enough, maybe I can achieve that special air of truthiness. Looks like I'm making some progress. A uniformed meter maid pushes through the throng and stands beside me. Maybe *she'll* talk some sense to them.

Holding up her iPad for all to see, she speaks with clear authority.

"He *did* do it! It's right here on YouTube! He stole that puppy from an old lady in Queens and brought it here to kill it!"

On screen, I see a long shot of me and Aunt May playing tug-of-war with Benny.

"No! That's a totally different puppy! Benny was a Maltese. Mr. Snuffles is a Labrador!"

Even though I know the truth, I somehow still feel like a slimy politician confronted with the selfies of his privates that he sent his underage intern.

"How many puppies have you killed?"

"None! And that video is out of context. If I was going to kill a puppy, you think I'd drag it all the way here from Queens?"

Thought I had them with that one, but lovely Rita the meter maid knows better: "Then you admit you've *thought* about killing puppies."

"Who hasn't thought about it? But that's not the point. Mr. Snuffles was a noble creature. Sure, he had the potential to become a rampaging beast that would eat you all, but I did my best to protect him! I just couldn't do it, okay?" My throat clenches. My voice cracks. "I…failed. I just…failed."

Someone in the back calls out, "That's as bad as if you killed him yourself!"

"Is not! It's totally different."

But they start chanting: "Just as bad…just as bad."

I manage to get all indignant. "Wake up, you knee-jerks! Between food, vets, and grooming, the U.S. spends $56 billion a year on pets. All that money could've been spent building girls' schools in the Middle East, or on domestic-surveillance drones right here at home!"

St. Francis the bike messenger doesn't skip a beat. "Dogs are people, too!"

The one-percenter with the *Wall Street Journal* hmphs. "That's corporations, you hippie!"

The meter maid gets all school-marmy. "Pets remind us of the innocent, natural part of ourselves, so we care for them. What's wrong with that?"

I bet she's an Internet troll. "You call keeping a predator in a Manhattan studio apartment 'natural'? You call taking control over the fate of a living thing that doesn't have a choice about it an 'expression of caring'?"

Who knew you thought about this stuff?

Please. He's just biding his time until he can heal.

Yep. And I'm just getting started. "Ever been to a puppy farm? It's not like they plant puppy seeds that grow into puppy trees! They're raised in cages smaller than the ones used for chickens. After suffering through that, do you know how many get abandoned every year?"

My strength is returning. I get to my feet.

The crowd gasps. "He can walk!"

"He was only *pretending* to be handicapped!"

"We've got to do something!"

"Get him!"

They're coming for me, but I won't go down easy. I grab the nearest weapon, which happens to be Mr. Snuffles. What? He loved me. I'm sure he'd still want to help me out—like the way the stump in *The Giving Tree* helps that kid.

I swing Snuffles like a cudgel. The crowd backs off—if not in fear, then in disgust. But I know in my heart that deep down, some of them are wondering: What would it feel like to get hit by a puppy?

As it turns out, miracles do happen now and then. When I pull back for a second swipe, what we all thought was a lifeless corpse twitches, inhales, and barks. The bike messenger's coat falls away. Two dark, watery eyes look up at me. His tail wags as he pants. It's my turn to gasp.

"Mr. Snuffles?"

"Yip!"

Maybe the Hulk petted all the air out of him, knocking him out for a while. Maybe Labrador pups have a survival mechanism that makes them go dormant when confronted by gamma-irradiated scientists. Or maybe—somewhere in this crazy, messed-up world—someone made a wish that just happened to come true.

But what does any of that matter? The sonofabitch is alive, I tell you, ALIVE!

"Mr. Snuffles!"

The crowd cheers. Teary-eyed, we all hug. The rich hug the poor, the old hug the young, and best of all, no charges are pressed.

Then I pull my guns, fire a few shots in the air, and they all go running.

But not Mr. Snuffles. He stands at my feet, barking like he chased them off all by himself. Does it get any cuter?

√-1

WHEW! After that emotional roller coaster, I'm a little sick of the monster-dog thing, so I 'port myself and Mr. Snuffles to Cancun for a little mercenary me-time. The beach is busy, but once I swap the ol' work suit for an asymmetric man-thong, I don't have to fire a shot. The whole place clears out.

Mr. Snuffles doesn't mind what I wear. He just likes the sun.

It's a beautiful afternoon. I'm sitting in a beach chair with a fancy umbrella drink, watching the warm waves lick the fine white sand way up into the cracks and crevices of my scarred toes.

Don't get me wrong. I'm totally into getting to the bottom of the whole Dick-and-Jane thing. But no matter how much you love something, your palms are gonna get sweaty if you hold hands with it for too long. Better to let it all go every now and then, step back and recharge, then go back in with your best game.

Right, Mr. Snuffles?

Wow. I'd almost forgotten what silence was like. Sure, there's the sound of the steady surf, some birds, and the breeze rattling the fabric in my beach umbrella, but none of it is as loud as the quiet. Perfect place to kick back, watch a puppy chew on driftwood, and stop thinking for a while.

Why can't you just admit you like him?

That you want a dog of your own?

Hush up. You two are spoiling my buzz. Just… ahhh! Lemme finish this drink, and let the sun and sand work out the kinks in my back.

Why did you pretend you didn't care when you thought he was dead?

Because I didn't care, and I don't, okay?

Then why get all weepy when it turned out he was alive?

Eh, I was swept up in the moment.

You've bonded before, you know.

Yeah, but that's almost always about sex, with a lady—like that MMFF, Jane. And that sort of pleasure only *feels* like it's forever. Eventually it goes away.

Is that how you felt about Sophie watching you at the game?

No. Yes. Maybe. I mean…

Oh, great. I'm trying to take a break here, and now even Mr. Snuffles is looking at me like I'm crazy because I'm sitting here arguing with myself.

Hold your cell phone to your ear.

That way it'll look like you're chatting with someone.

This is not the time for self-contemplation, okay? I've got a drink and a chair and a beach to myself! Can't you both make like white noise for a little while?

Like Radiohead?

But we love you!

(Because we are you!)

Ooo. The parentheses are new!

Parentheses? For the love of…how many of you are in there?

Relax, Wade. We've got lots of tricks.

Huh. What's that new typeface? Bodoni? Never mind. Don't want to know.

The real question is *why* we're here.

(Is it because you're crazy…)

…or just because you need someone to talk to?

Crap. Don't mind me! I'll just sit here, sip my drink, and count the waves.

It used to be called Multiple Personality Disorder. Now it's Dissociative Identity Disorder.

(Technically, it's not even DID, since we don't take over his body.)

Ah! So we're not so much different personas as the same one reflected over and over.

One Wade Wilson warped in a hundred funhouse mirrors.

Not listening! Don't care! Can't hear you. Can't hear any of you at all. La-la-la-la. Not Boldface or Italics, Parenthesis or whatever. Chatter your typefaces off all you want. I'm alone and happy on a gorgeous stretch of sand. La-la-la. Look, Mr. Snuffles, is that a dolphin out there?

So basically, he's pointing out things he knows he should pay attention to, but doesn't want to, because it's either outside his immediate focus or too painful to face.

(Like…did we have a dog once?)

Did we?

Yeah, did we?

Not all dogs who wander are lost.

Oh, is Arial supposed to impress me when Bodoni couldn't? And don't think for a second you can bait me with a Tolkien reference. Sure, the road goes ever on, but so do some of his passages.

(Can you remember if you had a dog?)

What difference does it make? I remember all kinds of crap. When push comes to shove, I have no idea whether any of it's true. Can't do anything about it, so why not keep on keeping on?

We cross our dogs as we come to them and burn them behind us, with nothing to show for our progress except a memory of the smell of smoke and the presumption that once our eyes watered.

Is that another reference?

Yeah. Tom Stoppard, translated into Dog.

As Gregor Samsa awoke one morning from troubled sleep, he discovered he'd transformed in his bed into a large schnauzer.

(That was Kafka. Could you try to remember, Wade?)

Gaze long into a doggie, and the doggie also gazes into you.

That one even I know. Nietzsche. Nietzsche is peachy, but liquor's quicker. How about we compromise, fellas? I'll stick my tongue in a light socket for a day, and you'll all leave me alone for an hour.

He who does not remember the dog is condemned to clean up after it.

I keep telling you, my memory's useless! Whenever I get whacked upside the head, skull-cracked, brain-traumatized, or whatnot, the little gray cells grow back differently—sometimes a little, sometimes a lot.

Dog present and dog past are perhaps both present in dog future.

So what? Even when I hang on to a thread for a little while, eventually my own head gives me a personal retcon. Why bother?

So you can have a story.

Any story is better than none.

If I gave two frigs whether I had a story, I wouldn't be hanging out in Cancun, would I?

Yet story is the basic mode in which we communicate self to ourselves and others. It can be defined by a basic structure of character, conflict, and closure. Some feel conflict isn't necessary, but clearly some sort of desire is required to propel any narrative. Even waiting for an elevator is a type of conflict. Likewise, the desire not to remember is as much a conflict as the desire to remember, and hence part of your story. It is inescapable.

Think you're so smart just because you have that fancy dollop at the end of your lower case f, don't you, Bodoni? I went to elementary school, pal. Block letters can spell all the big words, too.

You just said you can't trust your memory.

So how can you be sure you went to school at all?

All dogs, except one, grow up.

Look, even if this is part of my story, can't it be a

part where I just chillax? What's wrong with letting go and winging it?

Some writers make things up as they go along, surprising themselves or letting the characters take over. While the end justifies the means, strategically this is like being a magician who doesn't want to know how his tricks work. When building castles in the sky, isn't it better to know where the bricks came from so the castle can be built again, if need be?

No, because IT DOESN'T MATTER. Really. I know I'm in a fictional reality. While that might freak out most folks, it makes me feel better. It means that even if the Hulk *had* killed Mr. Snuffles, he wouldn't have gotten hurt, since he doesn't exist. On the other hand, it means there's hope for the real world, wherever it may be.

Either way, IT DOESN'T MATTER.

The most merciful thing in the world is the inability of the canine mind to correlate all its contents.

Thank you, Arial! Exactly. So what's the point of getting connected?

Because stories not only exist, they hold everything else together.

We are such stuff as dogs are made of, and our little life is rounded with a woof.

Oh, for the love of… Fine! Listen up! Want to know what I remember? I remember losing my mother to cancer.

All happy doggies are alike; each unhappy doggie is unhappy in its own way.

I remember Dad hitting me as often as he hit the floor. I remember, even as a kid, feeling crowded into my own skin and wanting to punch my way out. I remember really, really liking to take things apart.

(Garçon! Can we get a drink here?)

Shh! He's sharing.

It was the best of dogs, it was the worst of dogs.

I remember him calling it tough love, the way the righteous wield a sword of justice. I remember being okay with the justice, but more interested in the sword—in fighting back. I remember, by the time I left high school, having a bunch of angry psychos as friends—a gang of punk Dads. I remember one of them shooting real Dad with his own handgun.

And the dog said, "Nevermore."

And, okay, yeah, sure, I think I remember a dog somewhere along the line, in middle school—before things went really crazy. Something that loved me without talking back, or hitting me, or asking anything at all, except maybe for food and a walk.

What a piece of work is dog. How noble in duck-hunting. How infinite in stick-fetching. In action how like a squirrel.

Real or not, I remember wishing it could last forever. It didn't, but I did. I lasted forever. Even when I'm supposed to die, I keep coming back. And that's all I've got on that! Happy?

Because I could not stop for dog, it kindly stopped to pee.

Did I have a dog? For real? Or do I just feel like I should've?

All dogs happen, more or less.

But I *also* remember, just as clearly, being the richest man in the world. Having lived to a ripe old age, I lie in an expensive bed surrounded by countless treasures, clutching a framed photo of a boy and his puppy. Before I pass into the great beyond, the frame slips from my feeble fingers, cracking against the floor as I whisper my final word: "Rosebud."

That's *Citizen Kane*.

Exactly! Half the time I remember being Leonardo DiCaprio in *Titanic*. I don't want to explain myself because I can't, not really, not ever. So I just want me to shut up. I just want…

The dog died today. Or maybe yesterday. I can't be sure.

Come on, guys, can't you see he's hurting?

This is freakier than seeing the Hulk cry.

(We're sorry, Wade. Go on, take your break.)

Yeah, we'll be quiet for at least a chapter. Promise.

No! Y'know what? Too freaking late! Come on, Mr. Snuffles. I'm dropping you off with Preston. Then it's time to get back to work.

EIGHTEEN

IN THE 1950s, New York's SoHo was called Hell's Hundred Acres. It was all sweatshops, factories, and warehouses—packed with underpaid labor by day, empty by night. By the 1960s, the businesses were gone. A bunch of bohemian artists saw all those tall-windowed buildings and said, "Oooo! Natural lighting!" In the 1980s, Yuppies saw all the Bohemians living there and said, "Oooo! A justification for our conspicuous consumption!" These days, the converted lofts are mostly up to code. The few genuine townhouses in the area go for between three million and why-would-one-person-ever-have-*that*-much-money?

I can't imagine that the next address on the list would go for anywhere near that kind of cash. A worn-brick Federal with a red door painted black, it looks less like a crib for the rich and famous and more the sort of rundown haunted house you'd expect to be inhabited by a 1970s-horror-comic host. The owner's name, Cruston Withers, matches the ambience nicely.

I'd assume Cruston Withers is an alias, but I live in a world where people have names like von Doom. Here's the really weird thing—and you've gotta use the word weird loosely in this book—Cruston Withers didn't receive just one suspect puppy, or two, or ten.

He got *thirty*.

Meaning we may not be talking pets in the traditional sense.

Oh, I could burst in, katana swinging, and let God sort out the guilty. But oddly enough, I'm feeling mellow (A.K.A. psychologically drained) after my beach break. Could be more fun trying to guess what the hell he's up to in there first—make up a story myself for a change.

Going with the horror-comic theme, I picture a lonely old guy sitting in a chair by a roaring fire, regaling his dogs with terror tales to blow their minds, like "The Lurking Fear at Shadow House" (for you Steranko fans!).

Or…

He could be a male variation on Cruella de Vil, planning to use the dogs for a bathrobe.

Nah. The pups are different breeds. Skins wouldn't match.

Maybe he's a recent immigrant who misses the old country, and he's preparing a stew to remind himself of home. They still eat dog in lots of countries: China, Indonesia, Korea, Mexico, the Philippines, Polynesia, Taiwan, and Vietnam. Hell, a few hundred thousand folks in Switzerland like to chow down on Tabby and Spot around Christmas time. No lie.

Does Withers sound Swiss? No idea.

Besides, thirty pups would feed a lot of people, and this place does not look crowded.

Let's try the needlessly optimistic route. Cruston

might be a stand-up guy, misunderstood because his name is as freaky as his house. He may be planning to give all those puppies to disadvantaged kids.

No, no, no. I've got it. Check this out:

Sick of humankind and its cruelties, the lonely Cruston Withers wants to be a dog himself. He gets a bunch as puppies so they'll be more likely to accept him as one of their own. Then he dresses himself up in a dog costume and… Feh. Bored now. May as well walk up and ask. I can always start shooting later if I feel like it.

The place has one of those old-style manual doorbells. Real old style—no electricity needed. You twist the knob, and an actual bell actually rings. So I do that a few times.

I wait. I hum a little. I look at my feet, up at the sky. Then I twist it again.

It's not very loud. He might not hear it if he's on the can or watching TV, or breathing. If he's an older coot with failing ears, he may never hear it. But there I go again, making assumptions. Just because his last name is Withers doesn't mean he's old. He could be in his twenties for all I know. Besides, we already did the senior-citizen thing with Aunt May.

Though I would have preferred cash, my patience is rewarded by the steady swish of slippers sliding on a wooden floor. The knob twists and pulls, but the door won't open. Like I'm supposed to believe he forgot it was locked. I get a few clicks and clacks while the bolt draws back and the chain's undone. The black-painted door creaks open a crack.

You knew it was going to creak, didn't you?

I end up looking into two squinting eyes peering through Coke-bottle glasses.

Yep. He's old. He's even wearing a plaid bathrobe and using a wooden cane. So we're repeating ourselves. But this is no spry, vivacious Aunt May. We're talking Methuselah. Wrinkled skin on a bony head, white hair so thin you can barely see it. He's hunched, but just a little. To his credit, he's got a barrel chest that doesn't lend itself to easy bending, as though he was a dock worker once upon a time.

There's a long, dim hall behind him with, yep, a ticking grandfather clock sitting at the end. No sign of anything moving, aside from the clock's pendulum, but the puppy smell is thick.

"Hey there, Mr. Withers? Cruston Withers?"

"Go away."

No "What is this, Halloween?" or "What do you want?" Just "Go away." Points off for being stereotypically crabby. He tries to close the door, but I shove my toe in.

"Now, now, this'll just take a second."

"It's not a good time."

The floppy bathrobe hides his arms, but they're strong enough to slam the door and nip the end of my big toe. Not an easy thing to do. Plus, it hurts. Maybe he's *not* so clichéd, after all.

Admiring my bruised foot, I notice something else near the ground, something wedged in the jam.

It's the sort of thing Sherlock Holmes might call a clue. It looks like a dried piece of skin, a wrinkle that got sick of living on Cruston's face and decided to make a break for it. I bend down and try to pick it up, but it's stuck in the door. It stretches, but doesn't come free until it snaps.

Huh. Latex—as in a makeup appliance, the kind they'd use to set someone up as an extra from *Beneath the Dignity of the Apes*...or...to make someone seem old. Hmm. This is suspicious. People usually go out of their way to look *younger*. Then again, it's a big world. You have to figure there are a few trailblazers who try to look old. Maybe they think it makes them look more respectable.

But Withers seemed ancient. When it comes down to it, there's only one sort that makes himself up to look like a particularly frail old man. Someone who isn't frail.

Y'know, I'm starting to think maybe Withers *isn't* his real name.

The door has an old crack down the middle. I apply a little pressure, and the wood groans, ready to give. Easy to crash through, but he could be anywhere in there—why warn him? Must be a sneakier way in.

Manhattan townhouses never have decent alleys, so away to the rooftop I fly. En route, I pass a first-floor window, where I spy with my little eye a set of heavy-duty weights. Second floor, I see a room full of bowling trophies, which doesn't seem to have much to do with anything. No doggies, though.

The roof's a disappointment. No skylight. It's overdone, but I *love* crashing through those things. Nothing much to speak of at all up here, other than that black tarpaper stuff that covers most flat roofs. When I peer down back, I spot one cool feature you might not expect: an actual yard. It's tiny. I wouldn't raise sheep there, but it does provide those special moments of privacy for the mercenary on the go.

A hand to a windowsill, a drop, and I'm down. All the rear windows are dark except for the one in the basement. It's one of those thin jobs, low to the ground, so I have to get on my knees for a look. At least now the bowling trophies make sense. Cruston's got himself a lane down here—complete with a pinsetter, a digital scorekeeper, and an alley that's been polished to perfection.

Doesn't leave much space for thirty puppies. The rest of the place looks as vacant as Sophie's face that time I asked her to a movie, so where the hell are they?

Cruston steps in. Not seeing me, he chucks his cane aside, throws off his Coke-bottle glasses, and slips into his bowling shoes. Then he straightens, flexes his arms, and cracks his knuckles.

It's like I'm watching him change into his secret identity as…Bowling Man?

But which is his *true* self? Old man or young bowler? And does he have a sidekick named Gutter Boy?

He grabs a ball and steps to the line. When he grins, I think he sees me, but he hasn't. The end of the alley is below the window. He's looking at the pins.

I can see how he earned all those trophies. When he moves, he uses a classic stroking form, favoring finesse and accuracy over speed and power. Shoulders square to the line, up goes his backswing, his arm about parallel to the ground, leading to a smooth, almost silent release.

See what I mean about my memory? I've been married like four times, but for the life of me can't remember their names right now. This crap, I know— and I have no idea *how* I know.

From here it looks like the ball's headed straight for the 1-3 pocket. I can tell exactly when it hits, because Cruston's face lights up, cracking a bunch of that old man latex.

Only, instead of clacking pins, I hear…yapping.

Sweet Lord.

Why would I bother making up stories when the world keeps throwing things like this my way? He's not Bowling Man. He's not a hero. He's a…

The basement window is thick, a metal mesh sunk into the glass to discourage intruders. I'm not discouraged—not by a long shot. I'm in, landing feet first in the center of the alley before a broken shard can hit the ground.

A look back at the pins confirms the sickening truth.

-choke-

They're not pins, they're puppies! OMG, they're puppies! He's using puppies as bowling pins! Held into shape by Velcro straps! Sweet mercy!

He did get a strike, though. Got to give him that. All ten pup-pins fallen and whimpering, they're nearly swept back into the sorter. I tear out the guts of the machine, revealing that their twenty brothers and sisters are being held in the device. I free them so quickly and furiously, Cruston doesn't get the time to move.

When I turn to face him, he's still staring at me in shock.

"Not a good time, huh? Is *this* a good time?"

I clock him in the gut. His abs are nice and hard, probably from all those workouts, so the second time I drive my fist into him, I don't feel any need to hold back.

"How about *now*?" A right to his jaw.

"Is *now* a good time?" A left to the chin.

What remains of the latex and fake hair sloughs off. He's no retiree—he's a bruiser in his prime. Even so, I have to wonder how he's still standing after the sixth blow. Then I realize I've been punching him at just the right angle to keep him up on his feet. I guess even my instincts don't like him.

I stop for a second. Down he goes.

He tries to crawl away. His voice is pained, but macho deep. "You don't know what it's like!"

I shove my mouth against his right ear and scream:

"Bowling with puppies? Why would *anyone* know what that's like?"

"I don't hurt them!"

Figuring there are two sides to every story, I try to calm myself by kicking him in the side. "You tie them up in little shapes, run them through a pinsetter, and hurl a sixteen-pound bowling ball at them! How can you not be hurting them?"

"I...I think they like it!"

Bunching his plaid robe in one hand, I lift him so we're face-to-face.

"Like it? LIKE IT? How about I run you through all that and see how YOU like it?"

"Okay! Maybe they *don't* like it. But I swear, I don't hurt them...much."

I pull back for another go. He puts up his hands and pleads.

"Please. Didn't you ever have something you felt like you *had* to do, even though most people would think you were crazy for doing it?"

I narrow my eyes. "Like killing bad guys for pleasure?"

"Well...uh...if that's where you want to go, sure, I guess. You gotta believe me, I wasn't always like this." His eyes get all weepy. "I was a bowling champ, playing in the big leagues. Had a trophy bride to go with the trophies and all the money in the world. Night of the big match, I'm one frame shy of a perfect game and making my approach when this kid's puppy gets loose from his birthday party. It goes running across the lanes. I see it heading toward mine, but I'm in the zone. I didn't want to break focus, and I figured it would see the ball coming and get out of the way, but then…then…"

He closes his eyes and lowers his head. "I was kicked out of the league. My gal left me for a foosball champ. I became a pariah. Oh, I tried to move on, I swear. I even thought I had. Then, one afternoon, I chucked a rock at a squirrel—and in some weird way, out of nowhere, I felt better. All the pain I'd been carrying around disappeared for a while. But it came back, worse than before, and I realized what I had to do to keep it away."

"Oh, you poor thing." I punch him again a few times, but stop before he passes out. "One question. Why do you dress like an old man?"

Face bruised, teeth loose, he offers a feeble shrug. "That, I just kind of like."

Well, I'm not going to judge someone for how they dress. The puppies, though? Holding him up by his robe, I smash his face, letting go at just the right moment so he flies a few feet before hitting the ground.

I'm deciding how best to continue our little chat when a rumbling down by the machinery turns me around. Damn it! Thought I tore out enough of the guts, but the pinsetter must still be working. All this time I've been busy having fun, those poor pups have been in danger of resetting.

"Quick, how do you kill the power?"

Cruston points to a circuit panel. I yank the main breaker, and all the lights go out—but the rumbling continues.

"That should've worked, I swear!"

It gets louder. So loud, it's obvious now that it's not the pinsetter—or any machinery at all. It's one of the pin-pups, a cherubic beagle half wedged in the gutter. He's thundering against the lane like he weighs a ton. He falls and rolls toward us in a wobbly bowling-pin way. As his furry form begins to enlarge, the Velcro straps holding him in pin shape crackle and snap one by one.

He's free, on all fours, almost still looking like a dog, but the malevolently glowing eyes are a giveaway. The thing he's becoming rises up on its back paws, like it's begging. The hindquarters thicken into decidedly un-doglike legs and feet. The front paws throb into formidable four-fingered hands. The chest widens, rib cage cracking as it grows. Its ears become less floppy, more goblin-like. The snout—heritage of the proud breed that inspired Snoopy—pulses and warps into a grotesque porcine parody. Horns sprout on its head—not huge, but no less attention-grabbing thanks to the hawk-shaped black patches of skin leading up to them.

Color? Mostly two shades of green, with a black raccoon mask around the eyes.

Being fifteen feet tall prevents it from standing in the low-ceiling basement, but it tries. As it flexes, it cries out in a hollow, aching voice that speaks of the infinite stretches of the empty abyss of space:

"I AM GRUTO, THE CREATURE FROM NOWHERE!"

Nowhere? Can't let that one go.

"Is that a beatnik reference? Like, Nowheresville, man?"

The big lug looks around, puzzled, genuinely lost. "How came I to be here? And from where did I come? Why cannot I remember?"

Hey, I've been there—waking up disoriented in a bowling alley, lousing up my sentence structure. It's like staring into a mirror. But this isn't the time or place for a metanoia.

Cruston crazy-crawls for the door, hoping to get lost in all the excitement. Torture's kind of a sore spot with me, falling squarely in that "deserving" category. So I point at him.

"Oh, Gruto! I know how you came to be here! It was him! That guy, the one on his knees, wetting his pants! He's the one what brung ya!"

Gruto's head snaps toward the bowler. He puffs air from his nostrils like a big bull with a raccoon mask. "I...hunger!"

"No, please! No!" Cruston picks up his pace and scuttles out into the hallway.

I try to give Gruto some space, but it takes him a long time to squeeze through the door. By the time he's out, Cruston's nowhere to be seen. And the rest of the basement's a long, wide, cluttered mess: old weights, a steamer chest, a dress dummy, an old birdcage, a haunted Ouija board—you know the drill.

Poor Gruto. You can tell he's no good at hide-and-seek from the way he's forlornly squirming around, halfheartedly pushing stuff out of the way. That leaves it up to me. The stairs are the only way out, and I haven't heard anyone on them, so he must still be down here. Hm.

I slink up to Gruto and whisper, "We're a team, right?"

The Creature from Nowhere nods.

"Okay, then. I'm going to creep over and hide by the stairs. You stay back here and make a bunch of noise, so he thinks the coast is clear. Got it? Let's do this."

I creep back to the stairs, find myself a shadowy spot, and motion for Gruto to do his thing.

"Where could that human be? I hunger!"

Sure enough, some boxes shudder, and Cruston skulks out, trying to reach the stairs.

I'm on him. "Going somewhere?"

He gets on his knees, begging like a you-know-what. "Don't let it get me!"

I almost feel bad for him. "Sigh. Do you promise to never, ever bowl again?"

Even if he says yes, there's no reason to believe him. But if *something's* going to make a sadist reevaluate his life decisions, having one of his victims turn into a raging monster and try to eat him may be just the thing. So, yeah, I'm thinking about letting him go, but then he goes and ruins it all.

"I'll…I'll use squirrels! I swear it!"

"Here he is, Gruto! Right here!"

"Noooooo!"

Before long, Gruto's belly is full. I'm already fond of the big guy, so I hate to think about it, but what if Withers was like Chinese food and Gruto's hungry again in an hour? By rights, I should spritz him into oblivion here and now. But when he eyes me with that creepy look of gratitude, I can almost still see the puppy in his face. If he stays docile, maybe I can get S.H.I.E.L.D. to study him?

Have to be sure, though. "Gruto, let's head upstairs and talk a minute, okay?"

The living room ceiling is taller; the afternoon sun pleasant. Gruto manages to slump into a loveseat without hitting his head. I pull up a chair, sit, and look at him.

"We're not so different, are we? You lash out due to genetically programmed aggression. I enjoy killing, but not inflicting senseless pain. Usually, anyway. They call us monsters, but it's the sadistic creeps like the one you just ate who are the real monsters. Oh, buddy…" I point to his teeth. "You've got a little piece of Cruston right…there."

He's civilized enough to look embarrassed. As he picks his teeth, I'm thinking this could work.

"So we've got that in common. And the amnesia thing? I don't tell everyone this, but even when I do remember something about my past, I can't exactly trust it."

It looks like I'm getting through. "Do you… hunger for living flesh, as well?"

"No, but different strokes, right? Thing is, since

you and I can't define ourselves by our memories, maybe we can define each other through, you know, mutual trust. I guess I'm saying maybe we could be… you know, buds. Or we don't even have to put a name on it. If S.H.I.E.L.D. gives you some downtime from their testing, we could just hang out sometime."

I'm not sure if I'm making him misty-eyed or bored, but his eyes drift over to the window. A gassy, boiling sound erupts from his torso.

"Heh. That your stomach growling or an earthquake? Wanna order some pizza?"

He's still not making eye contact, so I slump back in the chair.

"I get it. I'm being pushy. I totally understand. I get the reluctance, the disorientation, the rage that comes bubbling up out of nowhere. Nowhere, that's where you're from, right? I'm only saying, I'm at a place right now where I feel like I'm from Nowhere, too. Maybe we could be from Nowhere together?"

CRASH!

All fifteen feet of him go out the window. Well, mostly the window. He takes out a hunk of wall, too. See that? I put myself out there, and even a freaking monster only wants to get away from me. It's middle school and Sophie all over again. It's like my life is just another cheap monster story.

Maybe you should check out what he was staring at.

Thought you were going to leave me alone for a chapter. But why bother?

You have to stop him.

Plus, it'll make you feel better.

How? Is this what I've come to? So pathetic I have to go chasing after some self-centered creature to get some attention? He's no prize. Why doesn't *he* have to stop *me*? If I'm such a loser, why are they making a feature film about me? A much-*anticipated* feature film, I might add. Anyone elevator-pitching a *Gruto, the Creature from Nowhere*? What does that tell you?

No, listen to us.

You have to stop him because he's a monster loose on the streets.

Oh. I get you. A metaphor. Solving his problems is like solving my own. Funny, you'd think I'd be more in tune with subtext when I'm talking to myself.

It's not subtext!

Look out the window!

Oh, my. And I've got a great view, too. Kids again. Right across the street, twelve little girls in school uniforms are marching along in two straight lines. Sounds familiar, but what really matters is the opportunistic apex predator headed straight for them.

"Gruto hungers!"

Oh, Gruto. We *all* hunger, don't we? In another place, another time, we might've been friends. As it is, I hop out with my ADD and zap him into goo.

NINETEEN

TheRealWade16: Cleanup's here. Where're u? How's Mr. Snuffles and the collie?

Preston2.0: Stuck w/paperwork, meaning the paper they use for their business. These dogs are like a water cooler w/broken tap. ☹

TheRealWade16: So…room for more? ●●

Preston2.0: ×ב ?! How many?

TheRealWade16: Uh…29.

Preston2.0: ×ב They *have* to go to the lab.

TheRealWade16: NVM. I'll work something out. ●● BFN.

UNDAUNTED, I trot back down to the whimpering crowd in the private bowling alley. Soulful eyes trapped in pin shapes stare at me, sad as sad can be. You know the drill: I dunno which are actual pups, which may go super-sized, yadda yadda yadda. I'm no expert on dog breeds, but I see an Afghan, a malamute, foxhound and spaniel, shepherd and schnauzer, basset and boxer, retriever, Doberman, deerhound and pointer, setter and Dane, mastiff, Newfoundland, sheepdog, Pekingese, poodle, pug, rottweiler, husky, whippet, vizsla, Shiba Inu, Weimaraner, schipperke, and I think that little fellow is a Samoyed.

Like I said, I'm no expert, but I already had the smartphone out to text Preston, so I looked them all up. And despite whatever weakness I may have previously displayed toward the magical Mr. Snuffles, I remain a pure professional, offering calming words as I do what I must.

"Don't be afraid, little ones! The mean Bowling Man is gone, and I'm here to save you!"

A few tugs here and there, and they're off scampering. Thankfully, being bound up has done nothing to stifle their youthful enthusiasm. It's like overwinding spring toys and setting them down to run amok. They bounce off this, skid on that, crash into each other, tear into cardboard and old clothes.

You'd think the overflow of delightfulness would tug at my wounded heart, but the sheer numbers make it easier to keep my emoticons to myself. One puppy is adorable. Twenty-nine is a statistic. Still, rather than subject them to a lab, I'm thinking I'll take them along on the next job. Question is, how? Mr. Snuffles, I could hold in one hand. Sigh. Mr. Snuffles.

Cruston left a collection of bowling-ball bags, but if I figure four pups to a bag, I'd wind up lugging seven bags with one dog left over. Boxes? Bulky. Backpack? Maybe. There's a pile of burlap sacks that could work. Has to be better than the Velcro.

I lay one sack down, hold an end open, slap my thigh, and point inside. "Here, guys! In here!"

You probably think that'd never work. Shows what you know. Dogs and sacks are like toddlers and cardboard boxes. It's their favorite thing. The closest pup, a pug, is a little hesitant at first, but his curiosity wins out, and he heads on in. After that, the others follow. Soon I've got ten rolling around in there happy as you please, with the others waiting for a turn.

By the time I get the last of them into the third sack, the first group's gotten a little quiet. Remembering the ugly Hulk incident, I peek in. No problems. They're all cozy, lying on each other, keeping warm. A few have even fallen asleep, probably exhausted from trauma. And the fabric lets in plenty of air. Seal them off with a gently tied bow, hoist the bags over my shoulder, and I'm ready to roll.

Where does our next lucky contestant reside? The wilds of Westchester County. Yeah, it's famous for Charles Xavier's School for Gifted Geeks—A.K.A. the X-Men—but that's in Salem Center, so far north it's practically Putnam. This early dog-adopter is in Briarcliff Manor. Google Earth shows me a recently constructed home sporting a lush 0.6 acres of lawn.

Without further ado (did we have ado earlier?), I 'port into a wooded patch behind the Double Quarter Pounder with cheese. That's a McMansion joke, btw.

Don't know if you're keeping track of time—I'm not—but when I arrive, it's dark enough for the owners to have the lights on. I gently lay my puppy-love-sacks down on soft earth covered by pine needles. I'm on my way to a manicured backyard when I notice a little marker stuck in the ground among the junk trees. It's all of two popsicle sticks glued together in a cross. A single word, nearly faded, is written on them, scrawled by a youthful hand in purple crayon:

Goldie

A grave some kid made for his pet fish. Hate to think I'm here to add to his losses, but that is part of the reason people give their children pets. The marker is pretty old, anyway. The kid must be over it by now; with any luck, it's prepared him for the loss he's about to experience.

But then I notice another marker: Gerry the Gerbil.

And another, with better penmanship: Mehitabel the Cat.

And another: Gef the Mongoose.

It's like a pet necropolis. They're all over. That's a lot of bad luck for one kid. His pet care may not have improved over the years, but his funerary design has sure picked up. The newer graves sport ornate designs. There's even a Play-Doh stele for Oscar the Ferret, with an inscription:

> Remember me as you pass by,
> As you are now, so once was I,
> As I am now, so you will be,
> Prepare for death and follow me.

Brrr! There's something about all these silent little graves, the hollow chirps of insect minds, the gray trees with long-fingered branches. It's not easy for someone whose skin oozes multicolored pus to get the willies, but at this point, one lone wind whistling through the trees behind me is all it takes. I snap my head around, expecting the Blair Witch to jump up with a shaky camcorder.

Leaves crunch. Or is it more wind? A branch snaps. A squirrel? A shovel chucks in the dirt, and I almost leap out of my cancer-scarred skin.

It came from behind me, away from the house and deeper in the small wood. Taking a few steps closer, I see a flashlight poke dying yellow light along the ground, hitting even more grave markers. How big *is* this junior cemetery?

The shovel chucks again. The yellow light wobbles and threatens to fade. You just can't get a decent flashlight these days. I can see the digger, but barely. He's a silhouette in the dark, a shadow against shadow, a blacker black hunched over a bunch of grayness. There's a hiss. Around where his mouth should be, a horrid, swelling pink mass rises into the dying flashlight beam. The glowing orb grows, then disappears with a pop.

Bubble gum. It's a kid chewing bubblegum. Of course it's a kid. Heh. What else would it be? And the graves? Maybe this is where *all* the neighborhood kids bury their pets. Nothing strange about that.

Much.

If he's digging that hole for the dog on my list, it's not going to be turning into a monster. Have to be sure who the deceased is, though. Maybe he waited to bury his previous pet until he got a new one. I move closer, loudly, so he can hear me coming. No need for both of us to be scared, right?

As he comes more clearly into view, I feel pretty stupid for getting spooked. He's a pudgy, Harry Potter type, maybe seven years old, in jeans and old sneakers. He couldn't look more harmless if he tried. Unless he's a vampire, I guess. Even then, I've got him on weight. Speed too, judging from the way he's moving that shovel. It's heavy for him, but he doesn't stop digging.

Chuck. Chuck. Chuck.

Think he'd have noticed me by now, but aside from being totally focused, he's got flecks of soil on his glasses. While I'm waiting, I catch a whiff of fresh-cut pine and earthy clay. The pine's coming from a coffin-shaped box on the ground behind him. The hinges are mismatched, and a nail pokes out, but it's not bad woodwork for a kid. The clay smell is coming from the headstone he's got propped up against a tree. It's a wafer-thin, slate-colored copy of an old Puritan marker, complete with a crudely etched angel of death on the tympanum— and underneath, the words:

HERE LIES
RUSTY

Kid has talent. Hate to interrupt. It's sort of a sacred moment, after all, and, well, he's almost done with the digging. Giving him another half a minute won't hurt. Besides, I'm so close, I have to figure out how to let him know I'm here without making him crap his pants. I'm already a masked man skulking around the back of his house. If I say something like "Don't scream," it'll only make it worse.

The kid's done now. Still not seeing me, he drags the box into the hole, settles it in straight, and starts pushing the loose earth back in. No way to avoid it anymore. I clear my throat.

"Hey, kid."

He doesn't even look up. "You sure dress funny, mister. Are you a burger?"

"I think you mean *burglar*. Me? Nah."

He gathers a shovel-full of dirt and tosses it in the hole. "If you are, you should try next door. They've got much more stuff than we do."

"Really? What kind of stuff? Do they have a fourth-gen gaming console?" I clear my throat again. "Uh…never mind. So…not a lot of luck in the pet department, huh?"

"Mom says it's a question of perspection. It 'pends how you look at it."

I nod sympathetically. "Perspective. Right. When you lose someone you care about, you're better off relishing the happy times than dwelling on the loss."

"Plus, she says you don't have to feed it or clean up after it anymore."

Okay, then, moving on. Better try to ease him into it before I ask any unpleasant questions about the pooch. "It's nice here—peaceful. Very natural. These graves all yours?"

"Uh-huh." He sticks the shovel in the dirt, then rests his chin on the handle. "I've been making them since I was little. Popsicle sticks got boring, so I started copying hiscorical pictures."

"Historical."

"Uh-huh."

I look at the clay marker lying against the tree. "Cool headstone. I'm sure Rusty would like it. He a doggie?"

He sighs. "Just a puppy. Mommy and Daddy got him for me yesterday."

"Yesterday." That's my target, then, so no hurry. "Wow. Uh…how'd he die so quick? He get sick? Hit by a car?"

He shakes his head. "Oh, he's not dead, mister."

Thinking there may still be some Goom in my ears and I didn't hear him correctly, I whack my head. "What'd you say? Not…?"

"But he will be. All living things need…oxy-tin."

"Oxygen."

"Uh-huh. Even fish. It's in water, so they need gills to breathe it. People don't have gills, so they drown in water, but a fish drowns without water."

"Back up a bit, Mr. Wizard. You bury your pets alive?"

"Mostly."

"Why?"

He shrugs. "I like making the little grave markers,

and my mommy said I can't make 'em anymore unless I have to. The mean school counselor said it was too… moo-bid?"

"Morbid."

"Uh-huh."

I dive toward him. "Are you related to a guy named Cruston, you miserable little…?"

I grab him and yank him toward me, but stop myself before I do anything he'll regret. The shovel falls, hitting the flashlight and sending it rolling into the dark. He's not like Cruston. He's just a kid. A psychopath, sure, but just a little one. Brain's not developed enough yet to have a moral compass. This could be a phase. He could grow up to be a CEO. Or Hitler.

I put him down and pat his clothes all nicey-nice. "Listen. As someone who gets a kick out of taking lives in interesting and, yeah, I like to think poetic, ways, part of me's impressed by all your hard work. The thing is…" I look around, hoping to see the right words carved on a tree trunk somewhere. No luck. "The thing is, I draw very specific lines about who does and doesn't deserve it. Your poor pets, they…wait."

The flashlight settles, its beam slicing across the new markers on two more freshly dug graves. One says, "**Mom**"; the other, "**Dad**."

I go into a standard pose of extreme shock and frustration. You know the one—hunched over, hands out, fingers curled, head thrown back.

"Holy crap! Did you…could you…? A little guy

like…? How'd you even…?"

He shrugs. "I used chora…flora…"

"Chloroform!"

I grab the shovel. He looks like he's afraid I'll smack him with it, and I admit it crosses my mind, but I step past him, toward the mom-and-pop plots. Some quick chuck-chuck-chucking of my own—and yep, there's truth in labeling. They didn't get boxes. He just bound and gagged them. I got to them in time. They're alive and squirming, staring up at me, unsure whether to be grateful or even more afraid.

"Pretty strange day for you two, huh? Knocked out and buried alive by your Bad Seed, and now you wake up staring at my masked kisser? Funny old world, ain't it?"

The kid tries to tug the shovel from my hands. "Please, mister! When my mommy saw Rusty's coffin, I heard her tell Daddy she couldn't take it anymore! She was going to call the social cervixes—"

"Services."

"—and they were going to take me away, and I got scared!"

We all get scared. Thing is, after seeing all this, there's something on my mind. It's a little dark thing, hard like a crumb, but a perfect dot. It's right over… got it.

What the hell is that? Some kind of bug? A poppy seed?

Honestly, I'm relieved when the loose soil above Rusty's resting place gets the shakes. Clumps of soil roll down the sides of the small mound, more and more, until whatever's giving off all that energy down there can't contain itself any longer.

Bright, blinding light stabs upward in white spears that stretch from the grave to the stars. The earth shakes and parts. A hand reaches up—a giant hand wrapped in flax linen. Ripping through the dirt, it spreads its fingers as if touching the air for the first time in millennia. The huge arm follows, pulling the wrapped body to the surface with it, head and all. The linen is ancient—some dangles in shards—but the vile body remains completely covered, save for the dead yellow eyes.

The kid gasps. "Rusty?"

The parents cry out: "Mmf?"

They're answered by a voice like a dry desert wind: "I am Gomdulla, the Living Pharaoh! Tremble, mortals, before my awesome might!"

Norman Bates Jr. ducks behind me like all of a sudden, I'm his best friend. I put my hands on my hips and stare up at the towering form.

"Living Pharaoh? Oh, please. First of all, we've already had Goom, Gorgolla, and Gruto! I'm sick of the G-names, okay? Second of all, you don't really expect me to believe you have an actual political title like Pharaoh, do you? Which dynasty? Old Kingdom or New? No answer? Thought so. Third, wait for it…you call that living?"

Rimshot.

Between the trees, the parents, the bagged dogs, and that lone whistling wind, it's too risky to use the

ADD. The sensor only lets me fire it at a monster, but if anything else gets in the way...

I whisper to the kid, "Run."

"Can't I please get some better names here? How about Gravitas, the Thing that Must Be Taken Seriously? No, wait, that's another G. Hold on. Maybe Toe, The Thing that Went Whee, Whee, Whee! All the Way Home?"

I hear crickets. At first I'm worried the audience doesn't like the jokes. People are crossing their arms. Even Sophie isn't laughing. Then I remember there is no audience. I'm outside in a patch of woods, and there really *are* crickets chirping.

Another costumed character might use his witty patter to distract his foes. Not me. I never could stop talking. At least Gomdulla's still staring at me, unsure how to react. The running kid, who really should be on some watch list somewhere, almost gets out of sight, but then stumbles over one of his own headstones. The mummy's eyes squint. He raises a wrapped arm and points a bony finger the size of a foot-long hot dog—meaning it's about a foot long.

"You buried me!"

Mini American Psycho looks over his shoulder, terrified. "I'm only six! I'm not restonsible for my actions!"

I cup a hand around my mouth and scream, "Responsible!"

Big mummy legs cover ground fast. Before I finish thinking that last sentence, Gomdulla's over me, swatting trees out of the way to reach his former owner.

"Dude! Cut him some slack! Didn't you ever bury stuff alive when you were a kid? Oh, right. You weren't a kid. You were a dog. My bad."

I jump, sliding out my trusty and not-at-all-rusty katana, landing on that broad, linen-covered back like it's a 3,000-year-old futon. The swords' points dig in, going deep and deeper. No idea what he's got in there, but the blades don't seem to register.

He tries to shake me off, but I ride the blades' hilts down his back, opening up a wound wide enough to drive a truck through. Okay, maybe not a truck, but a Prius, easy. I hop off somewhere around the waistline, expecting that to hurt, at least. It doesn't.

He reaches down for Lil' Hannibal Lecter. Based on what Gomdulla's done to the trees, it won't take more than two of those fingers to squish the kid. Well, if pain is meaningless, there's always physics. Since he's not as meaty as his G-name brothers, I go for the ankles, cutting away until both of his feet come free. He falls—toward the kid.

Arm outstretched, palms down, it looks like he'll crush him.

Time to take a risk.

The Pharaoh's open back wound hasn't sealed yet, so I toss in the ADD. Its green "active" light flips end over end as it passes into the gash, landing somewhere within his dry, dusty confines. I see it blink twice more before the tear heals up, covering it completely.

Huh. I was hoping it'd hit something in there that

would set it off and spray his innards. Oh, well.

His hand plunges toward the kid. The kid raises his own hand to shield his eyes from what's coming. For a moment, it's tiny hand against great big hand.

Then Gomdullah goes *bloop*. Like the others before him, the extra-large mummy rains his organic pinkness on the woods. A single drop hits the kid's index finger. He shakes his hand, flicking it off into the enormous puddle. With no more monster innards to hold it, the ADD clatters to the earth. Ha! Something *did* press the trigger.

Leaving us back at that whole who-is-the-real-monster-here conceit.

I take hold of the kid. "We really need to have a little talk about right and wrong. Like, suppose a runaway train is heading toward five people tied to the track, but you can flip a switch that'll send the train down a different track where only *one* person is tied up. Do you flip the switch, killing one person, or do you do nothing and let five people die?"

He can't answer. He doesn't get it. Or maybe he's frozen with fear. I think about taking him back to S.H.I.E.L.D., but I don't want him in the same building with Mr. Snuffles.

If I put him down to untie Mom and Dad, he'll book, so I carry him toward the house. "You got an aunt or a babysitter? Someone still alive in the neighborhood I can call?"

Nothing.

On the street in front of the house, squealing

brakes shatter the suburban illusion of peace. Kid under my arm, I'm doused by flashing white-and-blue lights. A tired man with an honest face runs toward us, panting. The three police officers behind him are armed and in better shape.

Once he's caught his breath, he asks, "Who're you?"

"Deadpool. I'm a mercenary, secretly working for S.H.I.E.L.D., and… Oh, damn. Uh…could you promise not to repeat that? And hey, who're you?"

He flips open his wallet, revealing an ID. "Social Services, responding to a call from the woman who lives at this address."

The boy shivers and clings to me. "Don't let them take me, mister! Please!"

"What're you, kidding?"

I toss him into the man's arms. The guy's so out of shape, he almost drops him. Once he lets go of the wallet, he manages to keep the kid from hitting the ground.

"Good luck with him, pal. That is *one* nutty kid. Well, gotta go. There are a few bags of puppies I've got to get back to."

As I race back into the comforting darkness of the woods and my own unknown destiny, a question haunts me. Should I tell them about the bound-and-gagged parents, or not? After all, what kind of people could raise a kid like that?

TWENTY

IN THIS line of work, you're always learning something new. Turns out that over time, carrying around three sacks of puppies stinks—in more ways than one. They need a place to run around, eat, and do their business. Someplace large and secure, set up to deal with a plethora of playful puppies and the monsters beginning with G that they might become.

Pretty specific, I know. Like shopping for a mansion that already has a Danger Room.

Then it hits me.

No, I'm not going to make some stupid joke about a truck hitting me. I actually have an idea, one that has my finger jabbing the speed dial.

"Yo-yo-yo! Preston, where'd you say that abandoned Weapon X lab was found?"

"I didn't. Why?"

"It's up in Canada, though, right?"

"No…but again, why?"

Fast-forward a bit, and she gives. Soon I'm on a lonely stretch of beach at the eastern end of the north fork of Long Island, doggie bags at my feet, enjoying a view of the Orient Point Lighthouse. Past that, it's a hop, skip, and a jump to Plum Island, which is probably why Weapon X picked this spot. See, Plum Island is home to the Animal Disease

Center. According to conspiracy theorists, it's also the birthplace of Lyme disease and a host of other tasty biological weapons.

Pretty cagey of the Canadians to hide a secret genetics lab so close to one owned by the U.S. Gives them someone else to blame if something goes wrong, eh? You'd never even notice the sandy dome I'm standing in front of unless you knew where to find it. I'd give you the Google Earth coordinates, but then I'd have to kill you, and I may need you to buy the sequel. The salty ocean breeze regularly sweeps so much sand over it, the entrance looks like one of a hundred dunes on an inhospitable beach.

I type in the access code Preston gave me, and the door hisses. I don't know why certain doors feel a need to hiss like that. Maybe the air pressure inside is different, or maybe it's just tired of being a door. Whether it likes it or not, the door opens to a cold, gray metallic inside that could barely sleep two. I've been around long enough to know this excuse for a phone booth can't be the whole lab. Sure enough, once I get myself and the doggies in, the door hisses shut, and the floor starts a-moving down.

It's an elevator—one that travels so smoothly, there's no way to tell how fast or how deep it's going. No Muzak, either. Smooth as silk on ice, it stops. We arrive dead center in a massive space with an open floor plan. Why open? Because study after study shows that evil-worker productivity increases up to 20 percent when everyone can keep an eye on each other.

The place is so tightly designed, you can't tell where the floor and walls end, and the endless array of uber-tech equipment begins. One object flows right into another: desk-like thing into giant laser-gun thing, laser-gun thing into pod-like storage device—all arranged in a weird forced perspective. Objects appear closer than they are, so it looks like something freaky is about to poke you in the eye no matter which way you turn. And the ceiling's covered with these glowing bulbous things that could be lamps or alien eyes.

Did I mention the constant power hum?

Ah, Weapon X, you old Canadian dog, you. Brings back memories, and at least these don't involve middle school. Not that my origin story resembles those of my fellow guys and gals in colorful suits— like one day I'm bitten by a radioactive spider, or find a magical hammer lying around in a cave—but there was one special moment when everything changed.

Already said that my terminal cancer diagnosis made volunteering for an experimental program seem like a good idea. Survival's always worth a shot, right? Felt that way right up until they started splicing those mutant regenerating genes atop my own. Forget all the sparks, crackles, and dark-energy fields, or the arched-back body with open-mouth scream. The real agony is much more intimate—like being forced into tight jeans four sizes too small, only the jeans are made of razors so sharp they barely exist. The sick, cutting feeling starts in on your skin, then works its way through the muscles and ligaments, finally wringing your internal organs so badly you can tell one from the other by how much it hurts.

From there, it moves into the bone—turtle-slow, because bone's tough. When it hits the marrow, that pulpy stuff you heard was in there but never really thought about? Surprise! That hurts most of all. And just when you think every one of your billion nerve endings are firing as hard and as fast as they can, well, then it gets worse.

I put down the sacks. "Welcome home, kids!"

"Kids? Smells like a bunch of mongrels crapping themselves to me."

The voice is as familiar and welcome as worn slippers. Heart in my throat (which could be a poorly healed wound from my last fight), my eyes eagerly zero in on the source. Leaning against what could be either a table lamp or a death ray is a sight for sore eyes: a blind, thin, scowling old woman. Her shock of white hair flows back in short, sharp tufts, like clipped raptor feathers. Rectangular black glasses wrap around her skull like an oversized visor from a Halloween costume. All across her face, wrinkles wrinkle about in a decidedly wrinkly fashion.

"Blind Al! You look exactly the same as the last time I saw you."

"So do you, Wade. So does everything."

"You old kidder. You came! You're here!"

She crosses her arms. "What nonsense are you spewing? Ten minutes ago I'm sipping lemonade on my porch. You show up, grab me, and 'port me here!

Now I'm supposed to pretend I came by myself, of my own free will? You want that kind of cooperation, hire a hooker."

I admit it, gentle reader. I left out the part where I tracked Al down and brought her here. In my defense, I felt it made for a better narrative introduction. Like I said back in Chapter 5, I don't have many close friends, but Al's the closest. Doesn't really matter how or why she got here, does it?

She shakes her finger in my direction—sort of. "Better not be thinking of trying to keep me here. I'll kill myself, I swear it. If I can, I'll take you with me. If not, I'll haunt you."

Don't let the cheery façade fool you. Al, short for Althea, used to be with British Intelligence. While she was stationed in Zaire, I was hired to kill her. Never could color inside in the lines, so I killed everyone else instead. Once I got all Deadpooled, I ran into her again. Long story short, I really needed someone to keep the place tidy and point out what was and wasn't real, so I decided to keep her around—and, yeah, I pretty much refused to let her go.

Kidnapping, or a complicated-but-loving relationship? You decide.

Kidnapping.

Kidnapping.

I step closer to give her a hug.

She rears up and grabs a mean-looking lever behind her. "One step closer, and I'll blow us all to kingdom come!"

"Al, Al! What's a guy got to do to get a little Stockholm Syndrome going? Besides, I think that's a light switch."

"You only get Stockholm Syndrome when the hostages mistake a lack of abuse from their captors for kindness. No lack of abuse, no Stockholm Syndrome." She spits. "As for the light switch…damn."

I gently pry her hand from the lever. "Oh, who was the real prisoner, you or me?"

"Me."

Her.

Yeah, her.

Same old gal. I try the lever just to be sure. Yep. Light switch. "I did give you a roof over your head, food, and all the *Matlock* you could watch."

Her sneer deepens. "When I finally escaped and made it to a friend's house, you were there waiting. You nearly tortured him to death in front of his dogs!"

"Nearly. The key word is *nearly*. So that means you're good with dogs, right?"

Speaking of which, they've been pretty quiet. Funny that they're not trying to get out. Maybe I should have untied the tops when I set them down.

"No. The only dog I ever fed was that seeing-eye mutt, Deuce, and I hate him more than I hate you."

I undo the bags. "How is old Deuce?"

Al's not like me, not so far from the realm of normal human feeling that she's locked herself off from love. That's why I kept her around, to ground me.

"How the hell should I know? I left him chained up in your yard years ago."

Wonder if I still own that yard… Anyway, I know that once she gets a lick from these little big-eyed animals, her heart will melt. "Well, you won't want to chain up these darlings."

Like an emo Santa, I pour puppy after puppy out of the sacks. She can't see them, but I know she hears them as they tumble over one another. One by one, with life-affirming yips, they right themselves. They're all over the place in no time, getting into all sorts of mischief in the nooks and crannies of dangerous equipment the purpose of which I can't begin to guess.

At first Al is expressionless. Then they start swarming all over her feet, jumping on her legs, pressing their noses into her varicose veins. And that woman with the harsh, unfeeling mask? Well, she tosses her hands in the air and starts screaming in utter dread.

"Help! Oh, sweet Lord, help me!"

In seconds, she's down on the floor, buried in a living mound of fur. I almost want to get down there and play with them myself, but I can't open myself up like that again. Mr. Snuffles might get jealous. I'll have to content myself with watching.

"You bastard!" she cries, but it's clear she doesn't mean it. "You sick bastard!"

"That's what I like about you, Al. Sometimes you sound just like the voices in my head."

I want it to last forever, but nothing ever does—not the good, or the bad. Before I can take a picture so it will last longer, the hissy elevator returns.

Six S.H.I.E.L.D. agents are crowded on the platform, looking all shiny in their stylish black field outfits as they heft that containment tank. You know, the one that contains all the monster-goo from the creatures I've zapped so far. The one that's perfectly safe. Like in *Ghostbusters*.

Preston steps up from behind, holding the collie and…Mr. Snuffles! The collie seems indifferent, but Snuffs recognizes me and barks. My heart skips a beat, but I try to play it cool.

"You're not bringing that tank in here, are you, Em?"

As the expertly trained, physically and mentally fit men and women in black set down the tank and start running wires, Emily rubs Mr. Snuffles' head. "Makes as much sense as having all the puppies here. This is where they came from. Once Tech assured me the place was secure and under our control, I realized you really did have a good idea, Wade. We'll keep the tank out here. There's a kennel area just past those double doors, if you haven't found it. It's comfortable; there's plenty of potable water and dog chow."

From under the puppy pile, Al screams, "Give me a gun with one bullet! I'm begging you!"

Preston looks down. "Is someone under there?"

"Where are my manners? Preston, Al. Al, Preston."

"She okay?"

"Agk!"

"She's fine. There were twice as many dogs on her a second ago."

It's true. At least ten of the pint-size devils are leaping on the consoles, nosing the levers, and chasing all the blinking lights on the touchscreens.

Preston looks around nervously at all the pointy, energy-gun-like objects. "Uh…maybe first priority should be getting them all into that kennel."

"Right. Want to get on that, Al?"

"Mfff!"

"Okay, okay, crybaby." I gather up a wriggling armful and follow Preston across the lab. It just sort of tickles, and they're a little cute. No biggie. I'm okay with it. Not worried, not…falling in love.

As for the kennel, I picture it as clean and humane, but basically a bunch of cages. Hope they're roomy. I've got that thing about tight prison spaces, so I'm bracing myself a little—telling myself it's for their own good, they're just dogs, etc. But when the doors do their hissy fit, I'm so stunned I drop my jaw. And the pups.

Wow.

It's like the scene in *Willy Wonka* when those brats first see the chocolate factory. It's a freaking indoor field, full of rolling hills, balls, and chew toys. And that grass? It's not AstroTurf—it's *real*! Cages? There are rows of little doggie *houses* on either side, each with windows and little flowerbeds and fluffy mats inside.

It puts a smile on my face so wide I have to slap it

off before anyone can see it.

After I carry in my second puppy load, Al can almost stand. Yeah, this time I'm giggling a little from all the scratchy tongues. And sure, there's a friendly tingling running up and down my spine. But I've got this.

On the third trip, when the pups see where I've brought them, they get so excited I feel it in their shivering little bodies. I can't stand it. I go to pieces. I fall on the ground with them, hug them while they lick me, and laugh like a little kid.

Puppies! Puppies, puppies, puppies! Wheeeeeee!

I hear Al ask, "He's hugging them, isn't he?"

"Yeah."

She *tsks*. "There are some things—just a few—mind you, that I'm glad I can't see."

BOOK 3

I WILL
DROWN YOU
IN MY
BLOOD!

TWENTY-ONE

HERE we are in Book 3. No big scene transition or anything. I'm still on the lush hills of the underground kennel, rolling around, luxuriating in my living canine quilt. What does that Book thing mean, anyway? Isn't the whole thing a book? Cheap effort at structure, if you ask me. Better yet, don't ask me—I'm having too much fun. I know Preston's staring, and Al would if she could, but I can't stop myself. This is better than Cancun—and no voices or flashbacks!

"Wheee!"

"Wade? Didn't you say something about keeping some professional distance?"

"I'm cold and distant as a star! I swear!"

Eventually—too soon, if you ask me—Em and Blind Al pull me up. The puppies tumble in a waterfall of delightfulness, then scamper off to explore their new digs.

Preston eyes me, brow as ruffled as the loose skin on a shar pei. "Glad to see your soft side. At least, I *think* I'm glad. You do have a job here, Deadpool. Some of those puppies may change, and then you'll have to…"

I cough out some dog hair. "I know, I know. Can we not talk about that right now? I'm fine, promise. It was only…you know, an instinctual physical reaction. Means nothing to me."

Em's "yeah, right" look stays plastered on her face until one of her techie minions marches in to report that the containment tank's been installed.

"Okay. I've got to head back to the office to complete downloading the offsite databanks into our secure mainframes, and sync the file structures to buttress our control of this facility," she says.

"Heh. Buttress. Is that code for some hanky-panky with the mister?"

"No. It means I've got to head back to the office to complete downloading the offsite data banks into our secure mainframes, and sync the file structures to buttress our control of this facility, but I'll let Shane know you were thinking of us. Once you get past the encryption, the operating system here is one of the most straightforward I've ever seen, so I shouldn't be long. Meanwhile, I'll have some staff onsite here within a few hours."

Though loathe to leave the dog version of Shangri-La, I follow her back into the main laboratory to make sure she's clear on a key point. "*Nice* staff, though, right? No cut-up-the-doggie types?"

She pats my shoulder and gives it a squeeze. "PETA supporters to a man. You *can* keep things together here for an hour, right?"

"Sir, yes, sir, ma'am!"

By the time I finish saluting, she's on the elevator platform with the other agents. Don't know if they practice that formation, but it sure looks like it. They're all at attention and staring at the same distant point, as if posing for a movie poster. The bright backlighting makes them look like they're a gift to humankind from some pagan sun god. I *assume* they didn't bring that lighting along with them.

I snap a pic and make an "okay" sign. "You got it, chief. I'll get back on that list pronto while Al keeps an eye on things here."

Em doesn't hear that last part, because the elevator's already rising. In a wink, she's gone. I know, because I wink, and then she's not there anymore.

Al heard me, though. I keep forgetting she can hear.

"What the frick, Wade?! Never mind I can't keep an eye on anything, you're going to leave me with a bunch of flea-bitten mongrels that can turn into *monsters*? Where the hell *is* here, anyway? Can you at least tell me which state I'm in?"

"Oh, Al. It wouldn't be a secret base if I told you where it was, would it? You'll be fine. They would've turned into monsters by now if they were going to. Probably. And you heard Preston, it'll only be for an—"

"Yip! Yip! Grr…."

Looks like we missed one during the kennel roundup. A Rottweiler pup is sitting up on a little raised platform beneath one of those ray-gun-shaped lights, gnawing away on the lever. Look at him go!

"Grrr…"

All that teething's important, and not only for his growing choppers. Gnawing is a big part of the way dogs explore their world. They don't call those beauties right and left of our incisors canines for nothing. When he growls like he's some badass wolf, I can't help but pick him up and take in the wriggling cuteness.

"Hey there, little guy!"

Are you bonding again?

You know you shouldn't.

Guys? I really don't need the internal voices with Al here. She can do that stuff now.

"Are you bonding again?" she says in the real world. "You know you shouldn't."

Hmph. Don't mind us.

We'll just sit here and try to remember the last book you read.

"You know me better, Al." I press him to my face. "But I am gonna name him Pop-pop!"

Living up to his new name, Pop-pop pops out of my hands, landing with a meaty plop and a grunt. Then he hightails it back to that lever and starts gnawing at it again.

"Aw, look! Pop-pop thinks he's an evil scientist working on his death ray!"

Al ducks. "Death ray? What death ray? Crap! Where's it aimed?"

"Oh-ho! Better watch out, Pop-pop. You don't know what that lever will…"

The world goes electric blue. When the platform fades back into focus, I see—choke—a bunch of dry bones standing there. They tumble into—sob—the most adorable little pile you ever did see. It's no use pretending that he's fine. I go to my knees and pound my fists into the floor.

"Nooooo! Pop-pop, no!"

Al puts her arm around me. "Come on, you ruthless mercenary, pull it together. I'll get you a goldfish. At least that won't be able to operate weaponry."

"That…you…know of…."

I crumble into her arms. Now I know how the Hulk felt. "I didn't mean…I didn't mean…"

She rubs the back of my head. "There, there. I know, I know."

"See why I need you here?"

"Yeah, guess I do." She feels her way over to the bones. "Somebody's got to clean this up. Don't worry, I'll find a nice resting place for Pop-pop. Where's the trash bin?"

"The trash? You wouldn't do that, would you?"

She gathers the skeleton in her arms. "He's too big to flush down the toilet, isn't he? And I'm not gonna… hold on." She gets a funny look. Not the same funny look she used to get when I passed gas, but in that ballpark. Puzzled, she rubs one of the ribs with her fingers. It's just weird enough to snap me out of my funk.

"Al, just so you know, what you're doing there looks pretty gross."

"Shut your pie hole." She tilts her head and focuses. "There's a pattern on this thing. Damn. Not braille, but it's some kind of raised writing."

"Huh. The monster pups were genetically engineered. Maybe the architect left some kind of signature?" I walk over. "Where? I can't see a thing."

"That's 'cause you're looking with your eyes."

"That some sort of Zen metaphor?"

"No, you idiot." She tugs my glove off and grabs my index finger. "Yeesh. When was the last time you washed your hands?"

"Been busy."

She presses it down into the bone. "Check it out. The human finger can discriminate between surfaces patterned with ridges as small as thirteen nanometers. So say your filthy finger was the size of the Earth. Push down on the planet like some giant freak that needs to finger everything, and you'd be able to feel the difference between a house and a car. My other senses work overtime to compensate for my lack of sight, so I could probably tell a Prius from a station wagon. And *I* wash my hands."

She's right. "I feel something rising up in a line. Cool, but it doesn't help me read it."

"You said this is a lab. Any microscopes around?"

"I don't think the best microscope in the world would help you, Al."

"Not for me—for you! So you—or better yet, someone with brains—can see the pattern!"

"Right."

It takes a while to sort the measurement devices from the death rays, cleaning equipment, and what I think may be a toilet. At least, I hope it was a toilet. Neophyte though I am, I manage to find a Scanning Transmission Electron Holography Microscope, because it has a label on it saying just that.

The big power lever reminds me of...Pop-pop. Sniff. Even though the tag means he was a monster pup, and I would have had to put him down anyway, it still hurts.

But Preston was right—the operating system that runs everything in this place is pretty straightforward. The hard part's centering the bone under the sensors so it can pick up the itsy-bitsy, teeny-weeny writing.

Al's extra-sensitive finger pads help with that. Sure, there's some shoving and hair-pulling, because *I* want to do it, but we get there. In no time, Al's still kicking me, but I'm staring at a video readout on a hi-res monitor. If my mask wasn't holding my chin up, I'd be slack-jawed. Sensing my shock, probably because I gasp loudly, Al stops kicking and nudges my shoulder.

"Can you read it? Is it English?"

"It's better than English. It's a website. Dirtydealingdick.com."

"They put a porno site on a dog's bone?"

"I wish, but no." I tap a finger to my chin. "I'm afraid, old chum, that I didn't tell you this before, because repeating story details is boring. But I have reason to suspect that the sick, twisted mind behind these killer dogs is, like this website, named Dick."

"Why?"

"A really hot MMFF named Jane told me."

"And you didn't tell that nice lady from S.H.I.E.L.D.?"

"Not yet. I'm on retainer with Jane, and I wanna see how things play out."

I type the URL into one of the terminals. It's not much of a website. No clickbait, just one of those placeholders:

Coming Soon!
Orders from Your New Global Leader!
info@dirtydealingdick.com

This is big. I feel like I'm close to cracking this thing, but I need more to go on. I can't just write to the guy and ask where he lives so I can come kill him.

Got to think. I look at the microscope screen. I look back at the doors to the kennel.

"Say…Al? You think having a look at some of the other puppies' bones might tell us more?"

"Maybe, I guess, but how you gonna do that without killing them?"

I slip the glocks from their holsters and cock them. Steeling my pounding heart, I move toward the kennel. I will not bond, I will not bond. There is a job to do.

TWENTY-TWO

DID I have you going? At least a little? Of course I'm *not* going to kill the dogs. Haven't you been paying attention? I'm going to grab one and see if I can find an MRI around here to scan him with. Al, not having been with the story as long as you, doesn't know better. I've rattled her. I can hear it in her voice.

"You sure run hot and cold toward those pooches."

I play it up. "Pop-pop was special, but he's gone. This is a war, and in a war, people die—even if they're dogs."

I'm almost to the door when her cane trips me. "Why don't you at least try sending an email first?"

"Damn it, woman, don't you think I've thought of that? What kind of idiot would answer a random email?"

I'm almost up, but she trips me again. She's gotten fast since the last time I saw her.

"Same kind that'd try to take over the world by breeding puppies that turn into monsters and write his website on the bones."

Hm. Maybe she's right. Eager to avoid exposing the pups to needless MRI radiation, even if it is considered safe, I crack my knuckles and head back to the terminal. "Email it is, then. But we've got to be clever about it. I can't just send him one of those spam messages from Nigeria offering to transfer millions into his bank account. Last time I did that, it cost me millions."

"You created fake spam from Nigeria…and *sent* the money?"

"Let's just say for once in his life, Dr. Yabril Omotayo was true to his word." Thanks to the intuitive OS, a few clicks get me to an email client. "This caper requires more finesse. To start, I've got to create a false digital persona—something that looks real, but bounces across servers all over the globe so it can't be traced. Oh, there's a button for that right here! Great. Now I just have to pretend to be someone Dick will want to meet, like a female admirer."

Al sticks her nose over my shoulder. "How do you know he's not gay?"

"Nah. They'd never make the only gay guy in the story the villain. Sends the wrong message. Besides, Jane said they dated. You're a woman, right? What do you say when you're flirting?"

Her lips crinkle in a devilish smile. "Couldn't tell you. The men always came to me."

I nudge her. "In droves, the way I heard it, Mata Hari, but help me out. I need an in."

"I dunno. Tell him you liked the website?"

I read aloud as I type. "Hi there. I'm strangely aroused by your email address. Is *info* your real name?"

"Sure. Why not? But ask him another question,

too—something open-ended so he can't answer yes or no."

"Good, good, good. How about: What's your idea of a perfect day? Mine would be meeting you."

She pinches my cheek. "And who said psychopaths are only superficially charming? You want to keep it short, so end it there with something flirty, like: Feel free to respond inappropriately."

I giggle. "You are so *bad*! What do I sign? Can I be Vanessa? I've always liked the name Vanessa. It's classy but alluring at the same time."

"Knock yourself out."

"And…SEND."

Then comes the waiting. The awful, terrible waiting, the waiting that can send the best of us right back into our awkward years.

I'm a pimply faced pariah on a Friday night, huddled by the phone. Sophie swore she'd call back when she was done with her homework, but I don't know whether to believe her or not. She may have been trying to get rid of me. There was something I had to talk to her about. Something really important, but I can't remember what it is. Couldn't be planning to tell her how I feel, could I? Nah.

Frustrating as it is staring at the phone, it beats listening to Dad get mad at the television. Starts out better, anyway, but my fear and longing build with every swing of our moving-eyes cat clock. Self-doubt and self-control vie for a hold on my soul. Self-doubt's about to take it, but at the last instant, long-seething resentment sneaks up and takes them both down.

It's seven, and Sophie hasn't called. The emotional teapot of my being boils over into rage. I smash the phone. It splits in two, already a useless hunk of junk, but that's not enough—not nearly. I want to hit it so hard Sophie will feel it all the way on the other end of the line—which makes no sense, since if she *were* on the line, I wouldn't be mad in the first place. I pick up the pieces and smash them again. I stomp on them, over and over, until all that's left is a crackling heap of plastic bits and circuit boards.

For the first time in my life, I'm making more of a ruckus than Dad. Might be jealousy, but when he stomps in and spots the mess, he puts down his drink and pulls out his belt.

"You have any idea how much that phone cost?"

I shouldn't answer, but I do. "Doesn't the phone company pay for those?"

He goes at me, Hulk-furious, beating me within an inch of his worthless life.

A digital tone from the Weapon X computer terminal yanks me back to the brittle present. The soft, squishy past disappears like blood stains scrubbed clean with bleach.

There on the screen, I've got my answer.

"OMG! OMG! He likes me! He wants to meet! Al! Al! What do I do?"

When I tap her shoulder, she nearly falls over. She must've fallen asleep during my hallucination. Before I decide whether to let her hit the floor, she catches herself and sucks in a waking breath.

"Huh? What?" Groggy, she smacks her lips and sucks some stuff out from between her molars.

I snap my fingers in front of her. "Dick wrote back. He wants to meet! What do I do?"

"Do I have to tell you everything? Offer to jump his bones and get his address. Head on over; catch the bad guy. Can I go home now?"

I shake my head. "Nah. Don't want him thinking I'm that easy. I'll suggest coffee. Vanessa's a class act. The high-octane swill I drink wouldn't be her style, so it can't be just any place." I do a quick search for popular spots. "Here we go. A chic open-air café on Amsterdam and 112th. Perfect. I only hope I don't start babbling. Caffeine makes me babble."

"Breathing makes you babble. At least a drink will give you something to stick in your mouth a while." She makes a face. "Ain't you forgetting something important?"

"What?"

"Well…never thought I'd be asking this, but do you look like a woman?"

"That is so cisgender. Does my body define who I am inside?"

"Anyone else, no. In your case—given the way I've seen your brain rearrange your personality when it heals up—yeah, pretty much."

"Mind/body point taken. Will you help me do a makeover?"

"The blind leading the bipolar? Sure."

The first hurdle is finding the right mix to smooth over my facial lesions. We settle on a concoction that's more plumbing caulk than pancake. Long as I don't move any of the twelve muscles in my mouth, or the four in my nose, I should be fine. I was going to go with my real hair, but that only grows in patches, so a wig it is. Finding the right outfit is the toughest part. Every time we 'port to a clothing store, Al tries to make a run for it.

But it's got to be right. New York gals know how to dress, and I don't want to come across like some Midwest hick. Not too this, not too that; revealing, but not too revealing. I want to look appealing, but not like a slut. It's half art, half science.

With minutes to go, we finish. Al steps back and runs her fingers along my face, judging her work.

"Well? What's the word?"

She inhales. "I am really, really sorry I'm blind."

At first I think it's a compliment, but then she starts laughing.

"You think it won't work."

"No, no, no."

She slaps her sides hard, barely about to contain herself. "Anyone desperate enough to meet someone after one email is going for low-hanging fruit, so I'd say you have a shot."

Already sociably late, with Al's laughter echoing in my ears, I 'port a block from the café. I try to regain my self-esteem, but a look at my face in a store-window reflection confirms the worst. Maybe if I get there first, I can buy a hot espresso. Then, when he does show up, I can hurl it into his eyes so he doesn't see me. I sigh and move on. Wouldn't you know it? There he is, seated with his back to me at the corner table I mentioned in my last message, looking out at the street.

I step up and lean over. "Dick?"

"Vanessa?" He gets up, but doesn't start running yet. A good sign.

He's about my height, so I'm glad I wore flats. He's dressed casual: sport jacket over a collared shirt, dark, fitted jeans, and pricey leather shoes. It's hard to describe his face, though, because he's got this black mask on—kinda like the one Jane wore back in Chapter 8, only more…manly.

He takes my hand—not in a creepy way, politely—and walks me the two feet to my chair.

We exchange a little small talk—the weather, the menu, our seats. Once the waitress brings our drinks, we hit our first real silence. Good a time as any to bring up the elephant in the room.

"So, Dick."

He perks up. "Yes, Vanessa?"

"You wear a mask?"

He looks down at his latte, a bit deflated, and taps the spoon against the rim, making a quick series of little clinks. "Yeah. I do."

Now I've done it. I've made him uncomfortable.

"Sorry, I just—"

"Oh, it's okay." His body language says otherwise.

He crosses and uncrosses his legs, taps the rim some more. "It's not as if people won't notice, right? I'm just never sure when to bring it up myself."

It's already out there. No point in going back. "So are you...?"

"A super villain?"

I laugh. "*I* was going to go with burn victim. But *are* you a super...?"

"Burn victim? No. Luckier than that, in a way. I wear this to conceal my identity."

I already feel like I'm prying, and I don't want to push him too hard too soon. I stir my espresso with the little spoon and focus on listening.

"Everyone's entitled to their secrets, right?" he says. "I mean, we're all so wrapped up in knowing these silly little details about each other, like what we look like. But what does it mean, really? Why don't we just say, 'I like to be surprising,' and leave it at that?"

He's far from charming, terribly self-conscious— and there is that mask. Still, there's something about him. I can't put my finger on it, but it's *something* that speaks to me. I just...like him. By the time I put the cup down, I've decided.

I give him an opening. "I like to be surprising sometimes, too."

"Do you?"

I take another sip. "Uh-huh."

He leans forward and makes his voice low and husky. "How's this for surprising? Want to get out of here? Go someplace and…talk?"

Unable to move my mouth very much, I smile coyly. "You read me like a dirty book. I want to, but I'm not sure. Will I get to see what's under the mask?"

He winks. "Only one way to find out."

I pretend I'm still thinking about it. I look left, I look right. Then I meet his eyes. They're brown, like mine. I know what I'm supposed to say, but I can't do it. I can't lie to him anymore.

"I'll be honest, Dick: I like you. Not in a gay way, but I get the feeling we could be buds—share some brews, play some *Dragon Age*." I pick up my purse and open it on my lap. "Thing is, I just lost someone, a dog named Pop-pop. I thought I could just move on, but I can't. A big part of the reason is that this sweet little puppy was bred to become a monster. He was made that way by some maniac out to form an army. So you caught me on the rebound—meaning this, whatever this is, wouldn't last. Now, I don't really know you, and you don't really know me, but I'm going to go ahead and guess that neither of us really wants that." I reach into the purse and slip my hand around the gun inside. "I figure it'll be much better if I just kill you."

TWENTY-THREE

DICK'S smart. Well, smart is the wrong word. After all, he was ready to invite a strange woman back to his place. Quick. Quick is a better word. Not Quicksilver quick, but about as fast as I am.

No sooner do I say *kill* than he's jumping up from the chair.

That move takes him three feet into the air. By the time I've got the gun out, he's landing on the table. While I'm pulling the trigger, he's kicking. As the Glock discharges, his fine leather shoe connects with my chin, ruining the shot.

I go backwards. Dick goes running. Run, Dick, run.

Works for me. Having explored my feminine side enough for one day, I could use a shot of testosterone. I tear away the fabric of my tasteful dress, revealing the black-and-red battle suit that hugs my manly muscles and, yes, rides up in places you don't want to know about. All eyes are on me as I slip on my own mask. With a quick salute to my caffeinated admirers, I go after Dick, dodging skirts, ducking uniforms, racing around pedestrians, diving past suits.

"Out of the way, you lame chase-scene obstacles!"

But all the while, I'm thinking, calculating the

best possible joke about his name to use when I catch him. Because, you know, it's Dick. It's only when he reaches the crosswalk that I come to the sad realization that none of what I'm coming up with can possibly make it into print.

He's halfway across when the light changes. Traffic rushes through, filling the space between us. Typically, this is the part where the good guy almost gets hit by a car, and then watches helplessly as the crook gets away.

Not this time. First of all, I'm a half-block away. Second of all, Dick's the one who gets hit. A late-model Subaru lurches into him. From here, it looks like the smack-up had to be worth a few broken bones—but no, he shakes it off and heads for the Subaru. Stunned, but a fast thinker, the meaty driver manages to close the window. Dick gets his own gun out and uses the grip to smash it in.

He tries to do like Buscemi in *Reservoir Dogs* and pull the driver out the window to steal the car. Only— get this—the driver won't fit! Oh, he *tries* to yank the poor guy through, but it's not happening. When he sees me gaining, Dick gives up and goes back to running. Pretty funny, if you could see it. Plus, his little faux pas has managed to stop enough traffic for me to sail across the street without skipping a beat.

We reach a more residential area (which in this part of the Big Apple just means that the tall buildings have apartments, not offices). Dick trips his way around some girls playing jacks. Barreling along in all my glory, I leap over them.

Apparently, this reminds Dick he can jump, too. The lousy copycat bunnyhops across a line of merchant tables spread along the sidewalk. Postcards, old LPs, and African knickknacks go flying. Back on the pavement at the other end, he tries to stay true to the classic foot-chase trope by shoving a steaming hot dog cart in my way—but just like with the Subaru, his timing's off. By the time I'm there, the cart is clattering against a building and not in my way at all—unless you count that delicious smell as an obstacle.

I know I do!

I pause to grab a footlong with relish. The garnish, not my emotional state—though I admit some relish on my part, as well. After comparing it to what I recall about Gomdulla the Living Pharoah's finger a ways back, I return to the race, satisfied that my analogy was accurate.

We all know it wouldn't be a truly classic chase without two guys carrying a big pane of glass. And here they are. Trying to look cool about it, Dick ducks down and scrapes his side along the asphalt to slide under the plate glass. It's tight, but he makes it.

I give him an 8.7.

Or I will, when I catch him.

I'm too busy trying to reach him to imitate his slide, but I do manage to run around the glass. Sorry, guys, looks like we'll avoid that cliché where the glass gets smashed. Seems a shame. Clichés become clichés for a reason. Like the elderly, they've earned some respect.

What the hell. I spin back and give it a quick heel-kick.

I call to the poor slobs carrying it: "Couldn't resist, working citizens! But is there anything more satisfying than the sound of shattering glass?"

They don't respond. They just gesticulate like we're in a silent film. You never hear a peep from the guys carrying the glass. Part of the deal.

Dick turns at the corner. Since I'm running after him, I do, too. And what do you know? The whole street happens to be sealed off from traffic for a grand outdoor food festival! It's one of those scenes that really remind you how many people fit into all these buildings. There are blocks and blocks of booths and food carts, bands, and street clowns—even a few of those giant twirling Chinese dragon puppets.

Not so much a bull in a china shop as an evil villain in a hurry, Dick grabs and throws whatever he can at me: fried rice, shish kabob, empanadas, some kind of pasta dish, dough—you name it. Man, this festival is *totally* international!

I happily catch a few fresh-cut fries in my mouth. The hot oil he sends flying my way after it doesn't sit so good. It hisses where it hits my skin, which gives off a smell like broiled lamb that could use more seasoning. Sure, it hurts—but after getting pulped by Goom and his goombahs, and up close with Hulk butt, a little first-degree deep-fry only pisses me off.

I pour it on. Almost got him—but out of nowhere, Dick does this great cartwheel that takes him between two tightly packed vendors and out the other side. He's finally showing me something here. In answer, I do a double hand-flip and watch for his next move.

Eh. The cartwheel was a one-off. He's all dead-on running. It's artless—brutish, even.

He's easy pickings, so I go back to trying to come up with a clever Dick joke. I mean, do they all have to be about size? It *is* the popular choice, I grant you, especially since *that's what she said* is so overplayed.

Hoping to get far from the maddening crowd (as opposed to *The Madding Crowd,* the Hardy novel), he ducks down an alley. It's like he's never seen a foot chase before. Of course it's a dead end. The poor sap staggers to a halt in front of the only door—which, naturally, is locked. This was quick.

I strut toward him, slapping my fist into my open palm. "In case you don't get it, lemme explain. In a few seconds, my palm's going to be your face. And my fist—well, that'll still be my fist."

I figure it's over. *You* probably figure it's over. But that's what we're supposed to figure. Saving his best for last, Dick fly kicks the door like he's spring-loaded. He hits hard enough to buckle it, yanks it out like it's so much cardboard, and dives inside. Now we've got a nice interior thing going. We're hurtling through tight hallways; making quick, hairpin turns that take us from one long, dark corridor to another; flattening ourselves against the thickly painted plaster wall to slide past custodians and repairmen.

The trick with a twisty corridor run is to never go all

out. You don't know exactly when that hall ahead of you is going to throw you a turn.

Called it.

Missing a righty, Dick crunches into the wall and stumbles. He keeps going, but that dent he leaves behind gives me an idea. Standard drywall's half-an-inch thick. Figure the wall's made out of two sheets—so all told, I'm headed for half an inch of gypsum, with some air in between. Not much for a well-built bruiser such as myself. Ignoring my own advice (who the hell asked me, anyway?), I go full-tilt boogie—thinking I'll smash on through without losing any speed and, with a little luck, cut off Dick on the other side.

The first part works out. I smash on through the plasterboard without losing any speed. But I didn't figure the wall on the other side would be cinderblock. Rather than cracking a bone, hitting the concrete only makes my left arm pop out of the socket, causing what they call a dislocated shoulder.

If that's not bad enough, Dick didn't even go this way. He went in the other direction—the one that leads to an exit. With a little more than my pride hurt, I trudge after him.

It's a whole new alley, wider than the last, but blocked off by a sheet-metal wall topped with coiled barbed wire. Dick's almost at the top. His face is cut; he's getting blood all over the nice barbed wire.

I whistle.

"Hey, Dick! Looks like you might make it— but unless there's a sewer or some other kind of cool underground catacomb on the other side, I'm calling this chase finis."

The first katana pierces his casual jacket right above the shoulder and stabs through it to the metal. He tries to pull it out, but the second blade hooks his waistband, twisting him around.

Hanging his head, he wisely gives up. "Good shot."

"I wish. I was trying to gut you, but I missed. Hey, we'll talk in a sec, but I got my shoulder dislodged back there. Mind if I take a break to fix it?"

"I'm not going anywhere."

I slam my shoulder into his chest. Dick pops up a little; my shoulder pops back into place. Pop-pop. That's why I'm here.

I grab his masked chinny-chin-chin. "Richard— can I call you Richard?—I've seen some really screwed-up crap lately, but I've still got to ask: What kind of madcap loon makes monsters that look like puppies?"

"It wasn't my idea."

I drop his head and give his cheek a pinch. "That's not what Jane tells me."

"Jane? That lying—"

"Careful. I've got a sweet spot for her."

His laugh is sad and beaten. "Jane's using you the same way she used me—trying to keep you off track. Like *I'm* the mastermind. I'm no one. All I was supposed to do was design the website, and I haven't even gotten around to that! I'm just a dupe, trapped in a sexless codependent relationship, serving *her* monster-army plans. She's the evil one deserving of death! I can prove it. Reach into my pocket."

"No way. The date's over."

"There's a flash drive on my keychain. Get it."

I do. There is. "So?"

"It's security-cam footage from the lab. Look at it. That's all I ask."

"Let's say I do. What'll I see?"

"Jane."

"Naked?"

"No."

"Damn."

"She's with the puppies right after they were created. Right there on tape, she says, 'I can't wait until you're all monsters, and I can use you to take over the world.'"

"Think I was born yesterday?" I laugh. "That could mean a lot of things. She might be answering a trick question, like, 'What would a super villain say about these puppies right now?'"

"No tricks. It's just her, alone with the dogs, laughing and carrying on about the carnage. I couldn't see it before. I was distracted by her beauty, wrapped around her little finger—like you—but she's crazy. Nothing short of death will keep her from trying to carry out her insane scheme."

I narrow my eyes. "You wouldn't be lying to me, would you, Dick? Because you know, this is really, really serious."

He raises his head. I can see the tears welling up

in those brown eyes of his. "I swear! I only want to be free of her. That's why I responded to your email. I was so lonely. I wanted to hope." He looks up at the sky and swallows. "But now all the world sees who the real fool is."

"You, right?"

He nods. "You're a mercenary. I'll hire you to kill her. I'll give you anything!"

"She already hired me to kill you."

"I'll pay you double. Triple."

I tap his nose with the drive. "This doesn't pan out, I'll be back in touch." I'm about to leave, but something's nagging at me. "Oh, and thanks a lot for running out and leaving me with the bill on our first date, Mr. Dine-and-Dash. When you pay me, it'll have to be cash."

TWENTY-FOUR

BACK at the lab—you know, the one with that big overstuffed

containment tank—Al's leaning against the only thing in the place

that looks like what it is, a water cooler, as I fill her in. She's full of questions, questions I wished I'd asked myself, starting with:

"You just let him go? What the hell, Wade?"

I try to explain, but I don't really understand myself. "There was just…something about him that made me think he was telling the truth."

Balancing her hand atop the five-gallon bottle, she leans my way. "A twinkle in his eyes? His winning smile?"

Ignoring the sarcasm, I walk toward a terminal. I keep my voice low as I pass.

"I wouldn't know. He was wearing a mask."

She pulls a paper cup from the dispenser and fills it, careful to keep a finger over the rim so she knows when to stop the tap. Then she takes a big swig of water and does a spit take in my direction.

"A MASK? Didn't you at least take it off when you had him pinned against the wall?"

"I want to say yes, but…no."

"I'm really starting to worry about you. First

you're rolling around with those flea-bitten mutts, and now this. Lord knows you've screwed up before, but…"

I toss my hands in the air. "I didn't think of it, okay? I got all confused." I plop into the seat and pound the keys, hoping to restore some of my dignity. "It's not like I'm a complete basket case. I may not have mentioned it to our readers, but I did slip a tracer on him."

"Well, don't get cocky about it. Even broken watches tell the right time twice a day."

I try to wow her with fancy tech-talk. "It wasn't any old dime-store tracer, Al. It was a S.H.I.E.L.D.-issued doohickey, a trillion circuits on the head of a pin, with a range of over umpteen billion miles. I'm telling you, that sucker can sense signals right through the core of the Earth—through the natural magnetic shielding *and* the mole people. Not only that, I can access the signal on scores of popular digital-media devices."

She *harrumphs*. "You even paid for the coffee, didn't you?"

Ignoring the question, I puff up my chest. "I'm telling you, I can find Dick whenever I want."

After an awkward silence, Al starts cackling. Her cup is still half-full, but spilling from her spasms of hysterical laughter.

"Ohhh! Thanks for that. So, Lame Bond, where is he?"

"Grr. Gimme a sec." I hit a few keys.

"So?"

I hit a few more keys.

"Yeah?"

I hit *all* the keys.

Then I hit this one key over and over again. Finally, I plug in the keyboard and hit a few keys again. The tracer interface comes up.

"Huh. That's funny. It's dead."

"Not as funny as you being able to find Dick any time you want—but, really, how can you follow that up?"

I rub my chin thoughtfully. "He must have found it. He's good. Real good."

A bony elbow nudges me. "Wade?"

"Yeah?"

"Did you turn it on?"

I close my eyes. She starts laughing again. At least this time, her cup is empty.

"Fine! So maybe he's not that good. That only means it'll be easier to catch him."

At first I think she's patting my back, but she's only supporting herself so she can keep standing while she howls. "Right. Great news! Man, Wade, sometimes I just don't know how you've managed to keep me a prisoner for so long."

"Comes down to one thing, Al. I can't die, so I always win eventually, as long as I don't give up."

"Think so? Got a little logic gap there, right where your brain should be."

"Yeah? What's that?"

"What if somebody *else* dies, and you want them alive? Then you lose, don't you? What was the name you gave that dog? Spit-spot?"

I take Dick's flash drive and plug it into the USB slot. "Pop-pop. I only lose if I care, Al. Only if I care." As soon as it loads, the screen flashes. "See? There *is* a video file on this thing. So far so good."

The image is nearly all white. There's an electronic rush, a steady pulsing. A sultry voice drifts from the speakers.

"They all want me," it says. "They can't have me."

Al wrinkles her nose. "That your girlfriend?"

I shush her. "Not sure. Sounds like Jane, but younger."

The pulsing continues. It grows. "Move with me. Chant with me."

I slap my hands. "It's an arcane ritual! Jane must serve some demonic netherworld entity!"

As if made manifest by unleashed eldritch energies, two wizened figures appear on the screen and speak in a foreign tongue. The words, the cadence... it all sounds so familiar, like the ghost of a memory haunting the edges of my consciousness.

As if in a trance, Al starts moving. Her right arm goes straight out in front of her, palm down, then her left. She flips her right palm over, then her left, all the while gently bouncing her hips. Right hand to left shoulder, left hand to right.

And then, at last, I remember. "That's not Jane! This is the "Macarena" video! That son of a bitch!"

Al keeps dancing. "Look at the bright side. At least you *thought* he was telling the truth. That's got to count for something, right? You idiot."

"Geez. The voices in my head never call me an idiot."

Sure we do.

And worse.

I yank the drive out, but Al keeps up the steps even as the thumping disco beat fades into silence. "Oh, come on, lighten up! Put it back on! It's my new jam!"

Before I can refuse, we get a whole new soundtrack: flashing alarms and wailing klaxons.

"You got a disco ball in here? I can't tell, so I wouldn't mind if you lied to me about it. Wade, tell me there's a disco ball."

I look around. Control panels light up. Devices crackle to life. A massive thud shakes the lab. I catch Al before she falls.

"Wade, tell me that was the disco ball falling."

I look at the screen. "That video wasn't the only thing on the drive."

"You didn't scan it for viruses? Can you tell what it's doing?"

"It's not like there's a button on this thing that says, 'Tell me what the virus is doing'!" My eyes dance across the screen. "No wait, there is. You know, this is one helluva great operating system." I click it. "It's rerouting all the power, trying to cause some kind of overload. But where?" I bring up an energy-management floor plan and breathe a sigh of relief. "Whew. The kennel's okay."

Another clattering thud puts Al in my lap. "Then what's making all the ruckus?"

"Can't tell. The surges are headed toward a blind spot, like it's something hidden, or…"

"What?"

"Something installed too recently for the system to recognize." I shoot to my feet, dumping Al on the floor. "Like that containment tank!"

Yep. As I watch, the three-ton thing shakes like a big-ass metal baby trying to take its first steps. The pressure monitors are so far past the red, they're into some new color that indicates a level of imminent danger so high it hasn't even been named yet.

"I *knew* that thing was a bad idea."

This isn't steampunk, so no popping bolts or rending seams—just a shimmy-shimmy shake-shake warning me it's about to blow. Not like I can do anything about it, other than watch.

A bump—a kind of blister—rises on its smooth, sleek form.

I look at the screen, hoping there's a button that reads, "Stop virus."

There isn't.

"Al, we've got to move!"

She tries to get up, but she has trouble, what with all the quaking going on. Right before the tank ruptures, I jump on her, shielding her with my body. I'm expecting a huge explosion, a major blast, a kaboom that'll take us all out. Instead, there's a sound more akin to Galactus, Eater of Worlds, having a bad case of explosive diarrhea.

The pink goo of five (five, right?) giant monsters squirts out in a single stream, drenching the place with a thick coat of gross, writhing, liquidy fleshness.

Remember way back when I said I wasn't killing anything, since all that stuff is technically still alive? Don't know how, or why, or what could possibly be producing the sound, but an undeniable voice rises out of the icky puddle. It's angry, aching, and hollow all at once—as if simply *being* is causing it indescribable pain, and speaking only makes it worse. At the same time, it has no choice—it *has* to be, it *must* make itself known, and it says:

"We...live..."

TWENTY-FIVE

WE'RE surrounded by a distilled essence of life. It howls against a dark nothingness from which it is nearly indistinguishable. There, but barely. The amorphous, boundless, bubbling blob of confusion slushes around like an ocean tide, filling open spaces, slapping against walls and doors. Al and I are already drenched in the stuff and seem no worse for wear, but I really don't like the look of those undulating waves. Before they can touch us, I hoist Al onto what I hope is a table. Once I'm sure it's not another death-ray platform, I hop up by her side.

In a rare moment of vulnerability, she clings to me. "Wade, what *is* it?"

Like prisoners suddenly granted parole, words escape me. "Uh…hmm. Let's see. Uh…I'm going to go with an octopus the size of New Jersey trying to put itself together after being in a blender."

Good a start as any. It's pink, all pink. You already know that, but this isn't the kind of pink you'd want for a bow on a birthday gift for a three-year-old girl. This is more like the pink you'd see in the lighter parts of a gore pile. Oily pustules rise and burst, releasing more of the same, but in a slightly darker pink. The dimmer parts try to form shapes along the surface. Pulpy tentacles briefly form, only to vanish with a hideous plop. A few manage distorted, complex squiggles, like a series of membranes trying to keep their shape, but failing. Somehow the hissing, bubbling, croaking, popping, and baying coalesces into a single voice:

"Father...father..."

Al grips my shoulder. "It must mean you."

I whisper back. "That's a leap. It's probably speaking metaphorically, like to its creator, rather than to a literal, physically present father. I mean, we don't even know if it can hear us."

"Father...is that you?"

Smart-ass goo.

Al nudges me. "Go on. Talk to it."

I shake my head. "I dunno. I just went on a very awkward date where I put myself out there, and things didn't work out. Besides, what do you say to something that's loony-bird crazy?"

"You're asking me?" She raps her knuckles on my forehead like she's knocking on a door. "You're the one with the experience. How do you talk to all those voices in your head?"

Yeah, Wade. How *do* you?

Tell us! Please, Wade!

Inches beneath the platform, the viscous putrescence wobbles. "Father? Father?"

What the hell. "Yes...uh...son?"

"Father...why...are...we?"

Sure, start with the easy ones.

"Forgot...to use...protection...?"

"Does...our being...have...purpose?"

"Do…you…mean…?"

Al slaps me. "Stop imitating it! If it figures out you're making fun of it, it might decide to eat us."

I clear my throat. "Well, son, do you mean all beings, or just you?"

"Is…there…a difference?"

"Well, duh. You're a big pile of goop made from melted monsters. Al's a typical human being, and me—well, if you want that answer, you're going to have to go back to the start and read the book."

"Why?"

Kids reach an age where they love asking questions. Why's the sky blue? Why this? Why that? Why did Mommy leave us for that guy with the beard? It's a game. They don't want to know the answer—they just figured out that no matter what you say, they can always ask, "Why?"

Luckily, there's a standard answer my old man used on me all the time.

"Because I said so."

"Why?"

"Because I said so."

"Why?"

"Because…I said so."

The liquid splashes against the platform. The voice gets louder.

"Say…something…else!"

Yeah, that used to drive me crazy, too. I know what Dad would do, but it's not like I can use my belt on a big puddle. Before I can come up with a more satisfactory explanation for the existential nature of being (like, Why *not?*), it yowls piteously:

"Aghh! I...will...destroy...you!"

Al's fingers tighten on my shoulder. "Wade, what's it doing?"

"Not much. Really, Al, it's a bunch of goo. It lurched up maybe half an inch, then fell back to bubbling. What can goo do to you other than get you gooey?"

"Rarrr!"

"But it sounds so...hurt and angry. What did it do that time?"

"Rarr!"

"The same, but it's a little lower now. Basically, it's draining away."

I kneel down and put my face closer. "Who's a big bad pile of goo? Come on. Who's a big bad pile of goo?"

Al sighs. "Wade, don't taunt the big bad pile of goo."

I pull back. "Why not?"

"It's just tacky."

(That last one was for you Joss Whedon fans—paraphrased, of course, but what series, who said it, and can you name the episode?)

Al and I sit, and watch, and wait. Light from the globular ceiling lamps plays across the goo, forming weird crisscross lines on the rippling surface that almost remind me of sunset at a lake. It gets lower and lower until all that's left is a series of puddles.

"Hm. Seven maids, seven mops, maybe half a year."

Lewis Carroll?

Is he a maid?

All but gone, it gives itself one more go. "Must... hurt...you..."

I try not to laugh. "You're staying pissed all the way down to the last drop, ain't ya? Face facts: The only way you can hurt anyone is if they accidentally slip on you."

"You're...wrong...father..."

I want to chalk that up to a dramatic flourish from a dying life-form, but the bright lights that flash on one of the soggier consoles make it tough. The screen is way across the room, but even from here, I see monitor bars rising.

"Did you do that?" I ask.

No answer. Unless you call that farting noise from some of the remaining bubbles an answer.

I hop to the floor. As I slosh through the lingering goo for a better look at the terminal, it speaks in a diminishing whisper: "Ow....ow...ow..."

The closer I get to the console, the more I realize the puddles on it aren't so random. They're covering the controls. Somehow, it got itself together enough to drip onto the right keys and enter a few commands.

"What does this control, anyway? Crap!"

I get a gander at the screen: images of little doghouses, thirty occupied. Their biometrics are monitored, and about half are skyrocketing. The canine icons above them warp and grow.

"No! No, no, no! It's the kennel!"

I thought they were sealed off. I thought they were safe. But I was wrong, terribly wrong. A dreadful din erupts from beyond the kennel doors.

"I am Xemnu!"

"I am Grogg!"

"I am Zzutak!"

"I am the Titan!"

"I am Shzzzllzzzthzz!"

"I am Orrgo!"

"I am Rombu!"

"I am Fangu!"

"I am Droom!"

"I am Sserpo!"

"I am Monsteroso!"

There's like four more, but I figure you get the idea.

TWENTY-SIX

THE heavy drumming of creatures on the loose echoes from beyond the twin white doors. The kennel—secure, comfortable home of joy and innocence—is now a place where monsters dwell. Infuriated, I stomp on the remaining droplets of sentient goo. I kick at them. I squish them. I grind them under my toe.

"Damn you! You had to go and do it, didn't you? Didn't you?"

"Ha….ha…ha…"

The pounding intensifies. The doors, two-feet thick and made of a composite that I assume has been designed to withstand a small nuclear blast, begin to bend.

I rush toward them. "I've got to get in there!"

Al calls out. "You just said there are fifteen monsters in there!"

"Which means there are fourteen *real* puppies. Fourteen, Al! And Mr. Snuffles! I have to save them."

"Them? What about me?"

"Oh yeah, you. Well, it looks like that goop fried the only elevator I know about, and my 'porter can't handle you and the puppies at once. See if you can find another way out of here. An emergency exit, or an escape pod, or a really big ant tunnel."

Al screams something about teleporting her out, then coming back for the puppies, but I can't quite make out what it is. Like I said before, the DP would never use my 'porter to ruin a good, tense action scene. So I'm declaring the transporter broken, kids. Unless another option turns up, we're here for the duration.

Why? Because I said so.

I hit the kennel access panel. The doors hiss open, they really do. The servos groan like the sex scenes in a cheap romance, but the doors are too bent to slide more than half a foot.

As the behemoths within continue to introduce themselves to one another, I find myself staring at a huge, orange, hairy thing wedged in the door crack. It's definitely a giant orifice of some sort. Hope it's a monster mouth, or nose, or ear canal. After that, the choices get dicey.

Whatever it is, it smells awful. Holding my breath, I force my hands against the doors and try to pry them apart. I strain, I grunt, I pull. When I adjust my grip for more leverage, I pinch a bit of monster mucous membrane.

"I am Rorrgg, King of the....YEOW!"

"Sorry!"

I try again. The doors won't slide, but between all my prying and the hammering from the other side, they bend out enough to flop onto the floor with a grand, ineloquent CRUNK.

What do I see inside? Picture fifteen monsters, each between twenty-five and thirty-five feet tall, crammed into the same space, and all too big to fit through the door. It's like a hairy, scaly, exoskeleton, robotic, extraterrestrial, cryptid game of Twister.

And nobody's wearing socks.

They're all in there, trying to stretch. They punch and kick, gnash their teeth, mince their mandibles, and click their pincers. Meanwhile, the whole underground base has become a deathtrap, shuddering like it's ready to collapse.

But above the howling din of things from here, there, and everywhere, a chorus of youthful yips reaches my ears.

"Puppies!"

They're still in there, still alive!

The moment Rorrgg moves his whatever out of my face, I dive in. Can't use the ADD. No telling what I might accidentally turn to goo. I shimmy under Orrgo, the Fiend With Two R's. I get up close with Shzzzllzzzthzz, the Creature With Eight Z's. I see a lot more than I need to of Xemnu the Titan. I nearly get my head stuck beneath the mossy armpit of Chalo, the Beast from the Bog, scramble through a tiny gap between the feet of Oog, the Frozen Terror, and barely escape the burning crotch of Dragoom, the Flaming Intruder.

All the while, I'm grabbing puppies, starting with the esteemed Mr. Snuffles (because he's special!). I snatch up shepherds and beagles, Rottweilers and poodles. Soon enough, I realize I can't hold more than three without dropping some, so I wait for a gap among the colossal limbs and toss them out the space where the door used to be. Three out of four times, I make the shot. When I miss, well, I have to try again.

And the smell. Oh, the smell! The smell, smell, smell, smell!

I thought Rorrgg's whatever was bad. But these things from space, from within the Earth, from other dimensions—all of them are sweating like crazy in the tight space, each in its own special biochemical way. The Bronx Zoo on a humid day, a fertilizer plant, a meat-packing factory, the hampers of the world's largest diaper service?

Perfume, all of it.

Can't take it much longer. I'm dizzy, losing it. I've got scores of dogs to go before I sleep, but the world doesn't care. It spins on me, and it's not like it was easy to orient myself in this mess to begin with. I'm ready to do a cross between puking and passing out when, out of nowhere, I feel something shoved under my nostrils.

It's strawberry, crazy sweet.

Sophie says, "Do you like it?"

It's a breezy morning outside school. We're with all the other kids, waiting for the bell to toll the beginning of our classless classes. I'm holding her books, she's holding her wrist under my nose. It smells so much like candy I want to bite it.

"Yeah," I say. "I like it."

"I tried calling back around 7:30, but the phone company said your line was out of order."

Desperate though I was to tell her something, I shrug. "Oh, that's okay."

"How's your puppy, Wade?"

My...?

Then I remember.

Near as our senses can tell, life plays out in time, one event after another. This total recall gives it to me all at once, and it takes my brain a while to sort all the images into a sequence. When I do, it goes something like this:

The dog. My dog. Mixed breed. I'm putting her down on the porch, holding her collar as she squirms and twists and I try to get the leash on. Then I'm letting go for half a second and watching the cheery white-and-tan blur shoot across the sidewalk, her colors so much like the cement that she's almost invisible. But when that blur hits the street's black asphalt, I see her oh, so clearly. I hear the squealing breaks, see the silvery bumper slowing, but not nearly enough to keep from making contact with the flesh and fur.

Then she's a blur again, flying sideways, soundless.

I wanted to tell Sophie about it last night, but now I don't want to cry in front of her, so I look down at my feet. "She…she…"

My dog. Mine.

The school bell rings. I look up. Sophie's gone, and all of a sudden, I'm not sure she was ever there. Now that I think about it, I can't seem to remember anyone else ever talking to Sophie.

The student mob wants to haul ass inside, and I'm in its way. They push me, pull me, shove me, and suffocate me. Furious, I push back.

But it isn't middle-school clothes or flesh I feel. It's alien hide, scales, and orange hair.

Whoa! Hallucinations like that really make a fellow wonder what's real—especially when I come back to a creature-packed underground kennel. Still reeling from the stench, I go back to scooping up puppies. I'm more determined than ever, like I'm gathering a furry bouquet on the puppy farm. I hurl them yipping and yapping through the monster maze, hoping to get them all out before everything everywhere comes crashing down.

My last count puts me at thirteen. I'm not great at math, but I'm pretty sure that means there's one more to go. I saved Snuffles first, but I've been saving another special guy for last—a pointer, because he's so damn frisky. They're hunting dogs: naturally fearless, lots of stamina, bred for sport, always raring to go. That's the problem. He won't sit still. I spot him easy enough, but the trick is getting ahold of him. He's running across Fangu's lava-lamp-like back, chasing one of Monsteroso's swinging tendrils, barking his head off like he knows what he'll do with it if he catches it.

Whenever he sees me coming, despite the hunks of metal and powdered rock tumbling from the widening ceiling cracks, he thinks I want to play. Each time I almost catch him, he slips through some thrashing creature crack too small for me to follow. On the lighter side, since he does want to play, whenever I lose track, he barks so I can find him. If I fall behind, he waits for me to catch up. It'd be great fun if he wasn't about to be flattened.

I hop onto the head of Grottu, King of the

Insects, figuring I always do my best thinking atop a giant ant. But Grottu's not having it.

"I am Grottu!"

He pokes me with his antennae, yammering about conquering mankind. Still, it gives me an idea. If you're squeamish about bug guts, you might want to skip this part.

What with all the shaking, it's tough to swing a blade, but I manage to sever a stick-sized bit of big ant antenna. Grottu does this insect screech, but it'll grow back in a flash, and at least that'll shut him up for a while.

The pointer sits on the rocky belly of Sserpo, the Creature who Crushed the Earth, wagging his tail. I shake the piece of antenna at him. "Here, boy! Here! Look what I've got!"

He shakes excitedly, wags his tail faster, and does that thing dogs do where they put their head down and keep their hindquarters up, ready to pounce.

"Fetch!" I throw the antenna out the door.

The good doggie goes diving after it. Just in time, too. I barely make it out myself before the kennel ceiling comes tumbling down. That doesn't make the monsters very happy at all. It doesn't damage them so much as rile them, and they weren't the peaceful sort to begin with. The entrance is too small for them, but the wall around it is creaking, and it looks ready to give. Once they get here into the lab, there's enough space for at least one of them to try to eat us.

I grab my sacks and start scooping the pups back

in. There's only fifteen of them now, so they all fit in two. Then I realize someone's missing.

"Al! Al! Where are you?"

In a single, completely unexpected moment, all the angst and agony, senseless death, ruptured memories, and buried remorse suddenly seem worth it. Blind Al staggers into view, the gooey end of the ant antenna stuck to the top of her head.

"Wade! Something hit me! Am I bleeding?"

It's all I can do to keep from laughing so hard I'll wet myself.

"No! You're fine." She starts to reach for it. "But whatever you do, don't touch it. You find us a way out?"

"I did! Surprise, surprise, that OS is handicapped accessible. Couple of voice commands, and that exit back there opened up!"

She points at a wall. A few yards over, there's a sleek gray corridor with a wide ramp heading down. Boy, that's one great operating system.

"Do you know where it goes?"

The floor shakes. Fissures open in the walls on either side of the kennel entrance.

"You want to ask questions, or you want to run?"

"Run, I guess."

I hand her one puppy sack and take the other, and we hightail it. As the wall collapses behind us, I turn back to see Grogg from the Black Pit and Zutak the Thing that Shouldn't Exist stuck in the breach, fighting like Abbott and Costello to see who gets out first. The pressure from the other thirteen gets to be too much, and they all come sprawling into the lab.

Another voice command seals the exit behind us, and we run down, down, down. The ramp turns on itself like a stairwell, but it's plenty tall and wide enough to carry all sorts of equipment, and maybe even let a monster or two through.

We're not out of the woods yet. Thuds and crashes continue from above, but the deeper we go, the quieter it gets. In time, the hum of the machinery ahead dampens the rampaging-monster sounds to about the volume of the bass speaker on that irritating car stereo owned by the jerk who pulls up beside you at the light, too stupid to realize not everyone shares his crappy taste in music.

We reach an open area that looks a lot like the one we left behind, but with no monsters and no damage. I lower the bag and let my doggies breathe.

"A secret lab beneath the secret lab? How'd S.H.I.E.L.D. miss this?"

Al puts a finger to her lips. "Wade, shh!"

"No. I will not shh! I know it's not 'politic' to criticize your employers, but come on! They're the smartest, best-funded outfit on the face of the Earth, and they don't notice there's a whole second lab down here? Preston ought to be…"

Her hand goes up, and she hunches over, listening. "Shh! You idiot! We're not alone!"

"Oh."

Once I quiet down, even I hear the heavy breathing. Sounds like someone's been in a fight. Al, who's much better with the whole audio-location thing than I am, points toward what looks like an examination table, but could be a really expensive reading chair. A pool of red liquid is seeping onto the floor from the space behind it.

Weapons drawn, I approach on tippy-toe. Slowly, the feet and shapely legs of an unmoving body come into view.

Oh, no.

I'd recognize those gams anywhere. It's Jane. She's hurt. I inch forward and see that the reddish fluid is flowing out from somewhere high on her body. Her neck. Why? Because her head isn't there to hold it in anymore.

And there, crouching above her lifeless form, is the source of all that exhausted, heavy breathing.

Dick.

He looks like a kid who's been caught trying to hide the hand of his murder victim in the cookie jar.

"This isn't what it looks like!"

"Good thing, because it looks like you're hovering over Jane's headless body."

"Well, yes, but…"

Emotionally speaking, I am having a tough day. At times like this—feeling raw because you just remembered how your dog died, and you're enraged that the love of your life has been decapitated—when you leap through the air wielding dual katana, all you can really say is:

"YEEARGH!"

TWENTY-SEVEN

THE katana strike Dick's arms. But instead of piercing muscle meat, the hardened tips are deflected. He must be wearing some kind of flexible, skintight armor under that suit. No problemo. His head's vulnerable—I remember it bleeding back in the alley.

"Let me explain!"

I unleash a flurry of blows on his smug, masked face—a *flurry*, I tell you again! The feel of flesh and bone is much more satisfying.

Hands up, he steps back, but I keep it coming. "You don't understand!"

After a count of eight, he finally gets the idea I won't be listening to any more of his BS.

"Have it your way!"

But by then good ol' Dick is backed into a wall. It'll take a desperate Hail Mary move to get himself out. He tries one. Clenching his fists, he raises his arms and tries to drive his pointy elbows down toward my upper chest. Peh. I see it coming a mile away. I'm already bending over, focusing my fists on his abdomen. His elbows hit my shoulders.

Hm. Those elbows aren't only pointy, they're hard as molded metal—the classy stuff. That's good armor. I may try to get his tailor's name out of him before I kill him.

Stupid. The two sentences I spent admiring his duds give him a chance to bring a knee up into my chin. It's as hard as the elbows, but bigger and driven by the stronger force of a leg muscle.

My head snaps back, but it's not as if I'm terribly inconvenienced. If this is going to be anything other than a slaughter, he still has to get himself out of this corner. Next, he tries a few feints, then throws himself to the side. My foot shoots out to trip him, but by then he's in midair, landing on his hands and cartwheeling onto his feet near the puppies. Damn, he's out!

That cartwheel at the food festival wasn't a one-off, after all. The piece of crud probably *wanted* me to catch him so he could slip me that flash drive. He was holding back.

The pups are underfoot, Mr. Snuffles leading the junior pack. They're all growling like they remember him.

Dick sneezes. "Stupid mutts!"

He looks at poor Mr. S. like he's about to kick him, reminding me in a funny way of my dad. Bad move. There are only three things I've even thought of caring about during this whole mess. One died from misadventure, Dick's already killed the other one, and now he's threatening the third.

I grab the nearest heavy object: the examining table. Sure, it's bolted to the floor—but I'm so amped, I pull it up and send it into the center of Dick's back with enough force to shatter a normal man's spine. That armor saves him again, but the impact pushes him forward. His arms and legs bend behind him, but he doesn't even have the decency to fall down.

When the table clatters to the floor, the puppies scatter, resuming their barking at a safer distance. Grateful for the extra space, I use my guns to lay down some suppressing fire—into his gut. Dick jiggles like a stripper as the bullets hit, but otherwise stays put.

Impressive.

He runs, but I'm not into another chase. Besides, other than the ramp leading upstairs to the monster convention, there's no way out. Speaking of monsters, it sounds like they're pretty drunk up there, trashing the place like a rock band stuck in a fancy hotel room.

I rush past Jane's body to get to Dick, but slip and slide when I hit the puddle. That's some *really* oily blood. Hasn't even started coagulating.

I'm nothing if not adaptable, so I twist with the momentum and slide right on up to Dick. Before he can offer to explain again, I grab his right hand and snap it back. I'm expecting to hear bone crack, but don't.

He does a full-body flip to break my grip, then takes a sweep at my legs. I jump and come down hard on an ankle. There are seven tarsal bones in the human ankle—but again, nothing cracks. The guns didn't work, either, so I holster them and try the katana again.

I swing for his head, and he blocks…

…with his forearm? They hear the metallic clunk all the way in Peoria.

Okay, so there's more to Dick than it appears. And again, no *that's what she said* jokes. What's the freak got under there? (See previous sentence about this sort of joke.)

In the half second I take to wonder why his arm isn't sliced, he goes into a jump kick, sailing three feet up from a resting position. Not waiting to wonder about it this time, I grab his legs. Holding him up, I run him across the floor—right into some built-in shelves. That back has to give at some point.

Shelf contents tumbling, he grabs the falling pieces and flings them at me. I get hit by a tablet computer, pens, and a coffee mug—all of which bounce off without stinging. But then he lucks out and latches on to a surgical saw. When I see that flying my way, I figure I should duck.

Good decision, too. It embeds itself about six inches deep in the wall behind me.

I rip it out and send it back. This time I don't aim at his body, since that hasn't exactly been working, but at his clothes, hoping for a peek at what's going on under there. The saw sheers off a nice slice of fabric. Yep. Robotics.

His head seems real enough, though. When I close the distance again, I grab his knuckleheaded skull under my arm and start slamming him into the nearest wall, over and over. This, at last, has the desired effect. Better yet, every time his head hits the wall, his robot arms snap out to the sides, like I'm yanking the string on one of those pull toys they put in baby cribs.

The location of that string always made me uncomfortable.

With Dick's body twitching and his head feeling pulpier, I'm starting to think I may actually knock him out. But he gets a second wind, like someone gave him a new battery, and wrenches himself free. We stand toe-to-toe, grabbing each other by the shoulders and pushing each other's chins up and away, trying to pull or push each other off our feet. Goes on like that a while, until we wind up breaking it off out of boredom and taking a few steps back.

He comes running at me. I'm expecting another kick. Instead, he *runs up my chest*, clamps his legs around my neck, twists, and takes me down. Nice move. I'd applaud if it didn't hurt so much. Before I can congratulate him, he picks me up and starts slamming me sideways, again and again, into another of those exam tables.

He's got me. He's got me good. He's slamming and slamming, harder and harder, until we both hear this loud SNAP!

No, not my spine. I'll give you a hint: It's something I'm carrying. Not the guns. I left those on the floor. Not the katana. They're sheathed along my back—hitting me sideways wouldn't do squat to them. Think a minute. What else am I carrying? No, not the 'porter!

That's right. The ADD. The deadly nano-catalyst in a supposedly indestructible container. But we've already seen S.H.I.E.L.D. containment at work on the monster-goo tank, right?

Between slams, I try to call a time-out. "Hold it! Wait!"

Not having it, Dick hurls me down again. This time, I do my own Hail Mary: I draw a katana and brace the hilt against the table, the angle just so. When he slams me down, he smashes into it, wedging the blade in his robo-shoulder.

It doesn't go in deep—maybe an inch—but it's enough to make him back off.

Less worried about him, more worried about ending up a puddle of whining pinkish glop, I yank the ADD free from my belt. The light's blinking like crazy, green-red-red-green, but I don't need a code book to see the problem. It's got a crack along the side. It's not seeping—not yet, anyway—but I don't plan on holding onto the damn thing much longer, let alone carrying it around in a fistfight.

I set it on the table and point. "Dick, we can keep beating the crap out of each other anywhere else, *with* anything else, but don't touch that, okay? It's like home base. You're gonna have to trust me on this. Got it?"

Huh. What do you know? Looks like there won't be any more fighting. I may already be a winner. The katana struck electronic gold. What would have been a flesh wound for a living body's got Dick twitching like a dancing machine. His head's flopping this way and that, like it's about to come off.

"Oh, never mind, then. You ready to say Uncle, Dick? I mean, Dick, do you want to say Uncle? Not that you're my Uncle Dick."

"No, Deadpool. Not just yet."

His internal mechanisms whine, metal clicking into place.

"Oh, Dick, you're not rerouting all your power for one final, all-or-nothing strike, are you?"

Head askew, he pulls the blade from his shoulder and levels it at me. "Yep."

I nod. "Then come to Papa."

We rush at each other. I was wrong about his speed before. He's faster than I am, at least on foot. But half the key in most martial arts is using your opponent's strength against them. I make it look as if I'm planning to butt heads with him, like we're a couple of freaking rams in heat, but at the last second, I drop and let him go flying over me.

The idea was for me to hop back up while his back was to me, then hit that weakened shoulder from behind. Didn't realize how long it'd take him to stop. Matter of fact, he doesn't stop at all—not intentionally.

He sails right into the base of the exam table holding the ADD.

"Oh, man! I told you to stay away from that!"

"Sorry!"

He stumbles away. His right arm's twitching, and his body takes to dancing again—but try as he might with his snazzy moves, he's no longer the most interesting thing in the room. That would be the ADD. With the table tilted from the impact, the canister wobbles, rolls, and then stops right before falling. I'm all set to breathe an exaggerated sigh of relief when I spot the gleam swelling at the crack. Clear liquid flows from it, down to the table's surface and onto the edge, where it beads into a single, clinging drop.

And who, of course, is right beneath this single drop, wagging his tail?

"Mr. Snuffles! Get out of there! Now!"

Either I didn't use any of those 165 words the average dog is supposed to understand, or Snuffles is below average. He stays put, twisting his head curiously up at his imminent demise, eyes wide, tail wagging, tongue lolling, as if saying:

"Oh, boy! Oh, boy! What is it? I can't wait to find out!"

Stupid freaking dog. But I still love him.

As I dive for him, everything goes slo-mo: me hurtling toward Mr. Snuffles and the deadly droplet dangling on a long strand, lowering toward him like a spider. I'm three quarters of the way there when the strand snaps. The nano-catalyst falls, nothing between it and Mr. Snuffles but air and gravity. I want to speed up, but being in midair, I don't think that's technically possible. I try anyway.

Almost there…almost there…me and the droplet. The droplet and me. The droplet and Mr. Snuffles. Me, the droplet, and Mr. Snuffles.

It's a game of inches, but it won't happen. I'm not going to get there in time to shove him out of the way. Fortunately for the dog, I'm good at quick decisions—real good. Unfortunately for me, they're not always very *smart* decisions. I stretch my arm out ahead of me, stick my open hand between his furry head and the nano-catalyst...

...and catch it!

Yeah, I can regenerate, but so could the monsters, and they splooshed into goo in under a second. So, hey, I just committed suicide for a dog.

Puts quite the look on my face, I can tell you.

I'm still in that slo-mo thing, so we can give this a couple of sentences. Neurons firing all over my body, the wordless word goes out, not only to every one of my major organs—internal or otherwise—but also to the little guys, the individual cells that make it all possible. The message careening at the speed of bioelectric reactions? This is it, gang: the last gasp of the molecular pattern that comprised the corporeal Wade.

Even the cancer cells are upset—but seriously, screw them. The rest of you? Hope you all kept your résumés updated.

And what does Wade Wilson get for his last selfless moment? A view of a mountain range? A field? Some porno?

Nope. Even Mr. Snuffles isn't in my field of vision. He's probably off licking his junk somewhere. Nothing to see here but a table edge and the flat wall behind it. Not even any color, just a white wall with silver trim.

Wish I could see him one last time. I wish I could tell him, "Earn this! Earn this, Mr. S.!" But there isn't time. There just isn't time.

I crash onto the cool floor. My hand registers a sharp pain, like my palm is being eaten by acid. I start to close my eyes, wondering if I'll be able to finish closing them before everything goes black. I do. I get my eyes closed. Then I slow-count to ten.

Hey—I'm still here. I open my eyes again to see what the &*@ is going on.

No, I'm not miraculously immune. There is indeed a hole in my hand, right where the nano-catalyst touched. It's about the size of a dime, and it is spreading, around and down, but...slowly. Because it was just one drop? The monsters all got a whole spritz. Could be a dosage issue. Or maybe it's like that transporter thing, and the nano-catalyst is suddenly obeying different rules in order to create dramatic tension. Can't say. All I know is, it *is* liquefying me, and while I may not be gone in seconds, this isn't the time to start watching an episode of *Murder, She Wrote*.

Besides, Dick's still here, and I doubt we have the same taste in TV.

I stand and point my remaining blade his way. His head's askew, like it's no longer properly attached, but he still has the nerve to nod at my dripping wrist.

"Your hand is gone."

I crouch into an offensive stance. "Or...is it?"

"Yeah, it is. And now your forearm's dripping pink goo. That is *so* gross."

"Look, smartass, I don't have time to argue about who does or doesn't have which limbs. Pretend I'm doing that Keanu Reeves thing and waving you forward with my fingers, and let's finish this up."

"You got it."

We eye each other like two mortally wounded Samurai, motionless but mentally playing out all the possible moves—the strikes, the counters, the combos—second-guessing then third-guessing until it's as if the fight's already over, and all that's left is to play it out.

Yes, it looks that way—but really, I make it up as I go along. He's expecting me to go for his weak shoulder again, and I'm expecting the same. But when it comes down to it and we move, I change my mind. I swing for his neck—right where that floppy head connects to his mechanized body.

See Dick. See Dick's head fall. Fall, head, fall.

The cyborg body hits the ground, landing in an odd cross-legged position that makes it seem quite thoughtful.

With Jane avenged, and no one left to try and conquer the world with dog-monsters, it's over. Well, except for the monsters tromping around upstairs, but that's someone else's problem now. All that's left for me is the melting. Arm's pretty much gone, along with a fifth of my chest—beautiful muscles, oozing scars, and all.

Woozy, I slump to the floor beside Dick's head.

Al comes out of hiding to kneel beside me. I look up at her.

"Puppies…out of…danger?"

She nods. "Want some water, or something?"

I've come back so often it's tough to *really* believe my own death is imminent, but the look on her face worries me.

"Nah. I think I'll just sit here, if you don't mind." As more of me dribbles off, I get to a place where it's easier to chat with the dead. So I turn from away her, toward the head.

"Good fight there, Dick. We really *could* have been buds."

I'm not expecting it to answer.

"I was hoping for a more physical relationship."

I'm *really* not expecting it to answer in Jane's voice.

TWENTY-EIGHT

WISH I had an extra minute or two to wrap my much-abused brain around this startling new development, but the liquefaction's reached my thigh. Not much longer before I wind up the Merc without a Mouth. But with my throat still intact and my eyes on the disembodied head talking in Jane's voice, I call out, "Al?"

She's beside me, so close it startles me. "Yeah, Wade?"

"I'll take that water now."

"Sure."

Somber, she hands me what'll probably be my last drink. Wish it had ice cubes, but there isn't even a freaking straw. Geez, Al, the condemned on death row get a better deal. Think you could have made some effort?

Bracing myself, I address the fallen head. "Jane... is that really you? Am I hallucinating?"

The lips beneath the mask crinkle into a smile. "It's really me, Wade, it really is."

Didn't realize how desert-dry my mouth was until I fill it with water. Instead of swallowing, I do a spit take all over the head. It wriggles and tries to shake off the water. Not being a dog, it can't.

"Hey! This mask isn't waterproof! And it's not like I can towel off!"

"Pardon me for a spontaneous expression of surprise! Jane, what-the-freaking-what are you doing in Dick's head?"

"It's not *his* head, it's...*ours*."

I throw the cup. It bounces on her forehead. "Like that explains it."

"Oh, Wade! I wanted to tell you from the beginning, I did, but I couldn't."

"Couldn't?" I turn away. "Or didn't want to?"

She opens and closes her mouth, using her chin to wriggle closer. "Please don't be like that. I was afraid if you knew the truth, you'd hate me. I couldn't bear it if you hated me."

I can't help it. I twist back toward her. It's not that I want to, but I can't control my melting body very well. It just sort of twists that way.

"Hate you? Babe, I don't even know what you are."

Al leans down between us. "Get a room, you two. Or at least a bucket."

"Some privacy, okay?"

Al *harrumphs*, but gives us space. Hip dribbling off, I search Jane's pleading eyes.

"All I want is the truth. Just gimme some truth."

"Can't you guess? You of all people?" As she speaks, her voice changes. It gets deeper, less flirtatious. "You know what it's like to have a psychological disorder, don't you?" I realize I'm talking to Dick. "A beehive mind that's always talking to itself?"

Oh! Oh! I get it!

They're a split personality!

Quiet, quiet! Let the readers put it together, will you?

My left buttock is half gone. I'm starting to list. "So…Dick is Jane? Jane is Dick? Does Spot know? Is *that* why Spot runs?"

One moment, Dick's talking: "You could say we're luckier than you. At least we have two android bodies to reflect our different gender identities."

The next, it's Jane: "Or…you might say we're not as lucky, since we're just a head now."

To keep from falling over, I use my only arm to grab the table. "Can we speed this up?"

"Wade…can you still love me?"

"Honestly, Jane, it depends—it depends on a lot of things. How'd you get like this? What's it got to do with the dog-monsters? And most importantly, is your female robot body completely anatomically correct?"

Another voice, neither Dick nor Jane, interjects. "*I* can answer that first question."

I told you guys to keep quiet!

Wasn't us.

Yeah, check the real world for once, will you?

"Uh…over here, Wade?"

I try to face the newcomer, but what's left of me does another twisty thing, and I end up looking half at a puddle of myself and half at a brand-new corridor that seems to have appeared out of nowhere. Standing in it, with a shiny cadre of grim S.H.I.E.L.D. agents posing behind her, is a sight for my sore and soon-to-be-melting eyes.

"Preston! And look, you brought an exit with you!"

She nods. "Once I had the mobile interface up, I found a tunnel that let us in from an acre away, avoiding the monsters upstairs—all from my smartphone. The OS here is a better find than the gene-splicing equipment. You don't look so good, as usual, Wade. Don't know why I ever expect different anymore."

"If I'd known you were coming, I'd have tried to stay in one piece. But to what do I owe the pleasure?"

Her face twists. "Your fight with Dick in New York attracted attention. Forensics did an analysis of Dick's blood samples, pulled from the barbed wire in the alley. I raced over here as soon the results were confirmed. I...wanted to tell you in person."

"You've ID'd our mysterious perpetrators? You know who Dick and Jane is...uh...are?"

Traces of confusion join the overall trepidation on her face. "I'm going to go with *sort of.* After the preliminary results, I thought the samples had to be contaminated, so I requisitioned a more complete diagnostic. The lab boys found a few markers to distinguish the genome from..."

Left buttock's gone now, and all I'm hearing is blah-blah-blah.

"Em, I'm already half-assed here. Can I have the short version?"

"There's no way to sugarcoat this, but..." The

perceptive agent finally notices my puddle. "Wade, are you melting? I'm just so used to seeing you in pieces... You *are* melting!" She puts her hands to her hips. "You broke the ADD, didn't you? You broke the damned ADD! I warned you, I said to be careful, but no—"

"Em, the news?"

She blinks. "Right. Dick, Jane—whatever that head calls itself—it's *you*. A complete genetic match."

A dark ache rises from the depths of my being. Could be the result of all these emotional shocks, but slowly turning to goo probably has something to do with it, too. "Nooooo! I don't believe it! I won't believe it! It's like Luke finding out Leia is his sister, only worse."

Jane coos at me. "She's lying, Wade. Don't believe her. She's jealous. They're all jealous of us. Look at them with their sad little lives, and then look at us— me a head, you melting. No, wait. Bad example. What does it matter? What does anything matter if we're in love?"

Before the sultry voice can take me into an adolescent hallucination, Blind Al slaps me. "For pity's sake! You don't have to believe anyone. Just take the mask off like I told you in the first place!"

Fear creeps into Jane's voice. "Wade, don't."

My body trembles. Or maybe *sheds* is a better word. "Why, Jane? What have you got to hide?"

"Nothing...I just haven't had a chance to do my hair or anything..."

"Quit with the lame gender stereotypes and hold still, toots."

I snag the bottom of the fabric. When I try to slip it off, the head just rolls around. I hold it down with my last leg, but it winds up rolling sideways.

"Al, hold the neck stump for me a sec, will you?"

"*You* hold the freaking stump. I'll pull the mask."

"Fine."

When I grab her neck, Jane giggles. "Ooo! Cold fingers!"

I'd promised myself that no matter what she looked like, I wouldn't be disappointed. But as the mask comes free with a moist plop, another fantasy ends.

Jane tries to make the best of it, offering me a wide smile. "Hiya, hiya, hiya!"

But we both know it's over—or at least it can never be what it was, whatever that was. Bottom line, if I had a little less body, it'd be like staring at a mirror. As it is, it's more like staring at my own head.

"Sigh. At least the pieces are finally falling together here." I look up and get a face full of plaster. "Or is that debris from the monsters crashing around?"

Blind Al clicks her teeth. "Oh, it's the monsters, all right. This mess makes about as much sense as going to a crack house for vitamins."

"Sheesh, Al. I'm dying here. You *ever* going to let that go? I didn't know it was a crack house when I dropped you off to shop, okay? But yeah, you're right. There's still the question of who managed to grow a genetic duplicate of my head, plus the whole swallowing-and-talking-without-lungs thing. Jane, you got anything on all that?"

The voice gets deeper again. "Dick."

"I don't want to talk to you. Put Jane on."

"*She* doesn't want to talk to *you*. She's too upset. But I can give you the backstory. Do you remember Bob, Agent of Hydra?"

Careful readers will recall that I mentioned Bob back in Chapter 3.

"Wow! Is he in there, too? Gee, this is like a series finale where they bring back all the old cast members who haven't moved on to better careers." I knock on the head. "Bob? Hello? Get on out here, you wacky bastard, while I can still beat the crap out of you!"

"You don't understand. You are our biological father—but Bob was, in a sense, our creator."

"You sure he's not in there?" I knock on the skull again. Knock-knock. "Oh, Bob!"

The Dick head wobbles. "Ow. Please stop that."

"Only if you say, 'Who's there?' Come on, I'll start again."

Knock. Knock.

"Sigh. Who's—"

"Interrupting Deadpool."

Dick gets all pouty. No sense of humor. "You want the damn backstory or not?"

I nod. He clears his throat—another questionable effort for a disembodied head—and begins a tale of most astonishing suspense. A journey, if you will, into mystery…

Focus BLURS as DREAMY MUSIC rises.
FADE TO: INT. WEAPON X LAB/DAY/
ESTABLISHING SHOT. The music quiets
as the image sharpens, its dreamy
tones replaced by the harsh crackle
and hum of insidious machinery. Think
Frankenstein, w/digital flourishes.

Oversaturated color gives everything
a subtle, ghostly aura: the ceiling
lights, the sleek machinery, but
especially the figure eagerly hunched
over a Scanning Transmission Electron
Holography Microscope (STEHM).

Close on the figure. It's sad-sack BOB,
his dingy HYDRA UNIFORM half-covered
with a slightly cleaner lab coat. What
he sees puts a grin on his face.

> BOB
> This is one **sweet** OS! I'll have
> a monster army in no time!
> (raises head)
> Then they'll want me back!

Wait. Hold it. That's a screenplay. Besides, Bob
doesn't talk like that. Sorry. We're going to put it all in
quotes now. Again, Dick somehow clears his throat.

"Fired from the evil terrorist organization known

as Hydra, after years of abuse, Bob—the man who was once your biggest fan—arrived at a crossroads. Who was he, really? What was his purpose? Was there anything he could hope for in life beyond quiet desperation and occasionally pretending to be a pirate?

"As if in answer to the questions vexing his soul, one night, on a long, lonely walk along the northern tip of Long Island, he found this hidden lab. At last, he thought: Here was a way to get back in Hydra's good graces—even negotiate the dental plan his wife Allison longed for! Suddenly, Bob, Agent of Hydra, felt transformed, more alive than he did that time the press mistook the H on his costume for 'Hero.'

"But simply leading Hydra here wouldn't be enough. He had to prove his value as more than a lackey—prove, if you will, his *agency* as an agent. Aided by the elegantly simple and incredibly intuitive OS, he was able to scrape some of your DNA from one of the many souvenirs he'd collected over the years. With it, he planned to create an unstoppable army of mouthy mercs, but…" Dick pauses. "…all he got was this lousy head."

He goes silent, lost in a shame spiral. When the head opens its mouth again, the voice has once again grown soft and feminine. "No, Dick, we're *not* just a lousy head! We're a good head, a *great* head! Remember how you suggested splicing in DNA from other species to make the clones more stable?"

Dick sniffs. "Well…you thought of that, really…"

Jane rolls their eyes. "You're being modest.

Whoever thought of it, *you* told Bob. He'd never have listened to a woman. It was only thanks to you he started to respect my voice."

I can hear the pleased smirk in Dick's voice. "Maybe, but you have your ways, strong lady. To continue, the computer modeling indicated canine DNA would make the clones more viable, but at the same time too domesticated. It was only when Jane found the mutagenetic patterns stolen from S.H.I.E.L.D.'s Howling Commando program that Bob's dream was realized."

Jane *tsks*. "Almost realized. Isn't it just like a man to create a life-form with a puppy-larval stage that'll become monster soldiers programmed to obey his every whim, but then have someone *else* care for them until they mature?"

Dick frowns. "That is so sexist. I'd never—"

"Please! You not only did that—you did worse! Did you think all that sweet talk would have me so dizzy in love that I'd forget what came next? Shall I continue? *Ahem*. Now that it was in Bob's interests for us to have arms and legs so we could supervise the kennel, he used the really fantastic equipment here to give us not one, but two prosthetic bodies—one for each persona. Relying on his friendship with you, he assumed we'd be grateful."

Dick chuckles. "Yeah, but clones don't have the same emotional history as the original. Once I secretly added that URL, Jane and I made the puppies. Then we killed him."

"You *killed* Bob?" I do another spit take, but I don't have any water, so it's probably my throat going gooey. "I mean, it's not like I never thought of doing it myself, but…"

"Oh, there's a DNA sample in the databanks here. Clone him if you feel bad about it, but he'll be a Chihuahua for a while. If you'll let me finish…once we had all these puppies, I realized I was allergic. I was sneezing my head off 24/7. A really bad reaction, I swear. I wanted out, but Jane…"

"I adored them! Loved each and every one!"

"And one day, while Jane was, you know, out, I uh…shipped them all off to those pet stores, making all the arrangements online. It was easy."

Jane's eyes go wide. "I was furious! I swore revenge!"

Dick guffaws. "She sure did! Naturally, I wasn't going to let her one-up me, so I swore revenge, too."

She sighs. "As you can imagine, I wasn't going to let him win out, so I swore double-vengeance on Dick, even though I was sick of all the swearing by then."

If Dick had shoulders to shrug, he would. "Looking back, I admit it sounds petty. We were a couple of confused kids stuck in one head. What did we know?"

Dick, or Jane, or both, offers a sheepish grin.

What do you know? Even the monsters have my DNA. It's been one big, crazy extended family. At least it explains my attraction to Dick and Jane. It may even explain why I've been so drawn to the puppies, so hesitant to kill the monsters.

It's really not like me.

For once, the Merc with a Mouth is speechless. Emily, too. Even the agents behind her are posing in variations of stunned-with-mouth-agape. Only Al seems to take it in stride. I nudge her with one of my squishy stumps.

"Hmm? What'd I miss? I fall asleep again?"

So it's been me, all along. Deadpool flowing from Deadpool into Deadpool, making Deadpool from Deadpool for Deadpool's sake—so that from the beginning to the very end, all there is, and all there shall ever be, is Deadpool.

And all the while, the pounding from my unruly half-children upstairs grows louder and louder. But kids always give you headaches, don't they?

TWENTY-NINE

SOMETHING heavy gives way with a sound like the sledgehammer of a mythic giant smashing down on our mortal world. The echo makes it placeless to the ear, and the raining debris hides the source. That crap coming down isn't even concrete or plaster. Old-school construction material crumbles in rocky bits and powder. This stuff has sharper edges, like shattered plastic. Even the smallest bits, still not tiny enough to count as dust, are skin-piercing and jagged.

No one has any problem figuring out where the next crash comes from. This one gives off a concussion wave that blows out from the ramp Al and I took to get down here. The force makes waves in the puddle I'm becoming. All at once, the guttural introductions of the monster crew are no longer quite so muffled. The individual names—like Droom, Grogg, Monsteroso, and so on—seem to cancel each other out, leaving the only recognizable words a chorus:

"I am…! I am…! I am…!"

I am This from That, the Thing from Anywhere but Here.

Melting must be mellowing me. A few minutes ago, I'd think saying your name over and over was totally lame. Like, who cares? Now it strikes me as sad. They're not even repeating their own names. They're clones, their brains a bunch of nerve endings grown in a certain way. But to them, that name's their only memory, the only thing giving shape to their crazy wild, screaming, flesh-eating rage.

I am, I am, I am.

They're announcing their existence just to prove to themselves they're really there.

That, I can sympathize with. Except for Orrgo the Unconquerable. That's just stupid. Ain't no amount of existential angst gonna save that sucker's pride. Am I right?

Does make me wonder what my own last words should be. I'd love to go for something cryptic, like I stare off into space the way a cat does, eyeing something invisible that the faithful assume is an entity from the Great Unknown, a spirit guide come to take me into that undiscovered country. With my last breath, I point at it and whisper:

"You're wearing *that?*"

Then again, I talk so much, I've probably already said everything. Just take all my quotes, put 'em in a document file, shake it like a magic eight ball, and you'll get everything from the meaning of life to how to replace the spring-loaded soap-dispenser door on a dishwasher.

Oh, but my mouth's only half the deal. Can't forget the merc, the muscled body moving through space—fists punching, feet kicking, guns blazing, blades swinging, breaking hearts and minds, and leaving exquisite corpses in its wake. Even if I come up with the last thing I want to say, what's the last thing I want to *do*? That answer's easier. Wait for it…

Kill something. Not just anything. Something that deserves it—something so screwed up, so beyond redemption, it's better off dead.

Now where, oh where, can I find something like that right now?

The puppies cower in a corner. The agents take cover, aiming their useless weapons toward the ramp. Em screams the obvious:

"They're getting through!"

There's only one weapon that isn't useless: the ADD. But it's leaking—a death sentence for anyone who touches it.

Blind Al surprises me. Face plastered with grim determination, she reaches for the weapon. I know what she must be thinking: "You're cowards, the lot of you! We're all going to die anyway, but I'm the only one willing to do what has to be done!"

I call to her. "No! Al, old friend. Let me do it. *I'll* take the ADD."

"The ADD? Crap! I thought it was a bottle of water!" She runs off, screaming, "Sweet Lord, why didn't someone *say* something? What is *wrong* with you people?"

Not so easy moving around with one arm and one leg, but they're still all muscle. A tug at the table edge gets me up. I hop for the gun. Seeing me, the agents and the puppies go silent. Preston calls out, unable to conceal the emotion in her voice.

"Deadpool...don't."

"Really? I mean, it won't be easy. A few of my internal organs feel ready to drop. But why not?"

She swallows. "Good point."

I wrap my hand around the fancy spray gun. The crack isn't oozing for the moment, but that'll change once I start bumping with the beastie boys.

"Get everyone out of here. Leave the kids to me. Bye, Em."

She says something, but the lab starts to shake again. The lights on the ramp are blocked by huge, writhing shadows. The monsters announce their arrival:

"I am...! I am...! I am...!"

After all, it's not like they could sneak in.

The last I hear from Agent Emily Preston are her commands to her agents:

"Grab those puppies and fall back!"

As they obey, the command is repeated: "Fall back! Fall back!"

It's down to me—yours truly, numero uno, the guy with his name in the title. I hop toward my destiny. Spring my way to kismet. Pogo myself to my fate. Between the falling rubble and my dying senses, I can't see what's going on behind me anymore. Have to trust that they're all getting out.

I sure see what's ahead, though—a double-page splash, at least. Hell, I'd blow the print budget and get something bigger for the full impact, like a *Playboy* centerfold. I'm facing a seething, struggling mass of gargantuan life gone mad. As it bursts out toward me, there's no way to tell where Fangu ends and Sserpo begins, if that's Droom's claw or Orrgo's foot. But them's the breaks.

Before too many missing muscles make it impossible for me to move, before my heart melts down, I crouch and leap, soaring through the air one last time as I embrace the world's largest monster stew, releasing the nano-catalyst as I go. I want to say I achieve satori, that special state of grace and enlightenment. That this—my last martial-arts move—is a sublime mesh of discipline, will, and form. That if nothing else, in my final moment, I achieve perfection.

But as I fly, I fart like crazy. We're talking major flatulence, with a smell that could knock a buzzard off a crapwagon. At least I think it's gas. Could be my intestines.

Doesn't matter. Gravity's already been defeated. As I hurtle toward several orifices whose nature and identity confound me, it's all about momentum. No need for thought, or will, or anger. The pain manages to hang around, probably because of the liquefaction thing. But we're the best kind of old friends, pain and I—and he always manages to surprise me.

I spray and spray and spray. As they melt, their final cries of being echo in my skull:

"I am…! I am…! I am…!"

I look at the ADD. A glistening drop at the crack seems to wink at me, beckoning me into the void. Y'know, in retrospect, I could've just cut off my arm before the nano-catalyst spread this far, but you can't think of everything while you're melting. Now, part of me wants to force myself fully into my last moment, to rage against the dying of the light. But then reality, or whatever you want to call it, decides to fade.

The hallucinations return for a greatest-hits parade, but they play out backwards. First I stand with Sophie McPherson outside school. Then I watch my dog slip from its leash. Then I'm home, waiting for the phone to ring.

And finally, I'm on the middle-school court, up and leaping toward the hoop.

Sophie's watching me, squealing my name over and over in girlish delight:

"Wade! Wade!"

It's just like before—the crowd, the lights, the cheering. Only it's different.

For starters, and this is strange, Sophie's voice changes into a bark.

"Yip! Yip!"

She's not the only girl I'll ever love anymore. Her name isn't even Sophie McPherson. It's Betty Farfield, a kid from Spanish class I strong-armed into dog-sitting during the game, because Dad said if I ever left that dog alone he'd kill it.

My puppy's in Betty's lap, barking like she's calling my name.

It's the dog I'm looking at while I make the shot.

Just as I remember I'd named her Sophie, the ball goes in.

I never touch down on the squeaky gym floor. The ceiling lights wriggle and disappear. The cheers become a hum. The salty sweat on my skin feels like acid.

I'm lying down, I think. A blurry Preston is holding the world's longest hypodermic needle. As she babbles some high-tech gobbledygook meant to explain why I'm not dead yet, the needle enters my neck. Her voice is like a buzzing mosquito—a mosquito well versed in biochemistry, but a mosquito.

"I used the equipment here to produce a serum that will either bind with the nano-catalyst, making it inert and allowing you to regenerate, or change you into a lemur."

I look down, trying to see what could possibly be left of me that still hurts, but I can't see anything. Where's the rest of me?

Al stands by, *tsking*. "You should've quit while he was a head."

I fade back to fantasyland.

I'm in our backyard, by Sophie's grave, feeling bad that the marker I made looks so crude. I dug the hole myself while Dad went bowling.

Sophie, the human version, is by my side, smelling like strawberries, her thin arm around my shoulder.

I look at her. "Don't know why I'd bother asking, but you were never real, were you?"

She giggles. "You might be better off asking if I was ever really alive."

"Okay. Were you?"

"No."

I nod at the little grave. "What about her? What about Sophie?"

"Well, Wade, that's the thing about being really alive—for most of us it means you can really die."

THIRTY

IN THE end, how do I know everything's not a dream? Some philosophical crap, like *I think therefore I am*? Never put Descartes before de horse? When it comes down to it, if even a nitwit like Bob can grow a new Deadpool, what the hell does *I* or *me* mean?

To sum up, what the #@&^ is reality?

I'll tell you, son, or daughter—or whatever version of me you happen to be—I've made a decision about that. I've decided that the whole what-if-life-is-*all*-an-illusion thing is total bull. Words only have meaning in context, and context is only the result of comparisons, so *everything* can't have a context. Say *everything's* a dream, and *dream* becomes meaningless.

It's as damn silly as saying everything's real.

Meaning, from here on in, I'll go with whatever's right in front of me and revise as I go along. Big monster? If I can stick my hand through it, sure, it may be a dream, or a freaking ghost. Whatever. As the GPS would say: Recalculating…recalculating…

Look at it one way, and Preston's deus-ex-machina maneuver worked—it saved me. Look at it another, and dying ain't all it's cracked up to be. Living sure isn't. It's taken a week for me to grow back all my pieces—a very long week. Every time a nerve ending regenerates, it's sure to let me know about it.

No wonder I'm nuts.

To review, Sophie the girl never existed. Sophie the dog did. At least that's the story I'm sticking to today as blue skies, cotton clouds, and green Central Park fill my eyes, and warm wind whistles through my scar tissue.

Tomorrow, who knows?

On the lighter side, I'm in one beautiful, healed piece again, and the late Agent Bob's dastardly plot for world domination has been foiled. Hard to believe, but here I am, Deadpool, perfectly content, maybe for the first time ever, hanging with Mr. Snuffles and playing catch with a certain disembodied head. Preston was so busy with the cleanup, she let me keep both of them.

Okay, maybe I 'ported out with them, and she's going nuts looking for us, but it's pretty much the same thing. Besides, whose head is it anyway? Is it Dick? Is it Jane? What's in a name?

As for Mr. Snuffles, well, let's just say he likes me and I like him just fine.

Sure, people keep their distance, and the sirens will wail sooner or later, but right now everything's perfect. And like I just said, right now is all you ever really have.

The head screams as I toss it. "Nooo! Not again!"

Snuffles and I move our heads in unison, tracking its arc way up in the air. Eager, he tenses, wagging his tail faster and faster, until it's moving so quick I pick up a breeze. But he's not going for it yet. Not Mr. Snuffles. He knows what most of humanity has yet to learn—that half the joy is anticipation.

The head peaks and begins to fall.

I slap my thighs. "Go get him, boy! Go!"

Zoom! He's off, pint-size legs moving so furiously they don't seem to touch the ground. He hits the head so hard he goes rolling over it into the grass, snout first. Quick as a lick, he shakes it off and barks at it, like the head hit him rather than the other way around. Then he opens his puppy mouth wide, grabs it twixt eye socket and cheek, lifts, and comes trotting back to me.

And all the while, the head is still screaming, "No! No! Sweet heaven, no!"

Heh.

I pick it up and rub Snuffie's back. "Good dog! Good dog! Again? Again?"

I know what he's thinking, so he doesn't have to nod, but he does. I throw it again, long and hard.

"Please! Stoooooppppp!"

We wait, and off goes the dog again, a streak of happy fur against the big, bad world. I tried to fight it, tried to keep my distance, to keep my heart shut—but in the end, if a dog can't be your best friend, who can? Maybe I was cruel to Bob and Blind Al, and Preston has her family to tend to, but Mr. Snuffles? This'll be different. I'm going to be there, stay with him, feed him, take him for walks, get him his shots, and…

Oh, crap.

Threw that one a little hard. It landed in Park Avenue traffic. Damn.

"Wait! Come back, Mr. Snuffles! Come back!"

He's still running. He can't hear me. I'll be damned if there's going to be a sad ending. Rested and whole, I streak across the field. The head hits the top of a bus just as Snuffles reaches the first lane. The roof of the bus is too high to reach, so he stops, waits patiently, and watches it roll off into the middle lane. Seeing his chance, Snuffles springs into action and races under the bus.

Pouring it on, I reach the sidewalk in time to see him pop out on the other side.

The falling head hits a Beemer's windshield. The cellphone-talking driver slams on his brakes. The luxury-class sedan swerves sideways, heading straight for the dog. For a second my heart's in my throat, terrified he's had it. I want to grab him and protect him with my body, but there's this big-ass bus between us.

Fortunately, there's a window open. I sail through, toss my Metrocard at the driver, wave to the puzzled commuters, then crash out the other side. Hitting asphalt, I scoop a cheery Mr. Snuffles up in one hand and use the other to stab a katana into the oncoming Beemer's passenger door. In a move that's pretty nifty if I say so myself, I use the hilt of the blade to propel us up and over the car.

We land safely in the crosswalk as the blinking sign turns to WALK.

I press Mr. Snuffles against my face. "Don't you ever scare me like that again! Don't you ever!"

There's the usual screeching and crunching as a couple of cars collide. Six, maybe. But who cares? They've all got airbags and insurance. If they were obeying the speed limit, no one was going over thirty. And everyone obeys the speed limit, right?

Better get out of here, though. I'm a bit on the lam, trying to keep it on the down-low.

Too late. I'm bending over to pick up the head when a S.H.I.E.L.D. hover-flier lands a few yards ahead of me. Preston steps out, her angry-librarian face already in place.

"Wade, what the hell do you think you're doing?"

I kick the head under a hot dog cart and hide Mr. Snuffles behind my back. "Emily! What're you doing here? Thought the job was over."

"It is. Just a little unfinished business."

"You already paid me. What else?"

"Once we completed searching the databases at the lab, we were able to track down the remaining monster pups. I also thought you'd like to know that the collie is back at the hospice, and all those real dogs you rescued from Withers are being placed in a shelter to be adopted. There is one puppy that has to go back to its rightful owner, though. A Labrador?"

"*Another* puppy? Nope. Don't think so. Think you got them all." I try to stuff Snuffles under my shirt, but he growls and crawls into my arms.

I really have to have this suit washed.

And then a certain little girl steps out from behind Preston.

"Santa! The nice lady elf said Snuffles is all fixed. She even gave me a ride in her sled." She leans forward and whispers, "It's a secret, but the reindeer are invisible!"

I glare at Preston. "Spoilsport! I bet you even told the Hulk he's not really a dog killer!"

"What? What are you talking about?"

"Never mind. I'm sure he's gotten over it by now."

"Can I have my dog back now, Santa?"

"*Your*…" I look at Snuffles. I look at the child, her small hands outstretched.

Preston looks at me. "Wade?"

"Look, I'll let him go, okay? But it's got to be *his* decision. Not hers, not mine—his. I'll put him down between us, an equal distance. We'll both call to him, and whoever…"

The little bastard leaps out of my arms and does a five-foot jump into hers.

"Mr. Snuffles!" she cries.

"Snuffles! Get back here, right…aw! Do you have to lick her face like that right in front of me?"

The girl giggles. "Thank you *so* much, Santa!" Then they both vanish into the hover-flier.

Preston blocks the entrance. I could take her easy, dump the girl, then fly off to live on an island for ten or fifteen years. How long do Labs live, anyway? Kid'll be in college by then…

But I don't. Instead I grab the head from under

the cart and give it to Preston.

"Might as well give this to her, too. It's…his favorite toy."

"Kill me! I beg you! Kill me!"

Holding the head like it's a big piece of snot, Preston gingerly places it in a biohazard case. "Not gonna do that…but I will take it back to the lab."

I sigh. "You know, Em. I was kinda hoping for a happy ending."

"This *is* a happy ending. You did a good job for once, Deadpool."

The head answers. "Thanks."

"Not you, him."

"Him who?"

"The real…oh, forget it."

Before they can go into a Señor Wences routine, the door does its hissy fit and seals them in. Whatever makes hover-fliers hover goes hum. It lifts and twists away.

I watch, the same way I watched with Mr. Snuffles a minute ago: arcing my head as the flier rises above the smoking pile of crashed cars.

Only it doesn't peak and come back down so I can go chasing after it. It just keeps going.

"Fare thee well, Mr. Snuffles. Fare thee well."

And then, for the longest while, even the city seems quiet.

I am alone. Alone as I get, anyway.

Who's a good boy?

You are, Wade! YOU are!

ABOUT THE AUTHOR

STEFAN PETRUCHA has written over twenty novels and hundreds of graphic novels for adults, young adults, and tweens. His work has sold over a million copies worldwide. He also teaches online classes through the University of Massachusetts. Born in the Bronx, he spent his formative years moving between the big city and the suburbs, both of which made him prefer escapism. A fan of comic books, science fiction, and horror since learning to read, in high school and college he added a love for all sorts of literary work, eventually learning that the very best fiction always brings you back to reality—so, really, there's no way out.

SPIDER-MAN
FOREVER YOUNG

Hoping to snag some rent-paying photos of his arachnidlike alter ego in action, Peter Parker goes looking for trouble—and finds it in the form of a mysterious, mythical stone tablet coveted by both the Kingpin and the Maggia! Caught in the crosshairs of New York's most nefarious villains, Peter also runs afoul of his friends—and the police! His girlfriend, Gwen Stacy, isn't too happy with him, either. And the past comes back to haunt him years later when the Maggia's assumed-dead leader resurfaces, still in pursuit of the troublesome tablet! Plus: With Aunt May at death's door, has the ol' Parker luck disappeared for good?